Chapter One

The mood on the bridge was still tense after their battle with the Ta'Akar warship while orbiting the small Haven moon. Although their current position put them a good thirty light minutes away from the warship's last known position, there was still the chance that their opponent might deduce their location and come after them in the very near future.

Because of this, Abby kept updating the escape jump plot every few minutes. In her spare time during the harvesting operations back in the rings, she had written an algorithm that would easily update the transition parameters and adjust the jump plot based on a given course and speed. It might be a little less accurate—she hadn't had time to validate the results—but as escape jumps were plotted to wide open areas, any slight discrepancies posed little risk, especially at such short distances. She would've preferred to be more accurate in her calculations, but the current situation seemed to favor speed over precision. As a scientist, it had been a difficult adjustment; after all, superluminal transitions required exact calculations. But as a wife and mother who desperately wanted to return to her family, she had found a way to overcome her aversion to shortcuts.

Tug and Jalea came out of the captain's ready room and were about to exit the bridge, when Nathan came out of the ready room behind them.

"You might want to stay and see this," he said to Tug as he passed. "Abby," he called as he stepped from the exit foyer onto the aft section of the bridge, "Commander Taylor says we're ready to jump to a safer position outside the system."

"Yes, Captain. To roughly the same position we originally jumped in from, give or take a few hundred kilometers."

"Very well. Prepare to jump," he ordered as he stepped aside to allow Jessica to take her position at the tactical console.

"Shall I kill the view screen?" Cameron asked as she sat down at the helm.

Nathan looked at Tug as he stepped up beside him near the tactical station. "Leave it on," he told her, a slight grin creeping across his face.

Cameron looked puzzled. "Sir?"

Nathan ignored her, instead speaking to Tug. "This is a graphical plot of the system," he explained, pointing at the main display at the center of the tactical console. "This is our current position— about thirty light minutes from Haven. We're going to execute a jump that will move us to here." Nathan moved his finger along the display all the way to the right, nearly to the edge of the map before double tapping the screen to emphasize the spot. "That's about two light days from Haven."

Tug looked intently at the display, comprehending its simplistic representations in short order. "I see. And this will happen in an instant?" The skepticism was clearly evident on Tug's face.

"Yeah, I know. I've done it six times now, and even I still can't believe it." Nathan turned to Abby at the jump control console on the starboard side of

THE FRONTIERS SAGA

EPISODE 3

THE

LEGEND

OF

CORINAIR

Ryk Brown

The Frontiers Saga Episode #3: The Legend of Corinair
Copyright © 2012 by Ryk Brown All rights reserved.

First Print Edition:
ISBN-13: 978-1480121133
ISBN-10: 1480121134

This is a work of fiction. Names, characters, places, and incidents either are the product of the author's imagination or are used fictitiously, and any resemblance to locales, events, business establishments, or actual persons—living or dead—is entirely coincidental.

the bridge. "Doctor Sorenson, if you'd be so kind..."

"Executing jump," she replied calmly.

"You might want to cover your eyes," Nathan told Tug.

Tug ignored him, wanting to witness the entire event. He stared at the main view screen, which wrapped around the entire front half of the bridge and up over the helm and command chairs located just in front of them. Only a moment after the physicist initiated the jump, a pale blue wave of light began to spread out from emitters located all over the hull of the ship. It seemed to dance across the hull as each wave of light reached out to connect to the ones next to it. As the waves of light made contact with one another, their brilliance increased immeasurably and they quickly grew into a blinding white flash of light. A moment later, after the flash subsided, the stars had shifted ever so slightly.

Tug rubbed his eyes, the flash of the jump leaving his vision littered with pale blue blotches that floated before him. He blinked repeatedly, squinting his eyes and then widening them again as if trying to clear something from under the lids. Something on the screen was different. To most people, the stars displayed on the view screen would still have looked the same. But for a man who had navigated them from the seat of a small fighter on numerous occasions, even the slightest change was noticeable.

Tug muttered something in his native tongue. Nathan could only guess at its meaning—"*Oh my God,*" or "*Holy shit.*" He was sure it was one of those two. Tug looked back down at the tactical display, locating the icon that marked their new position. It was just as Nathan had said—they were two light days away from Haven. Tug stared back up at the stars on the viewer once again. "Incredible," was the only *Angla* word that came to him. He turned to Nathan. "Absolutely incredible. It is no wonder that the Ta'Akar wish to capture your ship."

"Thanks for reminding me," Nathan said. Tug's last statement had knocked Nathan out of the wonder of the moment and back to the matter at hand. "Kaylah, any contacts out here?"

"No, sir," the ensign responded from her place at the sensor console to his left. "The area is clear. In fact, by direct imaging, it appears as if we haven't even entered the system yet."

"Huh?" It wasn't that Nathan didn't understand what she was talking about; it was that he hadn't expected it.

"The light is two days old," Cameron added. "It takes some getting used to."

"Yeah," Nathan agreed.

Tug understood only too well and was already analyzing the prospects in his mind. "Captain, do you realize the tactical advantages such a technology provides? Not only could you jump into range of your targets with complete surprise, but you could escape before help could arrive. And the reconnaissance possibilities..."

"Let's not get ahead of ourselves," Nathan warned. "We haven't committed to anything just yet. We're just *entertaining* the possibilities at this point."

"But Captain..."

"This drive is just a prototype; it's experimental. There's a *lot* it *can't* do. And so far, we know very little about what it actually *can* do. So let's just take it one step at a time, shall we?"

Tug regained his composure. "Of course, Captain."

"In the meantime," Nathan continued, "why don't you get your family settled into quarters. It's been a difficult day."

Tug looked around the bridge and then back out at the stars on the viewer. "Amazing," he muttered, shaking his head. He nodded to Nathan as he turned to exit. "I'll be available when you need me, Captain."

"Thank you."

Tug returned to the back of the bridge, exiting out the port doorway with Jalea at his side. Nathan watched as they walked away, discussing what Tug had just witnessed for the first time, again in a language that Nathan could not understand. He was beginning to think that if they were to spend much more time in this region of space, he might need to learn at least *some* of their language.

Cameron rose from her seat at the helm and stepped onto the upper level that encompassed the back half of the bridge. "So what do we do now?"

"We still need someplace safe to make repairs."

"Preferably someplace *safer* than Haven," Cameron replied with a hint of sarcasm.

"Hey, we got some molo." Nathan quipped.

"Yeah, and a bunch of rocks," Cameron added. "That reminds me; what are we going to do with all those workers stranded on board?"

The expression on Nathan's face made it evident that he had not considered that problem. "I don't know. I guess I'd better have a talk with them." Nathan turned to Jessica. "Can you round them all up and have them in the briefing room, in say, thirty minutes?"

"Sure thing," Jessica answered as she turned to exit.

"How long do you think we can hang around out

here?" Cameron asked.

"We're probably okay for a day or so," he admitted. "But to be honest, the sooner we get a few light years between us and Haven, the happier I'll be."

* * *

Nathan and Jessica entered the main briefing room located one deck below the command section. Large enough to hold fifty people in five rows, it seemed almost empty compared to how full it had been during his orientation briefing nearly a month ago. Now it contained only a handful of strangers—aliens, in fact—who were stranded on board his ship with no way to return to their homes.

Josh and Loki sat at the back of the room, their feet dangling over the chair backs in front of them. The two pilots of the now twisted and mangled harvester, still lying in ruins on the Aurora's flight deck, seemed to be enjoying themselves, despite all they had been through over the last couple of hours. Marcus, the harvesting crew foreman sitting next to them, did not seem as entertained by the situation.

The others, three men and two women, sat apart from the rest. They had all served as indentured workers under contract with the harvesting team that Tobin had hired during their brief stay in the Haven system. It appeared that they had no interest in socializing with the technical crew of their shared employer. They all appeared beaten and disheveled, having gone through more than a full day of labor, not to mention having watched their fellow workers die at the hands of Ta'Akar troops attempting to take over the ship. In fact, many of them still wore the blood of those who died around them during the slaughter.

Nathan stepped onto the platform at the front of the room. He chose to stand beside the podium instead of behind it, not bothering with the public address speaker system built into the room. There were only a half dozen or so of them, and Nathan felt that a more intimate approach would be appropriate. In retrospect, he wondered if it wouldn't have been better to have the meeting in the command briefing room on the deck above, as it might have been better suited.

"Good afternoon, everyone. For those of you who don't know me, my name is Nathan Scott, and I'm the captain of this ship. First, I'd like to express my condolences to any of you who have lost family or friends in the recent attacks that we have all endured. If there is anything that we can do for you, please do not hesitate to ask."

"Can you get us home?" one of the men asked.

"I guess that depends on where *home* is," Nathan began.

"Haven, of course," the man insisted.

Marcus shook his head, a sour expression painted on his weather-beaten face. "Haven ain't no one's home. Least ways not unless they're touched in the head," he chuckled.

"It was my understanding that most of you were indentured workers, forced to serve against your will."

"That's not entirely correct, Captain," the man explained. "While we may not have chosen to be there, we were required by law to repay debts owed to our creditors, by either indentured labor or imprisonment."

Nathan looked perplexed. He hadn't considered

the possibility that any of the workers would *want* to return to Haven.

"You *can* return us, can you not?" the man continued.

"Well, yes, I suppose we could. It's just that I can't guarantee your safe passage back down to the surface." Nathan felt all their eyes staring at him. "You see, there's still a Ta'Akar warship in the area. I mean, we think that it's still there. The images we're getting right now are two days old."

"Excuse me?" It was Josh's first words since Nathan had entered the room and began speaking. Nathan could tell by the looks on their faces that he was speaking for everyone in the room. "What do you mean, *two days old?*"

"Well, that's because we're about two light days out from Haven right now."

"What?" Marcus interrupted. "That ain't possible. I didn't feel us go to FTL. And even if we did, ain't no way we got that far out so quickly. Hell, it ain't even been an hour since the shootin' ended."

"Yeah, that's right," Josh suddenly realized. "And how the hell did you guys shake that Ta'Akar cruiser?"

Nathan realized the conversation wasn't exactly going in the direction he had intended. The tone struck by Josh and Marcus, although probably not intentional, was a bit accusatory.

"It's kind of complicated," Nathan offered, hoping to avoid the issue of *how* all together. Unfortunately, he could tell by the looks on their faces that they weren't going to let it go that easily. And to make matters worse, the workers—whose interests had previously been separate from those of their higher-ups—were looking like they were about to unite with them. Nathan looked at Jessica as if hoping for a hint at what to say or do to appease the group.

"Might as well tell them," she said. "They're going to find out soon enough."

"Well," Nathan began, "we have a device—we call it a *'jump drive'*—that allows us to instantly *jump* to another point in space. We can jump up to ten light years at once." Nathan looked at the group, all of whose mouths hung open. "So as soon as Josh and Loki got us back on board, we simply jumped away." There was no response. A second later, not knowing what else to say or do, Nathan made a gesture with his hands of a ship jumping from right to left.

"Bullshit," Marcus replied after a moment of silence.

Josh had a completely different reaction. "Hot damn!" he cried, the words nearly exploding from his mouth.

"Why only *two* light days out?" Loki asked.

"Well, to be honest, we were just trying to buy some time until we figured out what to do next," Nathan admitted. He could tell from their expressions they were not following his logic. "You see, we're not from around here."

"No kidding," Josh chuckled.

Marcus eyed Nathan suspiciously. "Where exactly are you from?"

"Well, pretty far away." Nathan took a deep breath. "Actually, we're from the Sol system. A planet called Earth."

Most of their expressions suddenly changed from disbelief to shock—except for Marcus, whose still appeared suspicious. "Earth? Even if it existed, ain't it like a hundred thousand light years away or something? You said your drive thingy could only jump ten light years at a pop. What did you do, make a thousand jumps just to get to Haven?" Marcus laughed. The whole story, jump drive and all, sounded preposterous to him.

"Well, how we got here is another story. One that I really don't want to get into right now."

"Captain," one of the workers interrupted, "if you *jumped* out here, can you not simply *jump* back and let us off the ship?"

"Ain't no way I'm going back to Haven," Marcus announced. "You can drop me off anywhere but that rock."

"*You* were there by *choice*," the men sneered at Marcus, apparently no longer fearing the wrath the surly foreman had once used to keep them in line.

"*I* was there for the *money*," Marcus argued. "Which was damned good, by the way. But after today, who do you think the owner is gonna blame for losing a harvester and half his crew?" Marcus shook his head in defiance. "Uh-uh, I ain't goin' back there. Not after all this. And you'd all be smart to do the same."

"Yes, we could jump back and let you off," Nathan began, choosing to ignore Marcus for the moment. "But I can't guarantee the Ta'Akar would allow you safe passage. In fact, I rather doubt they would."

"And why is that, Captain?" Marcus challenged, standing to emphasize the urgency of his request.

Jessica straightened up from her position against the wall, sensing the tension rise in the room. She took a step forward, her body language communicating to Marcus her intent to impede him should he step out of line. Just as Nathan was about to respond, Tug and Jalea entered the briefing room.

"Because of me," Tug announced in a commanding

voice.

"And who the hell are you?" Marcus asked, turning to glare at Tug and Jalea.

"I am the leader of the Karuzari."

"The terrorists?"

"They're not terrorists, Marcus," Josh argued, rolling his eyes. "They're freedom fighters."

"I don't care what you call them, kid. They're still trouble. And it's trouble that I don't care to be associated with. And if I were you..." Marcus suddenly stopped mid-sentence as he started to put it all together. "Wait a minute," he said, pointing a finger at Nathan. "Is this the ship we heard about? The one that appeared out of nowhere and helped them *Kazahooie* escape?" Marcus looked around the room again, his mind racing. "Yeah, that would explain all the damage to your ship, wouldn't it? And that would also explain why them Takar bastards came to Haven looking for you. Damn. On second thought, maybe it would be safer to return to Haven after all," Marcus concluded, scratching his head.

"He might be correct, Captain," Tug began as he and Jalea continued into the room. "It might be safer for all of them to leave the ship as soon as possible."

"Not me," Josh announced. "If you don't mind, Captain, I'd just as soon stay right here. I figure you're gonna need someone to pilot that shuttle anyhow." Josh nudged Loki with his elbow.

"Yeah, count me in as well," Loki added, somewhat hesitantly.

The offer surprised Nathan. The idea of adding civilians to his crew hadn't occurred to him. But the idea, although somewhat unusual, wasn't without merit. He was quite sure, however, that his XO would disagree. Complete with direct quotes from the regulations to support her objections. "Thank you," he answered rather automatically, surprising even himself. "I just may take you up on that."

It surprised Jessica as well, her expression reflecting her doubt.

"In fact," Nathan continued, "if any of the rest of you care to help out, I'd be happy to consider your offers as well."

"Nathan," Jessica mumbled under her breath, "what the hell are you doing?" She could imagine Cameron's reaction when she heard what he was proposing.

"Captain," one of the workers began. "I'm afraid that none of us would be much assistance in the accomplishment of your goals, whatever they might be. Perhaps you might see your way fit to put us off on the next inhabited world you come to."

Nathan was a bit surprised. "You don't wish to return to Haven?"

"I'm afraid I'm forced to agree with our former *supervisor* here. If indeed the Ta'Akar consider you associates of the Karuzari, they would probably look upon us in much the same way. As you said, it is doubtful they would allow us to pass unimpeded."

"And what about your contracts?"

"The terms of our contracts become null and void upon our deaths or by an inability to perform our duties, in whole or in part, due to reasons beyond our control." The worker grinned. "I believe *this* qualifies as *beyond our control.*"

"Let me guess; you were a lawyer?"

The worker nodded.

"Very well, if that's what you all wish, then we'll let you off at the earliest *safe* opportunity."

"If there is anything we can do to help in the

meantime, Captain, we would be more than happy to do so," the man added.

"Captain, if I might make a suggestion," Tug interrupted, "there is a rather large amount of molo that should be cleaned and prepared in order to keep it safe for consumption. Perhaps these good people could assist us in that rather pressing task."

Their overall lack of food had slipped Nathan's mind during the commotion of the last few hours. Nathan looked at the male worker who had been speaking on their behalf, waiting for an answer to Tug's proposal.

"Of course, Captain. We would be happy to help."

"Thank you." Nathan turned his attention to Marcus. Despite his having been the most vocal one of the bunch, he had yet to state his intentions.

"What?" Marcus asked when he noticed Nathan staring at him.

"And how about you, Marcus?"

"Don't get me wrong there, Captain. I'm happy to help out and all. But about all I'm good at is drinking, yelling, and getting in fights. If you need any of that done, then I'm your man. But I'm sure as hell not a *freedom fighter*."

"Marcus, you're a pretty fair mechanic," Josh insisted. "And someone's gotta help us keep the shuttles flying. Hell, you can be my crew chief."

"And take orders from you?" Marcus snorted. "Not likely, squirt."

Satisfied that they had all come to an understanding of sorts, Nathan prepared to conclude the discussion. "I think I should warn you all that just being on board this ship presents an element of risk. We're not *looking* for trouble out here. But so far, *trouble* is about all we've found."

"On a ship from a mythical world, equipped with a magical *jump* drive, and carrying the leader of the freedom fighters?" Marcus laughed. "What kinda trouble could we possibly get into?"

"What the hell are you doing?" Jessica demanded as they left the briefing room and headed down the corridor.

"Keep your voice down," Nathan hushed.

"Cam's gonna come unglued when she finds out," Jessica continued in a slightly more subdued tone.

"All I did was hire a shuttle and a crew to fly her. It's not like I asked them all to enlist in the fleet or something."

"Nathan, you can't just give these people the run of the ship. We don't know anything about them. Hell, we don't even know most of their names."

"Need I remind you that half those people just put their lives on the line for us?"

"They were just trying to save their own butts."

"As I understand it," Nathan defended as he stepped through the hatchway into the next corridor, "Josh and Loki *volunteered* to fly us out of there."

"The teenagers in flight suits? Please, gimme a break. They were just looking for some fun."

"Regardless, they got the job done. And they're right; we *are* going to need that shuttle *and* someone to fly it. And *you* know it."

Jessica could tell that she wasn't going to be able to change his mind. Nathan was impulsive, making decisions on the spur of the moment. She liked that about him, even admired it in some ways. And thus far, his command style *had* gotten them by. But as much as she enjoyed his direct, impulsive approach, she feared he might be taking it too far this time.

"Fine, you can keep the testosterone twins," she acquiesced. "But at least let me monitor them. I can give them all comm-sets. That way I can track their every move."

"What?" Nathan wasn't sure he liked the idea, as it seemed dishonest somehow.

"I can attach names to comm-set ID numbers and keep logs of their movements throughout the ship. I can even program the system to alert me if one of them ventures into a sensitive area. And I can assign them to the auxiliary channels only, so they won't muck up the command channels."

"I don't know, Jess."

"Come on, Nathan. I don't have the manpower to keep an eye on them. And for all we know, one of them could be a Ta'Akar spy."

Nathan stopped at the bottom of the ramp that led up to the command deck. "Yeah, I hadn't thought of that." He was a little embarrassed that, despite all that had happened, he still wasn't thinking in such terms.

"Of course not. That's why you hired me, remember?"

"Very well. Pass out the comm-sets," he agreed as he started back up the ramp.

"I'll get right on it."

"No, send someone else," he insisted. "And have them inventory all of their skill sets, in case we might need them later."

"Okay. But why not me?" she asked, a puzzled look on her face as she followed him up the ramp.

"We've got another meeting," he explained as he started up the ramp, "with Cameron. I need you there to keep her from strangling me."

* * *

"I think we should call Doctor Chen," Cameron said as she followed him into the ready room, "so she can declare you unfit for command due to mental disease or defect."

"Hmm, sarcasm. I should have seen that coming," Nathan said as he walked across the room to his desk. He had expected her to react poorly to the idea of using the locals to help out in a pinch. But he had hoped that she would at least object to the decision of her commanding officer in a more professional manner. He knew it would take time, just as Vladimir had warned him that morning.

"Well, obviously you've lost your mind."

"That's what I said," Jessica added as she plopped down on the couch.

"How could you have possibly thought it was a good idea to start using civilians—aliens no less—as crew?"

"Jesus, what is it with you two?" Nathan sat in his chair behind the captain's desk. "I asked them to cut up some molo, and you're both acting like I gave them the keys to the nukes!"

"It's just that you're *too* trusting, Nathan," Cameron insisted.

"Look, you and I both know that there is *no way* we can run this ship effectively with what little crew we have left. We don't even have one full shift staffed, Cam. And most of the crew has had less than a full night's rest in nearly a week. Hell, we're going to have to start using one-man watches in each department pretty soon, or else we're going to have people dropping from exhaustion."

"But these people don't have *any* training…"

"Which is why I'm *not* planning on using any of them in critical areas, Cameron. I might be impulsive, but contrary to popular opinion—amongst the women in this room—I'm *not* stupid." Nathan looked past Cameron who was standing in front of him, making eye contact with Abby, who had come in a moment ago and was sitting on the other end of the couch from Jessica. "Present company excluded, Doctor."

"Nathan…" Cameron tried to continue her argument, but was cut off when Nathan raised his hand.

"The decision has been made, Commander," he warned in a more official tone.

Cameron was slightly taken aback, as was Jessica. It was uncharacteristic of Nathan to pull rank on anyone, let alone the two of them. She took a deep breath and swallowed hard, letting her breath out slowly as she composed herself.

"Now, can we start this meeting?" Nathan asked in a more unofficial tone.

Cameron took a seat in one of the two chairs facing the front of Nathan's desk. "Yes, sir."

"I've called this staff meeting so we can decide on a course of action," Nathan explained.

"Captain, I'm not a member of your staff," Abby pointed out.

"You are now," he explained. "Since the jump drive is currently our only means of interstellar travel, every strategic decision now involves you."

"But I'm a civilian."

"It's not like I'm drafting you, Doctor. I just want your expertise available during any discussions that might involve the jump drive."

"Of course."

"What about medical and engineering?" Cameron asked, still fuming over Nathan's rebuke.

"Doctor Chen still has her hands full, and other than her department's state of readiness, she would have little to add to this discussion."

"And Vladimir?"

"He'll be here momentarily." Nathan leaned back in his chair, taking a breath and trying to relax for the first time since he had made it back on board from the surface of Haven.

Cameron could see his frazzled nerves becoming more apparent now that the adrenaline was beginning to wear off. "What happened down there?" she asked, in a surprisingly sympathetic tone.

"We got ambushed," Jessica explained.

"When Tobin came to pick us up, he surprised us with a team of Ta'Akar assault troops," Nathan said.

"I never did trust that skinny little shit," Jessica added.

"If it hadn't been for Vlad and Jessica, they would've taken us completely by surprise."

"They must've attacked you at the same time they attacked us," Cameron surmised. "They got on board using one of the cargo shuttles. We thought they were just returning from their run to the surface."

"Yeah, well, it's obvious that Tobin was in on the whole thing," Nathan said.

"What about Jalea and this Tug fellow?" Cameron asked. "You think they were in on it as well?"

"Doubtful. Danik was killed in the attack, and Tug lost his wife."

"Jesus," Cameron exclaimed.

"Yeah, and Tug was about to get executed, until we capped the remaining three all at once," Jessica bragged.

"Really?"

"Yeah, you should've seen it. Captain even put one right in the middle of one of their face plates. Blew the back of his head clean off."

Cameron looked at Nathan in disbelief. She knew there had been some sort of battle on the surface, but until now, she had no idea how serious it had actually been.

"Yeah, I was just as surprised as you are," he admitted.

"Surprised by what?" Vladimir asked as he entered the room.

"Nothing," Nathan said, not really wanting to relive the event just yet. "Have a seat."

Vladimir took the remaining chair, pulled it away from the desk, and moved it over toward the wall so as not to block Nathan's view of Jessica and Abby on the couch. He spun the chair around and sat down, his arms resting on the chair back.

"Before we start, I want you all to know how much I appreciate the tireless job you've been doing. I wish I could say that we're almost done, but I'm afraid we may have just gotten started." Nathan looked at their faces, each of them showing signs of stress and fatigue. Even Vladimir, who normally was stoic and smiling, looked beat. And poor Cameron, who always looked *military perfect*, looked like she had slept in her uniform, and for a very short time at that.

"When Captain Roberts placed me in command, his last orders were to get the jump drive back to Earth. At the time, I didn't understand the urgency of his request, but I learned a bit later—and correct me if I'm mistaken, Doctor—that this particular unit is not only the sole prototype in existence, but that all research in regards to this project is currently stored in the project's mainframe on board this ship. There is not a shred of evidence to be found anywhere on Earth that would reveal this project had ever existed. In fact, other than the researchers who came on board with the prototype, there were only a handful of people on the entire planet that were aware of its existence. That's how important this project was to the security of Earth."

"That is unbelievable," Vladimir exclaimed.

"That's exactly what I thought," Nathan agreed, "at first. But think about it. If the Jung ever got their hands on this research, there would be no stopping them. That's got to be why Fleet was so secretive."

"You are correct, Captain. And the paranoia of our leaders went far deeper than you could imagine. The few that knew about this project were willing to sacrifice their careers, even their very lives to protect it. We even had suicide devices implanted in our teeth, in case of capture."

Nathan stared at her, asking with his eyes if that included her.

"Yes, Captain, I have one as well."

"Does this mean we have to get them as well?" Jessica asked halfheartedly.

"I'm pretty sure medical doesn't carry suicide pills," Nathan assured her.

"Captain," Abby warned, "you do realize that if this drive were about to fall into enemy hands, you would be expected to destroy the ship and the crew in order to maintain its secrecy."

"I'm afraid the *secret* is already out, Doctor. The Ta'Akar have already seen us jump away on several occasions. I suspect they're hunting us for exactly that reason."

"Then we need to get out of this region of space as quickly as possible," Cameron insisted.

"Five or six jumps should put us well out of range of even their fastest ships, Captain," Abby estimated. "We could be out of danger and well on our way home in a matter of days."

"But earlier you said you had no way to tell how much longer the jump drive would continue to function. Has that assertion changed?"

"No, sir, it has not. But I also have no reason to suspect that it would *not* continue to function as designed. When I made that statement, I was doing so to *warn* you about the risk of *assuming* the jump drive would always be available to get you out of danger."

"So you think it *could* make the hundred or so jumps back home *without* any problems?"

"I have no reason to suspect otherwise. But admittedly, I have no evidence to suggest that it *could*, either."

"Which is exactly why we're *not* going to head home just yet," he announced.

"What?" Cameron wasn't surprised by his announcement, as she had suspected this would be his plan all along. "Nathan, it's not safe to stay in this region of space. You said so yourself. The sooner we start jumping home…"

"Cam, we don't know what lies between here and Earth," Nathan told her. "There could be other inhabited worlds—maybe friendly, maybe not. They could be even worse than the Ta'Akar. Or there could be nothing but empty space. That's more than a hundred jumps—any one of which could be our last. We could easily end up stranded in a far worse situation than this. And I'm just not prepared to commit to such a risky plan, at least not without more information."

"And if the Ta'Akar manage to hunt us down?" Cameron wasn't backing down this time, not without a fight.

"Well, we can always start jumping away then, can't we?"

"It may not be that easy, Nathan. They underestimated us once, maybe twice. They probably won't make that mistake again."

"According to Jalea, they're not that bright when it comes to tactics," Jessica recalled.

"You want to bet your life on that?" Cameron asked.

Jessica said nothing, but her expression told Cameron that she did not.

Nathan was getting tired of arguing with Cameron. It was beginning to feel like their days back in the training simulator. And he was exhausted. He'd been shot at all afternoon and had been bounced around in a tiny spaceship that crash-landed on the Aurora's hangar deck. He had too little energy left to waste it arguing with his XO. "Cam, I'm just saying I want to find out more before we make a decision one way or the other. That's all."

"That's all?" She was sure there was more to it that he wasn't revealing just yet.

"And maybe spend some time fixing a few things along the way, if you don't mind." Nathan knew that he didn't have to get her approval. He was in command, after all. But the nature in which he had ended up her superior officer had never sat well with her, and he knew it. Furthermore, he needed her on his side. Her unique organizational skills and attention to details, as well as her uncanny knowledge of procedure, made up for his weaknesses in those areas.

"Of course not," she assured him.

"And while we're doing all that," Jessica interrupted, "maybe we can find out a little more about this power source."

Nathan was quick to jump onto the new topic, wanting to leave the debate with Cameron using any excuse possible. "Exactly. At the very least, we need to verify its existence. I mean, if it really is as great as Tug implied, couldn't we use it to increase our jump range?"

Abby realized that his last question was aimed at her. "I suppose it's possible. But I'd have to know a bit more about it before I could give you a definite answer."

"Deliza seemed to know quite a lot about this research," Vladimir added.

"Really?" Nathan was a bit surprised to hear that Tug's teenage daughter was so well versed in the subject.

"Yes. She is actually a very smart young lady. I do not think she gets out much."

"What did she tell you about it?"

"Only that it is based on the principles of *zero-point energy.*"

"Captain," Abby interrupted, "there are references in the Data Ark to such research. In fact, we were very close to developing something similar on Earth just before the plague struck. It was one of the research and development proposals being considered in the defense of Earth after the Jung threat had been recognized. Had it not been for our accidental discovery of the spatial transition effect, it might even have been pursued."

"Would it be something that we could use?"

"Indeed. A zero-point energy reactor would provide more than enough power to significantly increase our jump range. It might also reduce the recharge time between jumps."

"Both of which would be significant tactical advantages," Jessica pointed out.

Nathan looked at Cameron. "What do you think, Commander? Does it warrant further investigation?" He knew she could not deny the logic.

"Of course," she agreed, frustration still evident in her tone.

"All right then. But let's not forget that our first priority is to make repairs. To that end, Cameron, I'd like you to put together a damage report and a repair plan. You can coordinate with Vlad on that. I think it's high time we got our repair priorities in order."

"Yes, sir," Cameron answered. Despite the fact that she preferred to jump out of the area as soon as possible, she was relieved that Nathan had listened. For once he had considered all the facts before making a decision, even if in the end his decision had remained pretty much the same.

"Doctor," Nathan continued, turning his attention toward Abby, "I need you to get your jump drive in as good a state as possible. And when you get the chance, see if you can't come up with some energy requirements for a super-jump home, just in case that power source happens to fall into our laps." Nathan looked at Cameron and winked. "Vlad, see to it that Abby gets all the help she needs. That jump drive is our only means of FTL travel at the moment, so we have to take care of it."

"No problem," Vladimir assured him.

"What about me?" Jessica asked, feeling a little left out.

"You and I have a meeting with Tug and Jalea. It's about time we got some straight answers about what's really going on in the Pentaurus cluster."

* * *

"Remember, don't tell them anything you don't have to," Jessica said as they approached the command briefing room.

"How am I supposed to get them to share intel with us if we don't share it with them?" To Nathan, it seemed an obvious flaw in her logic. But he was beginning to realize that Jessica's special operations instructors must have programmed her to be suspicious and deceitful by nature.

"It's easy. Just let them do all the talking. And only answer direct questions."

"Why do I feel like I'm about to go on trial here?"

"Maybe you should feel that way," Jessica added. "It might make you think twice before you speak."

Nathan recognized the jab. Jessica and Cameron had already become friends over the last week, and Cameron had been admonishing him for acting without thinking the situation through since their first day in the simulator together. But deep down inside, Nathan knew he was the type who preferred to operate on instinct. Information was always helpful, but in the end, he had to follow his gut.

"Look," he said, coming to a stop just outside the briefing room, "I appreciate what you're trying to tell me. In the end, it's my responsibility, and I have to do what I think is best." Nathan looked in Jessica's eyes, his tone becoming less official. "I understand where you're coming from. But this is not a covert spec-ops mission. This is more of a negotiation. It's politics—and politics, unfortunately, is in my blood. I'm a people person," he added with a smile. "You said so yourself," he added as he turned and entered the briefing room.

"I did say that," she admitted sheepishly as she followed him through the hatch. She was afraid of what Nathan might commit them to during this meeting with Tug and Jalea. And as much as she wanted to prevent him from doing so—as much as she felt it was her *duty* to prevent him from doing so—it was just as much her duty to follow the orders of her captain, regardless of how under-qualified he might be. But there was still a part of her—a small part to be sure—that somehow trusted Nathan to do the right thing.

"I apologize for being late," Nathan began as he sat down at the head of the briefing table. Tug and Jalea were already seated along the outboard side of the table, and Jessica took a seat across from them next to Nathan. "I hope you haven't been waiting long."

"Not at all, Captain," Tug answered.

Nathan instantly got the feeling that, unlike previous meetings, Jalea would not be taking the lead in these discussions.

"Last night, I shared much with you about Earth. In fact, you probably know more about our world than anyone in this sector."

"Yes, it was most enlightening."

"I was hoping that you might shed similar light

on the affairs in your part of the galaxy."

"That's a tall order, Captain. Could you be more specific?"

Nathan wasn't sure if Tug was trying to force him to ask more specific questions in order to avoid revealing information unnecessarily—as Jessica had advised Nathan to do—or if he was just wanting to know where to start. "I guess I'm primarily interested in two things," Nathan began. "First, about the rebellion, or more specifically, the battle we jumped into when we first arrived in the Pentaurus cluster."

Tug adjusted himself in his chair, as if preparing to make a speech. "As I explained last night, the battle you were caught up in was the last stand for the rebellion. In recent years, the Ta'Akar have become more ruthless in their dealings with both the Karuzari and those that support us. Entire communities have been erased from existence as punishment for offering aid to our people, and as a warning to those that might still consider such actions."

"Were you at that battle?"

"No. I was wounded some months ago in another engagement and was still recuperating. What I know of the incident I learned through Jalea."

"Any idea how the Ta'Akar knew where to find your people?"

"Unfortunately, no," Tug admitted.

Again, Nathan felt as if he were being forced to ask direct questions in order to get the information he needed out of Tug. "Is it possible that someone within your organization sold you out?"

Tug looked at Nathan, unsure of the meaning of his expression. Jalea leaned into him and whispered a translation. "There were only three people that knew the location of the new base: Marak, Jalea, and I," Tug explained. "Each of us was responsible for gathering the remaining cells and bringing them together for a last attempt to obtain a larger, more powerful ship—a tactical advantage that we have always hoped for but never achieved. Even the pilots did not know their destination until the final leg of the journey, at which point communication with the Ta'Akar would've been impossible."

"Couldn't a message have been sent after you arrived?"

"It is possible," Tug admitted, "but such a message would require specialized equipment, which we did not have. Any message sent by standard methods would've taken far longer to reach its destination. The attack came too swiftly for that to have been the case."

"Then that leaves only the two of you and Marak—who is dead—as potential suspects," Nathan pointed out. He knew that the statement would not bring a reaction from Jalea. In the past, she had proven herself far too disciplined for him to expect such behavior. But he had hoped for some telltale sign from Tug, who seemed a bit more open with his body language. However, Tug seemed to take the accusation in stride, as if it had been expected.

"Yes, this is true. Of course it goes without saying that I have complete trust in the loyalty of both Marak and Jalea."

"No offense intended to either of them, Tug," Jessica interrupted, "but such trusted individuals usually make the best informants."

"That is true," Tug conceded, "but neither of them had any motivation for betrayal. And I might add that such suspicions have also been an integral part of our tactics. And to that end, I had not revealed the location of our new base to either of my subordinates until the last possible moment, after which a communications blackout was put into effect."

"If you trusted your subordinates, why did you feel it necessary to take such precautions?" Nathan asked.

"While trust can be a wonderful thing, it can also be the most destructive of weapons," Tug explained. "Only a fool places complete trust in anyone, even themselves."

"They must have spies on the ground," Jessica concluded.

"That is the general consensus," Jalea agreed. "It has been suspected for some time that the Ta'Akar have developed an extensive network of spies with which to monitor every inhabited world within the cluster. We have even found them operating in fringe systems no longer under their control."

Nathan leaned back in his chair, contemplating all that he had heard thus far. "What concerns me most is how quickly they learned of your location."

"The Ta'Akar have recently developed a system of interstellar communications that utilizes a network of small, automated communication drones," Tug explained. "These drones use an advanced version of their standard FTL systems, enabling them to travel at several hundred times the speed of light. With most stars within the cluster being only a few light years apart, messages can now be exchanged in days rather than weeks or even months. When combined with strategically placed ships—say in between systems—it gives them a tactical advantage that is proving to be difficult to overcome.

"We believe that a nearby warship received information about the location of our base, and took immediate action without waiting for orders from the Ta'Akar home world. He undoubtedly saw it as an opportunity to advance himself in rank. Thankfully, your sudden arrival ruined his career plans."

The faint smile on her lips was the first sign of emotion Nathan had seen from Jalea since he entered the room. "That would explain the swift arrival of reinforcements," Nathan concluded. Jalea affirmed his conclusion with a simple nod. "So how many people survived the attack?"

"To our knowledge, other than the ships that came aboard the Aurora, only three other ships escaped. I would estimate there are only twenty surviving members of the Karuzari."

"Out of how many?"

"There were over two hundred Karuzari on the surface, not including families, which numbered twice as many. They too were exterminated."

Nathan could do little to hide his shock. "Why would they bother with the families?"

"Some believe it was to ensure that there were no survivors who might someday seek to avenge the deaths of loved ones," Jalea stated. There was bitterness in her tone that Nathan found surprising. He noticed Tug placing his hand on her arm, as a subtle warning.

"Captain," Tug interrupted, "the Ta'Akar have lost many ships and crew over the years, and it has put an increased strain on their industrial infrastructure. It has also forced them to require mandatory service for all of appropriate age. These two factors have led to a steady downfall in the quality of both their weapons and the training of the people that use them. Over time, they have gradually moved away from surgical strikes—which require more costly weapons—to more widespread assault tactics, with little concern over collateral damage. At first, this trend outraged their citizens. But as the aggressiveness of the Ta'Akar increased, the outrage was replaced by fear—fear for one's very survival. Although this may not have been by design, it has also led to a drastic decline in support for the Karuzari. In fact, on more than one occasion, the Ta'Akar have managed to place the blame for such collateral damage upon us, making the Karuzari appear more as terrorists than revolutionaries."

"Then your support is fading?"

"No one likes the regime of Caius, Captain. But after so many years of war, the people long for order once again, even if that order is delivered by an iron fist."

"But with this ship..." Jalea began, enthusiasm rising in her voice.

"Jalea," Tug interrupted sternly, "we are here to answer the *Captain's* questions."

It was obvious to Nathan, as well as to everyone in the room, that Jalea and Tug desperately hoped to get the Aurora, more specifically her jump drive, on their side. And although he thus far found Tug to be a brave and honorable man, his opinion of Jalea was quite the opposite.

"That's all right," Nathan assured him. "We'll get to that. Before we do, I'd like to know more about this power source you spoke of."

"The Royal Institute of Sciences on Takara conducts all manner of research under grants by the royal family. They claim to have created a working prototype of a zero-point reactor. The prototype itself, although reported to be a bit unstable, is capable of generating massive amounts of nearly limitless energy. They are reported to be working on a more reliable production model. Once complete, they will begin refitting existing ships. The ships will be faster, more powerful, and will have much better shielding than before. And their energy weapons will also be significantly enhanced. In a word, they will be unstoppable. And as you can surely imagine, this is just the tip of the iceberg. I believe that if they are allowed to complete its development, they will once again expand beyond the Pentaurus cluster and will eventually dominate most, if not all, of the galaxy."

"That seems like a rather far-fetched prediction," Nathan said.

"Captain, for a civilization to rapidly expand, it requires three key elements—infrastructure, resources, and energy. The Ta'Akar have the first two, and are about to have the third, in abundance I might add."

"There's one more element required," Nathan told him. "Desire."

"Oh, Caius has the desire, Captain."

"How can you be so sure?"

"You must trust me on this, Captain. Of this I am quite certain."

Tug's assertions only made Nathan more curious. This man had led a rebellion against *Caius* for more than two decades—maybe longer, as Nathan had no idea how their *years* translated into Earth years. But there was quite a bit of emotion evident in his assertion, and it made Nathan wonder if it was simply the result of so many years of fighting, or if there was something deeper to Tug's convictions.

After a brief pause, Nathan continued. "I feel it

only fair to warn you that we have not yet decided what our best course of action might be. Some of us feel we should immediately leave the area and begin the long process of jumping our way back home. Others speculate that this new power source might get us home much faster."

Tug considered Nathan's words before asking his question. "And on which side of this debate do you reside?"

Tug's diplomatic skills had not gone unnoticed by Nathan. The man who had once presented himself as a simple farmer was not a stranger to the delicacies of negotiation. Nathan had spent many mind-numbing hours witnessing such exchanges during summer internships with his father, the senator. He could recognize a skilled orator when he heard one.

"I believe we have insufficient information on which to base such a decision. However, as long as our individual goals remain compatible, I am not opposed to working together to our mutual benefit."

"What additional information do you require?"

"No offense, Tug, but we need to independently confirm your claims about this zero-point reactor."

"That should not be difficult, Captain. As I explained before, although the research facility is highly secure, information about its progress has been freely available, as a panacea for the masses. There are news broadcasts about its progress on a weekly basis at least throughout the cluster."

"We'll also need to know more about Ta'Akar forces."

Now there was an obvious emotional response from Jalea. "Then you'll join us?"

"Let's just say that I have not dismissed the idea

just yet."

"We will provide all that we know, Captain," Tug added.

"Thank you. In the meantime, I have other business to attend. So if you wouldn't mind discussing these matters with my security chief, it would be greatly appreciated."

"Of course not, Captain. We have recently become good friends," Tug said with a smile.

CHAPTER TWO

The medical department was once again in shambles. Although not as bad as before, the sense of order that Doctor Chen and her staff of mostly volunteers had establish was strained to the point of breaking. To accommodate the influx of additional casualties resulting from the battle in the hangar bay, the young doctor had been forced to move most of her still recuperating patients into nearby quarters that had been converted into makeshift hospital rooms.

The battle was nearly three hours past by now, and though the situation appeared to be under control, the main treatment area was again in a state of disrepair. The initial chaos that had immediately followed the battle was under control, and Doctor Chen had done what she could for the wounded. Now, as before, it was mostly a waiting game to see how many of them would survive.

As Nathan walked through the treatment area, the first thing that struck him was that most of the wounded were not his crew. They were the workers that had been hired to harvest the rings to maintain their cover. In fact, of the eight patients currently being treated, six of them were workers from Haven. Nathan was suddenly struck with a sense of guilt. These people had been wounded—many of them had died—because of his decision to bring the Aurora to Haven. True, he had been following the advice of Tobin and Jalea. But in the end, it was all his responsibility, and he had to wonder: was it worth it? Furthermore, did he even have the right to make that decision? These were not members of his crew, after all. These were civilians, and not even of his own world.

He braced himself as he made his way through the treatment area, expecting to be overcome with nausea just as before, but it didn't come. That's when he realized that, while he felt guilty for what had happened to them, he didn't feel responsible for their deaths. He hadn't known that he was putting them in harm's way. Tobin knew; it was he who was responsible for the fate that befell them. Suddenly, Nathan was no longer troubled by Jalea's execution of the *skinny little shit*—as Jessica had put it.

He reached the utility room on the far side of the treatment area, half expecting to find Doctor Chen sitting in the corner nibbling on dried fruit and nuts as usual. But the room was empty—a mess, but empty.

"Captain?" A woman's voice came from behind. Nathan turned to see a familiar face. She was a good four or five years younger than him, with short brown hair and hazel eyes. She looked tired, but determined. But as the young woman approached, he couldn't quite remember where he knew her from. She wasn't a member of his crew—or at least she wasn't wearing a uniform. Then he noticed the partially healed scar on her forehead, and he remembered. He had helped her in the corridor after the battle with the first Ta'Akar ship on his way to see Captain Roberts right before he died. She had been injured herself, the gash on her forehead, and had been trying to help a badly injured man more than twice her size, despite her weakened state. And he had seen her later, running around the treatment area with a data pad, taking treatment notes for Doctor Chen.

"Yes?" Nathan answered as the woman approached.

"You probably don't remember me," she started.

"The corridor," he said. "You were helping an injured man to medical. You called for help. Yes, I remember."

"That's right," she said, surprised that he remembered her. "My name's Cassandra. Cassandra Evans," she told him, holding out her hand.

"Nathan Scott," he said as he shook her hand. "You're on the jump drive project, right?"

"The what?"

"Oh, sorry. The superluminal transition something."

"Yeah, I guess jump drive is easier to say."

"What are you doing in medical?"

"I've been helping Doctor Chen. My job on the project was to study how the *jump drive* might affect human physiology. But with all that's happened, it made more sense for me to help out here for now."

"That's good of you. I'm sure Doctor Chen appreciates it." Nathan looked around for the doctor. "Where is she?"

"She's in surgery. She'll probably be in there for quite some time. She said to yell at you for '*bringing a bunch of unscreened foreign humans on board without prescreening them for pathogens.*'" Cassandra's face pulled into a slight frown. "I don't have to *yell* at you, do I?"

"I'll consider myself properly scolded."

Relief washed across her face. "She also said to tell you that everyone needs to undergo a full physical as soon as possible. That means anyone who went down to the surface and anyone new to the ship."

"I'll see to it, but it may be awhile," he explained. "Things are still a little hectic right now."

"Of course, I understand. I'll let her know when she gets out of surgery."

"Great, then I guess I'll leave you to your work then," he said as he prepared to leave. "It was nice meeting you, Cassandra."

"You too, sir." Nathan started to head back toward the entrance, when she called to him. "Captain?" Nathan turned back to her to see what she wanted. "I just wanted to say thanks."

Nathan looked a bit puzzled. "For what?"

"Doctor Sorenson told us how you stepped up and took over when Captain Roberts and Commander Montero were killed. She says you have probably saved us more than once already." Cassandra looked a little embarrassed by her statement. "So, I just thought someone should thank you; that's all."

Nathan was surprised, and at a loss for words, which was something that didn't happen to him very often. "You're quite welcome, Cassandra." Nathan looked at her for a moment. "And thank you for saying so."

The young woman suddenly felt awkward. "I'd better get back to work now," she said, taking a few steps backward before turning and disappearing into the utility room.

Nathan turned and continued out the door into the corridor, thinking, *Sometimes this 'captain' gig isn't too bad.*

* * *

The musky, overpowering aroma of the molo struck Nathan long before he reached the hatch to the mess hall. If there was one thing he had learned from his dinner at Tug's farmhouse, it was that molo smelled far worse during cooking than it did when you ate it. As he approached the hatch, he made a mental note to himself to make sure that all future molo cooking was done with the galley doors closed.

Nathan was unprepared for what he saw when he stepped through the mess hall hatch. The entire room, which was large enough to sit at least two hundred at once, was covered with sheets of raw molo. There were stacks of it, each piece about a meter square and ten centimeters thick. Tug was leading the workers from the harvesting crew, along with two of the Aurora's crew, as they removed the outer skin from each piece. After skinning it, they would quarter it and then move it into the galley for cleaning.

Across the serving counter, Nathan could see several large pots with steam pouring out of them as one of the female workers dumped bowls full of diced molo, as well as some sort of fresh herbs, into the pots of boiling water. While there was nothing appetizing about the smell, Nathan knew from experience that, when prepared properly, molo was a tasty and nutritious meal. He was just thankful that they had someone on board who knew how to cook it.

Nathan made his way over to one of his crew, a young technician who was showing one of the workers from Haven how to use the comm-set he was being assigned. "How's it going?"

"This is the last one, sir," the technician answered as he indicated to the worker that he was free to go. "I made a list of all their names, skill sets, and their comm-set IDs, just like Commander Taylor asked."

"Very good. Do me a favor, and make sure they all know that our doctor will be calling them in for physicals at some point over the next few days—if they're here that long."

"Yes, sir," the technician answered, looking somewhat dejected.

Nathan was sure that the smell of the molo was getting to the young man. "Don't worry; it tastes a lot better than it smells."

"It would have to, sir."

Nathan made his way across the room to where Tug was working. On one of the tables he passed, there were several boxes full of some type of prepackaged food, labeled in a language he didn't understand. "What's all that?" he asked Tug as he approached, pointing back toward the boxes.

"They were on the shuttles," Tug explained. "It was meant to feed the workers for at least a few days. We thought it might be useful. We might be able to combine some of it with the molo to stretch it a bit further."

Nathan looked around at the stacks of molo. "It looks like you've already prepped most of it. That was pretty fast."

"Actually, about half of the original shipment was ruined during the battle in the hangar bay. I guess a few of your men took cover behind one of the stacks, and it got pretty cooked by energy weapons fire."

Nathan grimaced. "So how long will what we have last us?"

"Including the extra people you took on board today, maybe two weeks. But I understand you have some emergency rations that you pulled from the escape pods."

"Yeah, but don't get your hopes up," Nathan told him, remembering the noodle and mystery meat that he and Vladimir had been forced to eat just before their trip to Haven. "Most of that stuff is barely edible." Nathan looked around the room. "Where are the fly boys?"

"Your new shuttle crew? They're down in the hangar bay, going over the shuttles to check for damage. I don't think they were comfortable rubbing elbows with the workers."

"Yeah, I can understand that," Nathan said. "I think I'll go check on them," he added as he turned to walk away. "We're going to have another strategy meeting in about an hour or so," he called back to him.

"I'll be there, Captain."

As he headed out the door, one of the female workers stopped him and offered a sample of a type of prepared molo that he had not seen before. They were small, round balls, brownish in color, and covered with a finely ground cracker or cookie of some sort.

"Would you like to try some, Captain?" the woman asked, holding out the plate in offering.

"Sure." Nathan picked up one of the small brown balls and popped it into his mouth. It was still warm, having recently come out of the oven. The outside was firm, almost crispy, with a slightly sweet taste. As he bit down, the outer crust broke open and the silky, creamy center spilled into his mouth. "Oh, wow! That's amazing," Nathan exclaimed. The woman beamed at his praise. "This is made with molo?" he asked as he grabbed a few more to take with him.

"Indeed it is," she assured him, pleased that he enjoyed them.

"Thank you. Be sure to give one to that guy over there," Nathan told her, pointing to the technician who was dying to get away from the putrid smell emanating from the galley. Nathan popped another one into his mouth as he left the mess hall, his eyes rolling at the wonderful taste.

* * *

"What were you planning to do," Josh asked, "stay on Haven forever? Maybe marry some dirt farmer's daughter and pop out a bunch of dirt babies?" Josh had to laugh, at least to himself. Loki had always been so starry-eyed every time an even moderately attractive woman smiled at him. He could easily see his friend surrounded by a wife and a bunch of grimy, screaming little kids.

"Don't be such a smart-ass, Josh," Loki snapped, as he continued entering commands into the shuttle's diagnostics system. "You know I have no intention of staying on Haven for any longer than I have to. I'm just not so sure that *this* ship is the best way off Haven. I mean, have you taken a close look at her? Sure, she's new and all, but the tech on her seems kind of outdated, even by Haven standards."

"Are you kidding me? I've never heard of anyone with a *jump drive*, or anything remotely like it. Besides, it's not so much the ship that interests me as where it's from."

Loki shook his head. "You've always been the

dreamer."

"Come on," Josh exclaimed. "You can't tell me you're not at least a little bit curious. I mean, these people came from *Earth*. That's where we're all supposed to be from. Surely you find that at least a little bit exciting."

"Just maybe next time you could *ask* before you volunteer us for something."

"What's the matter? Don't you trust me?"

"No, I don't." The diagnostics computer made an angry sounding beep at him, causing Loki to toss his data pad on the console beside him in frustration. "Damn, I can't even get the diagnostics system to work properly."

"Yeah, for low-tech projectile weapons, they sure do a lot of damage, don't they? Half the console is full of holes up here." Josh turned to Loki from his seat at the front of the shuttle. "I say we scrap her. The electronics and flight controls are just too shot up to be repaired, especially since we don't really have any spare parts."

"But the engines and the power plant are fine," Loki argued, "as are most of the actual flight systems."

"Then we can use them for spare parts for the other shuttle, if needed. But this one's not worth the effort."

"Yeah, you're probably right," Loki confessed, running his hands over his face and through his hair. It had been a long two days of nonstop work with nothing more than intermittent meal breaks. And the exhaustion was really starting to get to him.

"Right about what?" Nathan asked as he walked up the damaged shuttle's aft boarding ramp.

"That this crate should be scrapped for parts,"

Josh announced.

"Really? It didn't look too bad from the outside."

"That's because all the damage is in here," Loki added.

"Yeah, your guys shot up the inside pretty good. If it wasn't for their armor, I doubt any of those troops would've made it out alive."

"So it can't be fixed?"

"Maybe, if we were back on Haven and could pick up some parts. But aside from that rock, I doubt you'll find parts for this old bucket elsewhere."

Nathan felt a little embarrassed, as *'this old bucket'* had a lot of systems that looked like they were far more advanced than anything the Aurora had on board. "So I take it she's not *'state-of-the-art'* around these parts."

"Nothing on Haven is *state-of-the-art*, Captain," Loki explained.

"Yeah," Josh added with a grin. "Haven is pretty much where old spaceships go to die."

"I don't know," Nathan disagreed. "Your harvester seemed to perform quite well."

"That's because Marcus took care of her. He's really a much better mechanic than he lets on."

Nathan nodded, acknowledging Josh's claims. "How about the other shuttle?"

"Oh, she's fine," Loki promised. "She was pretty much buttoned up when the fight broke out. So other than a few nicks and scorch marks to her hull, she's ready to go."

"Well, at least there's that. Speaking of Marcus, where is he? I thought he'd be here with you."

"He's pulling the computer core and a few other usable odds and ends outta the harvester. He says the reactor is not looking good. He's afraid it'll get unstable and he wants to jettison the whole mess and be rid of her."

"Too bad," Nathan said. "I'm sure my chief engineer would like to get a look at some of its systems. You sure there's no way to make it safe to store? I mean, we've got lots of room."

"Naw, I suspect Marcus is right. Last thing you want is a core breach in the middle of your hangar bay," Loki told him.

"I suppose you're right," Nathan said. "And Tug's fighter? How's it?"

"You'd have to ask Tug about that," Loki told him. "I expect he wouldn't want anyone coming near it. Least I wouldn't if it were mine."

"What do you think of her?" Nathan asked. He had no knowledge of local spacecraft, and thus had no idea how well Tug's fighter would match up against others in the area.

"She's an older model, to be sure. But she's a beauty, that one," Josh said.

"Yeah, they don't make them like that anymore," Loki agreed.

"How do you mean?"

Josh may have been the natural-born pilot, but Loki knew the ins and outs of spacecraft, having studied them since he first learned to read. No one knew more about spacecraft than Loki. "The newer ones are smaller and more maneuverable, but they don't have the range, the speed, or the punch. They're harder to hit, for sure, but you usually only need a single hit to kill them. And the newer ones don't have FTL either. These were the last ones built for deep space patrol and intercept. The newer ones all have to operate from carrier ships."

"Captain," Josh began, "I was meaning to ask

you something. Why is it you've got so much room in this bay but no ships? It was obviously built for flight ops, but the only things in here besides our shuttles are a bunch of crates and junk."

Nathan took a seat on the bench running along the starboard side of the shuttle. "Well, that's kind of a long story. But the short version is we were just out on a test cruise, and things went wrong. Way wrong, in fact. We didn't have any of our flight wing on board at the time, as we were just supposed to be testing the jump drive. In fact, this ship isn't even completely finished yet. That's what all the crates are—more equipment that has yet to be installed."

"A thousand light-year test cruise?" Josh wondered aloud. "If that's your idea of a test cruise, where the hell did you plan on going on a real cruise, another galaxy?"

"Actually, we weren't planning on going much more than about thirty or forty light years."

"Well I'd say you over shot your mark just a wee bit there, Captain," Josh said.

"Yeah, just a bit," Nathan agreed with a smile. Nathan knew where the conversation was headed. They had to be curious about the ship, and the Earth in general, just as Tug had been the night before. But Nathan still had a lot to do before he could call it a day, and that was a conversation he didn't have time to get into right now. "Listen, I've got another guest I need to talk to. You guys get checked in to your quarters and get some chow and a good night's rest. I have a feeling you'll be doing some more flying soon enough."

* * *

Jalea stared through the one-way window at the Ta'Akar assault trooper as he sat in a metal chair, at a metal table, in the small, plain interrogation room. He had been stripped of his body armor and was dressed only in a plain jumpsuit from the Aurora's laundry. He wore a pair of thick, wide, metal bracelets that were locked around his wrists but he was free to move about the small room as he desired.

Jalea's gaze contained a seething hatred for the man before her, for all he stood for, and for the many atrocities he had probably committed and still had yet to commit—all no doubt in the name of Caius the Great, the leader of the Ta'Akar. Jalea despised that name almost as much as the man himself, for he was the one she held responsible for the deaths of her mother, her father, and her husband. He may not have done the deeds himself, but his legions had, and in his name—which as far as she was concerned made him just as responsible for their deaths as if he had pulled the trigger.

She continued to stare, her breath coming slow and regular, her chest rhythmically rising and falling. Her eyes only blinked once per minute, so intense was her gaze. The subject of her relentless attention was no more than a boy in her eyes, barely the age of adulthood. But he bore the ceremonial markings of a Ta'Akar warrior, complete with the serpent's tail that encircled his neck before disappearing down his back. He was trained, this one. Not just another indentured grunt, forced to serve or die. Somewhere along the line, this man had chosen to swear a blood oath to his leader. This one did not fight only as a means to survive. Men with such simple motivations were easy to kill, as they were more often than not unwilling to fully commit to the battle. Such men fought for glory, for their own as much as their leaders, which meant that they were not afraid to die in battle. In fact, they welcomed it.

Her rage was broken by the arrival of others, as Nathan and Jessica entered the observation room.

"Jalea, thank you for meeting us," Nathan said. "I hope you don't mind, but I thought we might need a translator."

"Of course," she said, her chin dipping slightly. "However, this one is Ybaran. And although young, he is old enough to have learned Angla in his youth."

"Ybaran?" Jessica asked.

"A small system just outside of the Pentaurus cluster. It was conquered just recently by the Ta'Akar—maybe ten years ago. Before then, all children were taught Angla, just as I was. It was only after the Ta'Akar came and enforced the Doctrine of Origins that the use of Angla was discontinued on Ybara."

"Then he can understand us?" Jessica asked.

"Most likely, yes, although he will not admit to such. To do so would be admitting doubt in his own faith."

"I'm not following," Nathan admitted.

"Ybarans, like those of any other Ta'Akar-controlled world, are required to serve in the legions. The best and most devoted of them join the *Ghatazhak*—a specially trained group of elite warriors. They have been brain washed into believing that Caius is a God, and that all humanity comes from Takara, not Earth. They are fiercely loyal to Caius. Admitting that he understands Angla would be like denouncing his belief in the Doctrine of Origins, which would disqualify him from service in the Ghatazhak, bringing him great dishonor."

"How do you think we should handle this?"

"He will not respond to questions. He might give you some simple answers meant to placate you and to feed his feeling of superiority. But he will offer no information of substance. To obtain such information will require more direct persuasion."

Nathan had a pretty good idea of what she meant by that. He wasn't sure he was ready to go to that extent just yet. After all, being from Earth, they really had no quarrel with the Ta'Akar. Whatever skirmishes they had been involved in thus far could all be attributed to a galactic misunderstanding, stemming from being in the wrong place at the wrong time.

"Let's just start with conversation, shall we?" Nathan turned to Jessica and nodded. Jessica moved to the door and pressed the intercom button.

"Hands on the table!" she ordered through the wall-mounted intercom. The prisoner looked up, indicating that he heard her words, but made no movement indicating compliance.

"I said, hands on the table!"

Jalea leaned over to the intercom and shouted something into the intercom in her language— presumably the same thing that Jessica had just said. Reluctantly, the prisoner put both of his hands on the table in front of him.

Jessica turned a small dial on the control panel and flipped a switch. The prisoner felt his hands suddenly being held tightly against the table, as powerful magnets built into the tabletop secured his metal-clad wrists against its now magnetized service, thus rendering his hands immobile.

"All clear, Captain," Jessica assured him.

Nathan unlocked the door and entered the room with Jalea and Jessica close behind, closing the door as she entered.

The prisoner's eyes narrowed with hatred at the sight of Jalea. "Karuzari," he seethed, as if describing something quite vile. A string of unintelligible words followed, to which Jalea responded in kind, although far more calmly.

"What did he say?" Nathan asked.

"He described a quite distasteful sexual act he was going to perform on me before killing me."

"What did you say?"

"I told him he would require a bigger weapon."

Nathan smiled. Again, it didn't seem to matter where you were in the galaxy; people were people just the same. "Feel free to translate at will."

"Why did you attack this ship?" Nathan began. Jalea immediately translated his question. The prisoner answered without hesitation.

"The Ta'Akar kill the Karuzari. You are with them, so we kill you," Jalea translated, offering nowhere near the tone and inflection that had been used by the prisoner.

"Guilt by association," Nathan muttered.

The prisoner continued his rant, each sentence becoming more enraged than the previous one.

"Because of your actions, you are doomed. You cannot help them," Jalea continued to translate. "Soon the Karuzari scum will be exterminated, as will all who dare to help them."

"I wouldn't count on that just yet," Jessica spouted off, unable to control herself.

Nathan, standing beside Jalea with his arms crossed, glanced at Jessica, one eyebrow shooting up in disapproval as he held up one hand, motioning her to control herself. "Easy, killer." Nathan turned his gaze back to Jalea. "What if we told him where we're from?" he suggested as he turned to his left and took a few casual steps forward, as if deep in contemplation. The steps took him just behind the prisoner's periphery, where he could no longer see Nathan without taking his eyes off Jalea. Nathan turned slowly back to face Jalea. "What if we went ahead and admitted we're from Earth?"

The prisoner's eyes darted to his right, to look briefly at Nathan, then back again at Jalea to watch her response. The prisoner's eyes had gotten a bit wider. *Just as I suspected,* Nathan thought. *You've heard of Earth as well.*

"But, Captain," Jessica protested, "You..."

Nathan held one hand up again, gesturing for Jessica to stop talking. He locked eyes with Jalea, winked, and said, "What harm could it do?"

"Nathan..." Jalea began to protest, purposefully using his first name. The prisoner's eyes became even wider.

"Go ahead," Nathan urged.

Jessica had been watching Nathan's eyes during the exchange and witnessed the wink. She didn't know what he was up to, but it was obvious that he had a plan. She only wished he had let her in on it before hand.

Jalea sighed. "As you wish, sir." Jalea turned to the prisoner and began speaking in low, calm, even, melodic tones. It was as if she were reciting a passage from a book, a poem, or even a psalm. She circled the prisoner, from his right side, around behind him, and to his left, talking softly as she did so. The prisoner appeared disconcerted, growing ever more so with each lyrical phrase that rolled off

Jalea's tongue.

Despite his inability to understand the Ta'Akar language, Nathan had a feeling that what Jalea was saying to the prisoner was familiar—to both her and the prisoner—as his eyes continued to widen with a mixture of doubt and fear. More than once, Nathan heard references to '*Earth*' and each time it seemed to make the prisoner slightly more uncomfortable. Finally, her utterances came to an end with a slight pause, and then the word '*Na-Tan.*'

The prisoner objected, calmly at first, but soon his objections grew more pronounced. Jalea continued to preach to him, repeating the same phrases over and over. As his objections grew louder, so did Jalea's. Within moments, they were shouting at one another.

Suddenly, Jalea's preaching's broke into Angla, still at full volume. "The *Legend* of Origins is no longer a legend! And soon *all* the people of Ta'Akar shall know the truth! That your king is a *liar*! That we are *all* from Earth!"

"No!" the prisoner protested yet again. Only this time it was also in Angla, and with tears streaming down his cheeks.

"This ship *is* the ship of legend! These people *are* the warriors of God! And this man *is* Na-Tan!"

"No!" the prisoner cried out, his words rising to the level of shouts, spit flying from his lips as he screamed. "It is not true! Caius is a God!"

Jalea's voice raised with the prisoner's, matching not only his volume but also his level of emotion. "Caius is only a fool *pretending* to be a God!"

"No! No! No!" the prisoner repeated at the top of his lungs. "Soon our new reactors will be available and our ships will be invincible! There will be no stopping the mighty Ta'Akar legions as we spread across the galaxy! Caius the Great shall rule supreme over all the stars in the sky!"

Suddenly, the soldier's voice changed, his tone and volume dropping. His conviction had returned. He had convinced himself once again that his beliefs were all that mattered and that his cause was just. His voice became more sinister, more lascivious, as his eyes wandered up and down first Jalea's and then Jessica's bodies. His words became guttural, his tongue lashing out salaciously between them, over and over again, until finally he stood abruptly, screaming out another vile string of words at full volume.

Jalea lunged at him, her right fist driving hard into his throat, knocking him backwards. The force of the blow drove him back so hard, his magnetically locked wrist restraints pulled the metal table they were attached to back and on top of him. Jalea nimbly dodged the falling table, knocking Nathan out of her way as she circled around the fallen table and came down with another blow to the prisoner's face. Surprisingly, despite repeated full-force blows to his face, the crazed man continued to spew lewd remarks at her at the top of his lungs, sprays of his own blood added to the spittle that flew from his mouth as he screamed. Jalea continued to strike him again and again, screaming out in rage with each blow.

Jessica jumped across the fallen table and grabbed Jalea by her hair, yanking her backwards and away from the prisoner. "Get her outta here!" she yelled at Nathan, who was grabbing at Jalea from behind to keep her from getting back on her feet to attack again.

The prisoner continued to scream, his curses now aimed at Jessica. She turned and looked down at him. "Fuck you," she said as she planted her boot in his face, knocking him out cold. She turned and watched as Nathan dragged the now crying and screaming Jalea out the door. Satisfied that the situation was under control, she squatted down next to the unconscious prisoner's head and checked his neck for a pulse. "Yeah, you're still alive." She reached up and tapped her comm-set earpiece once to activate it. "Medical emergency in the brig. Man down."

"What the fuck was that all about?!" Jessica asked as she stepped into the observation room.

"I don't know!" Nathan admitted. He too was stunned by what had happened. "I thought that if he spoke Angla, we could trick him..."

"And who the hell is Na-Tan?!" Jessica interrupted. She looked at Jalea, who was pacing back and forth across the opposite end of the room, rage still blazing in her eyes. "I mean, *Warriors of God?*" Jessica asked. "What the fuck?!" Getting nothing more than an angry glance from Jalea, Jessica turned back to Nathan. "I don't suppose you have any idea what she was doing."

"I think she was trying to get him to doubt his beliefs," Nathan tried to explain.

"How? By quoting scripture?"

"It's what she said earlier, that the guy was Ybaran, that they all learned Angla when they were young. Angla was always taught by some kind of priests of the order."

"What order?"

"I don't know, like some kind of religion or something. It's all based on the belief that they all originally came from Earth, and that the Earth befell a great evil. They believe that someday warriors from Earth will come and free them from their own evil."

"Oh great!" Jessica exclaimed, throwing up her hands. "So what, now we're the horsemen of the apocalypse?"

Suddenly, the hatch from the corridor swung open and two crewmen stepped in, followed by Doctor Chen.

"He's in there," Jessica said, stepping aside and pointing into the interrogation room.

The three of them rushed past them, Doctor Chen glancing at Nathan as she passed.

"It is all my fault," Jalea admitted, having finally calmed down enough to speak rationally.

"You're damned right it is," Jessica told her.

"I was only trying to..."

"I don't give a shit what you were trying to do," Jessica interrupted. She was about to lose her temper as well, and at the moment, if she did so, it would be at Jalea. "You know what; you'd better just go," she added, pointing to the exit.

Jalea looked confused. She looked to Nathan for support but received only his incredulous stare.

"Now!" Jessica shouted. "Before I smack you around the same way you did him!"

For a moment, Jalea looked ashamed. But it was only for a moment, as she regained her usual indignant composure and walked calmly out of the room.

"Jess, It's my fault..."

"Of course it's your fault," she said, cutting him off. "But more importantly, it's your fuckin' responsibility, Nathan."

"I know."

"No, you don't. You don't play the religion card so casually, or you might just start a holy war! And those kinds of things can spin rapidly out of control."

Nathan stared at the floor for a moment, trying to process all that had happened in the last few minutes. Finally, he spoke. "You're right; I don't know. Hell, Jess, I don't know anything," he admitted.

"Then next time, leave the interrogations to someone who has actually been trained to interrogate."

Nathan looked at her.

"Yeah, that's right. Me." Jessica shook her head as she tapped in her security code to open the weapons locker and pulled her side arm out, placing it into the holster on her gun belt.

"You're right," he said again, as he stepped back out of the way. Two crewmen carried the unconscious prisoner on a stretcher, moving past Nathan on their way through the small observation room.

Doctor Chen followed them out, stopping momentarily in front of Nathan. "You know, it's not like I don't already have enough patients to care for, sir."

Before Nathan could say anything, the young doctor departed. Jessica followed them out, also pausing in front of Nathan. "Jalea's a loose cannon," she said, her eyes still looking at the exit. She turned her head and added, "You know that." Nathan's head nodded ever so slightly in reluctant agreement as Jessica turned her head back toward the door, exited, and followed the doctor and her team down the corridor.

Nathan turned and looked back through the

open door into the interrogation room. The table was still on its side, the chair knocked across the room. There was blood splattered on the floor, as well as at least two bloody boot prints, presumably made by Jessica as she walked out of the room.

Nathan let out a long sigh. At that moment, he didn't think being captain was all it was cracked up to be.

The prisoner was still unconscious and was being carried on a stretcher by two crewmen. A bio-monitoring harness was attached to his torso and fingers and was sending a constant stream of telemetry to a handheld wireless receiver carried by Doctor Chen, who studied it intermittently.

"What happened to him?" Doctor Chen asked as they continued down the corridor.

"He became violent," Jessica answered calmly. She knew it was a lie, but the less everyone knew about what really happened in the brig, the better off they would all be. Jalea had crossed a line. It wasn't one that Jessica herself wouldn't have crossed, if necessary. But it wasn't Jalea's place to do so, nor was it Nathan's, as far as she was concerned. The man was barely able to pull off being captain. Interrogation was definitely something best left to those properly trained. *Maybe next time, Nathan will be more cooperative,* she thought.

"I see," Doctor Chen answered, noticing the mag-cuffs still on the prisoner's wrists. "Wasn't he restrained?"

"Apparently not as well as we thought."

"I'm afraid I need more details if I'm going to know what kind of injuries to look for..."

"It'd be best if you left it alone, Doc," Jessica warned, cutting her off.

"Can you at least tell me where and with what he was struck?"

Jessica rolled her eyes and sighed. "Several blows to the face, and at least one to the neck. In the process he fell backwards and pulled the metal table down on top of him, onto his chest, I think." Jessica knew that she was telling her a bit too much, but she needed this guy to survive so that *she* could interrogate him properly. She knew the head game Jalea and the captain had been trying to play on him. It had even appeared to be working to some extent. And if used correctly, she might be able to parlay it into some useful intel.

"Is that all?" the doctor prodded. "His nose is badly broken."

"There may have been a boot to the face," Jessica admitted sheepishly. She was starting to think she might have gone a little too far with that one, and she did feel just a bit guilty. "Is he going to survive?"

"His vitals are stable for now. I'm mostly worried about possible brain and chest trauma," she explained as they entered the medical section.

"Jess!" Enrique called out from down the corridor. He and another crewman, both carrying side arms and automatic close-quarters weapons came trotting down the corridor. "What's going on?"

"Had to rough up a prisoner," she joked, hiding the guilt that had hit her a moment earlier. "Go and keep an eye on him," she instructed the crewman.

"Yes, sir," the crewman answered as he followed the doctor into the treatment area.

"Did you kick his ass?" Enrique said, a grin coming across his face. He had been in a firefight with this guy and his cohorts a few hours ago. Seeing the sole surviving prisoner injured and suffering didn't bother him one bit.

"It wasn't me. Except for the boot to his nose in the end." Enrique gave her a quizzical look. "Jalea snapped and started pounding on him."

"Really?" Enrique was more than a bit surprised.

"Yeah. She was trying to mess with his head. I guess she got to him, because next thing I knew he was screaming something ugly at her and she flat-knuckled him to the throat and then took him down and started pounding away on his face."

"Damn!"

"Scary part is, it didn't even phase the guy. He just kept screaming at her. It was my boot that finally shut him up."

"Screw him," Enrique declared. "You should have kicked him harder."

Jessica's mind was already several steps ahead. "You get the comm-set tracking running yet?"

"They're setting it up now. It'll be ready in a few hours. It'll notify whoever has the duty the moment one of our *guests* goes someplace they don't belong."

"Good. These people are making me nervous." Jessica tapped her comm-set earpiece to activate the device. "Nash to Yosef."

"*Yosef, go ahead.*"

"Do me a favor and use Jalea's comm-set signal to figure out where she is at the moment."

"*Stand by.*"

Jessica noticed the metal chains and cuffs in Enrique's hand. "Make sure that guy is well restrained. And don't let the doc tell you otherwise."

"You got it."

"And I want someone watching him at all times

until his ass is back in the brig."

"*Jessica?*" Ensign Yosef's voice called over Jessica's comm-set.

"Go ahead."

"*Jalea is in her quarters.*"

"Copy that. Thanks." Jessica tapped her comm-set again to turn it off and started down the corridor.

"Where you going?" Enrique asked.

"I'm gonna have a heart-to-heart with the rebel princess," she told him as she walked away.

* * *

Jessica strode confidently down the corridor towards Jalea's quarters. Her cabin was not far away, since everything forward of the primary bulkheads was still closed off due to the hull breach that had occurred when they had rammed the Ta'Akar ship a week ago. That had given Jessica little time to think about what she was going to say to Jalea when she confronted her.

Arriving at her door, Jessica pressed the buzzer along the side of the doorway. A moment later, Jessica heard the sound of the metal latch releasing right before the door slid open to reveal Jalea. Her face still appeared angry, and the prisoner's blood splatter still decorated both her top and her right hand.

"We need to talk," Jessica ordered as she stepped into the cabin, forcing Jalea to step aside.

Jalea turned to keep herself facing Jessica, not wanting to turn her back to her. "I don't believe we have anything to talk about."

"Oh, I beg to differ," Jessica said, a slight chuckle following her words. Jessica stepped deeper into the cabin. It was a small, standard cabin meant to accommodate two members of the crew. Jessica herself had lived in one until only a few days ago, when she moved into a larger single occupancy cabin on the command deck. She had done so not because she wanted to, but because her new duties required her to be as close to the command section as possible, even when she was off duty.

"Very well," Jalea said, realizing that Jessica was not offering her a choice. "What would you like to talk about?"

Jessica smiled at Jalea's attitude and at how Jalea not only kept herself between Jessica and the exit, but had also chosen not to close the door. This lady was well trained. And the more dealings Jessica had with her, the more she was sure of it. The question was, *trained by who?* "What the fuck happened back there?"

"Nothing," Jalea lied. "I simply lost control. I apologize."

Jessica could tell in an instant that the apology was fake and was only meant to hasten an end to the confrontation. "That's crap and you know it. You've been cool as a cucumber since the moment you stepped on board. Hell, you didn't even shed a tear when your brothers in arms, one by one, blew themselves up to save us. And all of a sudden I'm supposed to believe that you just lost it?" she said, throwing up her arms. Jessica folded her arms across her chest as she recalled the events that had transpired in the brig only minutes ago. "You were pushing him, fucking with his mind, weren't you? You and the captain. Yeah, I saw the little wink he gave you. So what was it? What did you say to him?"

Jalea turned to her left and moved a few steps

away from Jessica while still maintaining a clear shot to the exit should she need a quick retreat. "I was trying to prove to him that the Doctrine of Origins was false," she said with indignation, "that Caius is not a God, and that his cause is not just."

"And the part about us being from Earth? And about Na-Tan?"

"It is just a variation of the Legend of Origins. One followed by many of the more spiritually inclined. Ybarans are such people, so I expected he would be familiar with the details of this particular variation of the legend."

"Well I'm not familiar with the details. Perhaps you'd care to enlighten me?" Jessica's tone demonstrated that it was more of a command than a request.

"If you insist," Jalea answered reluctantly. "Many of the societies in this part of the galaxy have been oppressed for countless generations. Caius himself has been in power for more than one hundred years. During this time he has also caused much pain and suffering and has oppressed billions. Believing in miracles, believing that salvation from such atrocities and oppression will someday come to be, helps keep hope alive. For many in the Pentaurus cluster, hope is all they have."

"And what about this Na-Tan?" Jessica prodded.

"One of the versions talks of one that will save them from evil. This one is called Na-Tan. He is said to come from a distant star called Sol, from the birthplace of humanity. Earth."

"Na-Tan," Jessica mumbled as everything fell into place. "You were trying to convince that poor, brain-washed schmuck that Nathan was Na-Tan, come to save the people from the evil Caius." Jessica shook her head. "And it almost worked, too, didn't it?"

"Almost," Jalea admitted.

"But it didn't. And you know why it didn't? Because it was stupid. You don't win somebody over by telling them everything they believe is wrong. All that does is solidify their beliefs and make them hate you all the more. And when done to groups, it galvanizes them."

Jalea's demeanor changed, softening somewhat, as her tone became less defensive and her posture more open and inviting. Jessica may not have been born with Nathan's natural ability to read body language, but she had been taught the skill in spec-ops training.

"My intent was only to make him question his beliefs," Jalea explained apologetically, "not to convince him to side with us. Making one question their beliefs puts a crack in one's armor. Over time, that crack widens and the armor weakens."

Jessica didn't much feel like listening to Jalea preach. And she had absolutely no patience to stand by while she tried to play her in the same way that she tried to play the captain. "Yeah, I don't really give a shit about all that. You see, your methods of persuasion don't work on me the way they might work on Nathan. So save it, princess."

Jalea tried her best to look confused and shocked. "I'm sorry. What is it you'd like me to do, then?"

"What I'd like you to do is to shut the hell up."

"Excuse me?" Jalea asked, continuing her charade.

"If someone asks you a question, you answer them. If someone tells you to go somewhere and do something, you go there and do it. Otherwise, you shut up. You don't make tactical decisions on your own. And you don't take action on your own. And if you do otherwise, at best you end up in the brig right alongside our Ghatazhak friend."

Jalea did not care for Jessica's threats and immediately changed both her posture and her tone to communicate her dislike back to Jessica. "And at worst?" she asked, as if challenging her.

Jessica's arms dropped to her sides, her gaze became cold, and her eyes became slits. "I end you."

"End me?" Jalea asked, feigning ignorance of the term.

"Yeah, end you. You know, put a bullet in your brain. Punch your ticket. Put your lights out. Plant you six feet under. No wait, those are all Earth terms, so you wouldn't understand them, would you?"

Jalea looked down for a moment. "No, I'm afraid..." When her eyes came back up, she found the business end of Jessica's sidearm only centimeters from the bridge of her nose, immediately noticing that Jessica had just finished thumbing off the safety. She froze in her tracks, not moving a muscle. Her first instinct would normally be to jerk to one side while smacking the weapon in the opposite direction. But there was coldness in the eyes of the holder of the weapon that told her caution was the more prudent choice of action.

"Do you understand this?" Jessica asked coldly.

"Yes, quite clearly, in fact."

"Good. Cuz the next time I catch you putting this ship or any member of this crew at risk, I will kill you."

Jalea said nothing in response, only staring over the top of the weapon into Jessica's eyes. She doubted she could disarm her without injury. And even if she could, she would have to kill her—and that would be difficult to explain.

After what seemed like an eternity, Jessica finally lowered her sidearm and replaced it into her holster in one smooth and quick motion, thumbing the safety back on as she did so. A second later it was back in its holster with the safety strap snapped back over it.

"We're done here," Jessica stated as she reached up and lightly double tapped the side of Jalea's cheek with her open hand. "There's another briefing in thirty minutes, princess," she added on her way out. "Don't be late."

Jalea stood still for several minutes after Jessica left. She heard the young woman's every foot step as she walked down the corridor away from her cabin. It had taken every ounce of self-control to keep from exploding and screaming out in sheer anger and frustration at the arrogance of the security officer. The woman had probably fought in less than a handful of battles—had witnessed only a few deaths of others. She had not suffered. She had not lost or felt the loss of loved ones. She had not witnessed the execution of hundreds or thousands of innocent lives. She had not walked the surface of planets that had been glassed from orbit by men in fancy uniforms sipping tea and eating pastries. And she would not prevent her from achieving retribution for the countless lives lost—especially for three of them.

CHAPTER THREE

"You're going to have to tell me eventually," Cameron insisted. "I am your XO, remember?"

"I promise, I'll fill you in later," Nathan told her as they entered the command briefing room. Nathan stopped at the doorway, letting Cameron, Jessica, and Abby enter first, Jessica casting a knowing glance at him as she passed.

Tug and Jalea were already sitting on one side of the conference table. Tug had his usual confident yet approachable expression. Jalea's expression, although as nondescript as usual, hinted at something more. Nathan attributed it to the events in the brig an hour ago.

"Thank you all for coming," he stated as they made their way around the table. Nathan took his usual place at the head of the table, with Cameron, Jessica, and Abby on his right, Tug and Jalea on his left. Nathan first addressed Tug. "I understand that you and Doctor Sorenson managed to translate your star charts into English and upload them into our navigation system."

"In a manner of speaking," Tug said.

"It was a bit complicated at first," Abby began. "You see, we use a coordinate system with Sol as a zero reference point. The Ta'Akar use their own star as the reference point for their star charts. But most other worlds outside of the Pentaurus cluster use a system that utilizes the galactic center as a reference point."

"It does sound complicated," Nathan admitted.

"It might be better to use the most universal of the three," Cameron added, "which would be the galactic-centered version."

"We came to the same conclusion. We got a copy of the galactic charts from the shuttle. But it appears that each chart has at least some information on them the other charts are missing. So we are attempting to use conversion algorithms that will merge the data from all three charts into one that is based on the galactic-centered version."

"Doesn't that mean we'll have to relearn our own navigation points?" Cameron asked, not looking forward to the task.

"Well, since we're new to this region of space, it shouldn't be that difficult. Besides, it will be more accurate."

"How so?" Nathan asked. Although he was a trained navigator, it had never been his strongest skill.

"Coordinate systems that use a moving object as a reference point must constantly be recalculated to accommodate the reference point's movement through space, as it travels out from the galactic center."

"Stellar drift?"

"Yes. The galactic center does not move, at least not within its own domain, so it provides a relatively *fixed* point in space from which to calculate the positions of all objects."

"How long will this take?" Nathan wondered.

"Days, perhaps weeks. Much of our core is still inoperable."

"We can't wait that long."

"Of course not. That's why we tested the idea by converting only the Pentaurus cluster for now. We now have a galactic-centered star chart for the cluster that is loaded into our navigation system. And thanks to the information contained in the charts from Mister Tugwell's ship, we also have planetary movements and even common shipping and patrol routes. We can navigate the cluster at will."

"That's great," Nathan exclaimed. He had not liked relying on Jalea's advice when deciding where to go.

"I am also working on providing details of each system and the worlds within them," Tug added, "so that you have a basic understanding of the socioeconomic and political structures that you might encounter."

"That will also be very useful," Nathan said.

"It was at the request of your security chief," Tug said, tipping his head toward Jessica in acknowledgment.

"Once the conversions are completed, how big an area will it cover?" Nathan asked Abby.

"An area of approximately one hundred light years, Captain. With the Pentaurus cluster roughly at the center."

"Not quite enough to link up with any of our own navigational charts, though," Nathan thought aloud, "not even the ones found in the Data Ark."

"No," she admitted. "But we are hoping that once the conversion is complete, we might find at least a few stars common on the fringe of both sets, ours and the galactic-centered charts, that will provide us a navigable route home."

"Then there is hope."

"Yes. I believe there is."

Nathan leaned forward in his chair, leaning on the table and clasping his hands together. "So, then. Any ideas where we should go next?"

"If I may," Cameron asked. Sensing no objections, she pulled out a small drawer built into the table to access controls for the tabletop holographic display system. The room darkened slightly as a three-dimensional holographic representation of the entire Pentaurus cluster, as well as several of the other nearby systems, appeared floating in the air above the table. "Forgive the graphics, as there wasn't much time to program a proper display. We just used existing elements to represent the objects for now. But at least it gives us a better understanding of the general layout of this region of space."

"This is the Pentaurus cluster," she continued, waving her right hand in a circle around the display. "There are five stars in the cluster." Cameron reached up and pointed at a five centimeter, glowing yellow orb floating in the middle of the display. "This is Takara—a G-type star, about three times the size of Sol. Its planetary system is somewhat similar to our own, with rocky inner planets and a few gas giants farther out. It does, however, have eighteen planets. Seven of them are rocky inner worlds, three of which are hospitable. The rest are a collection of mostly gas giants, as well as a few frozen rocky worlds farther out. Including all the various moons, there are over three hundred objects in the system."

"Many of the moons orbiting the gas giants are reformed worlds," Tug added. "I believe at last count there were a total of fifteen bodies in the system that can sustain human life."

"Impressive," Nathan admitted.

"Anyway, there are two binary systems nearby. Melbourne, about two light years away, and Taroa about three. Taroa is where we originally entered the cluster and had our first run-in with the Ta'Akar. Taroa's secondary component, Korak, is the red dwarf with the heavy asteroid belt that we hid in just after that."

"Yes, I remember it fondly," Nathan commented.

"Taroa has eleven planets, two of which are inhabited, along with three more reformed moons that are also inhabited. It was on one of those moons that the rebel's last base was located."

"It also was a reformed world. It was completed more than three years ago and was fully developed."

Nathan noticed the forlorn look on Tug's face, as well as his use of the past tense. "Was?"

"There were more than three million people living on that small moon. When they refused to reveal our location, the Ta'Akar simply obliterated them from orbit, as a warning to any others that might support us."

"They glassed the planet?" Jessica asked, shocked.

Tug looked at her for a moment, as he considered the terminology she had used. "Yes, I guess that is as good a term as any. There is undoubtedly little left on the surface."

After waiting for what seemed like a polite interval, Cameron continued. "Over here," she said, pointing to another pair of yellow balls orbiting around one another, "we have another binary system called Mellabore. It's similar in size and type to the Alpha Centauri system near Sol: two G-type stars, the B component smaller than its primary. The primary is called Savoy, and the secondary is called Darvano. Between the two of them, there are about eight inhabited planets and moons."

"Where are we now?" Nathan asked, looking over the hovering holographic display.

Cameron reached down and pressed a button on the slide-out control drawer, causing the holographic display to zoom out. As it did so, several more stars appeared about the fringe of the display. "We're about here." Cameron pressed another button and a small blue triangle appeared next to an amber colored star. "Just outside of the Haven system," she explained, as she pointed at the amber star. "Just a second."

Using both hands, Cameron entered several commands into the control pad, pressing the last button as she began to speak again. "As I stated before, we jumped in here, in the Taroa system." The blue triangle that had appeared next to Haven disappeared, only to reappear a moment later, overlapping the yellow star representing Taroa. "We then jumped to Korak." She pushed another button, and the blue triangle repositioned itself overlapping the nearby red dwarf star, a dotted blue line connecting the two stars. "Then we jumped to about the same place we are now, just outside Haven." Again, the triangle moved, drawing another dotted blue line. "From there we flew into the Haven system at sub-light." A solid blue line drew itself through the air from its starting point the last few centimeters to the amber star representing Haven. "After that, we did the mini-jump, and then jumped back out to here again." Finally the blue triangle returned to its position a few centimeters away from the symbol for the Haven star.

"So technically, we're still outside of Ta'Akar space?" Nathan surmised.

"Actually," Tug explained, "the Ta'Akar never formally released any of their former worlds from their control. They simply chose to withdraw their forces and cease their governance and taxation. This is one of the reasons that I fully expect them to quickly retake these lost worlds once they have put their new power source into widespread use."

"How many worlds are we talking about?" Nathan wondered aloud, noticing that only a few had been added to the display when Cameron had zoomed out.

"This was the area controlled by the Ta'Akar at the start of the rebellion." Cameron again zoomed out, this time more than twice the distance. At least two dozen more star systems appeared.

"Whoa," Jessica said under her breath.

"These are the inhabited ones," Cameron added, pressing another button on the control pad. More than half of the newly added stars in the display suddenly changed to a brilliant lavender. "Eighteen out of the twenty-eight additional systems are inhabited."

"And many of those have multiple bodies that have been colonized."

"I had no idea this area of space was so heavily colonized," Nathan admitted.

"Yes. This area of space is blessed with a great number of bodies that are hospitable by nature, and many more that were easily reformed. It is believed to be one of the main reasons that humans originally settled here."

"Believed?" Nathan was a bit surprised. "You mean you don't know?"

"We once did, of course. But remember, Caius has been in power for over one hundred years. During this time, adherence to the Doctrine of Origins required the destruction of all heretic historical documents. As crazy as it sounds, Caius was trying to elevate himself to the level of a God by removing all evidence to the contrary."

"Kind of takes narcissism to a whole new level, doesn't he?" Jessica commented.

"Surely out of all these worlds, someone must possess the truth of how you all came to be out here."

"There are many," Jalea interrupted, speaking for the first time since the meeting had begun. "They formed an order of sorts, partially spiritual, partially historical. But they maintain documentation of the truth of our origins. This is what Tug refers to when he speaks of the Legend of Origins."

"Shouldn't it be called the Truth of Origins?" Nathan suggested.

"Perhaps," Jalea agreed. "But the Ta'Akar began using the word legend in order to support their claim that the records were no more than fabrications created to further the agenda of the Order. Actually, we had hoped that you would be able to fill in some of the holes in the legend that have been created by the efforts of the Ta'Akar over the decades."

"Well, as I explained to Tug before, civilization on Earth fell apart because of the plague. Had we not discovered the Data Ark a century ago, we wouldn't even be back in space yet, let alone a thousand light years from home."

"Did this Ark contain nothing about the mass exodus from your world?" Jalea asked.

"Only that people fled the core worlds in order to

escape the bio-digital plague. We assumed that most of that migration had been to the few fringe worlds that were just being established at the time. We surmised that some expeditions might have struck out on their own, traveling deeper out into space. But early into the plague, the Data Ark was sealed off to protect it. So details about the aftermath are vague at best. The following seven centuries were brutal for the people on Earth. It took more than two hundred years just for the population to start to increase again. There were only a few million people left alive after the plague ran its course." Nathan sighed. "So, you can see how we would have very little information that might help you. Quite frankly, we were shocked to find out that some of us had traveled out this far."

Cameron looked around the room, waiting to see if they had finished their discussion. "If we can get back on topic?" Nathan nodded sheepishly. Cameron took his cue and touched the display control pad, zooming in again to show the Pentaurus cluster and a few of the systems on its borders, including their current location just outside of Haven. "Although I still believe that departing the area posthaste would be the most prudent course of action, in line with your orders, sir, Tug and I have discussed the best location in which to conduct repairs and take on more supplies." Cameron pointed to the second binary system she had described earlier. "The Mellabore system, or more precisely, the secondary component, Darvano."

"That's all the way on the opposite side of the cluster," Nathan pointed out. "Is it even within our range?"

"Technically, yes," Abby said. "However, I would

prefer that we travel there in two shorter jumps instead of one max-range jump. We have yet to test the drive at its maximum jump range."

"Other than the thousand light year jump that got us here," Nathan reminded her. He looked at Tug. "Why Darvano?"

"Several reasons," Tug started. "First, being so far away, it is not only the last place they would look for you, but it is also the last place that will learn of your existence. Even with the comm-drone system, unless they were to dispatch a dedicated drone, it would take nearly a week for the message to propagate through the system and reach Darvano. Second, the presence of the Order is strong on this world. This usually means that there is considerable support available for our cause. Although if news of our defeat has reached Darvano, then that might no longer be the case."

"Any other reasons?"

"Yes, and perhaps the most compelling. We have a rather unique facility hiding in the Darvano system. The system has a fairly dense asteroid field. It is heavily mined, using a method whereby the larger asteroids are hollowed out until they are nothing more than an empty shell. Then the shell is sent on a slow intercept trajectory inward where it will be captured by the primary world, Corinair. Once settled into orbit, it is further dismantled into nothing."

"How does this help us?"

"It takes decades for this process to complete. Therefore there are literally dozens of hollow asteroids scattered throughout the belt, waiting to be de-orbited. And there are hundreds more that have had huge caverns carved out in preparation for an eventual mining station to be placed inside to complete the harvesting. Nearly a decade ago, we prepared one such asteroid to act as a hiding place for a ship even larger than your own. We had hoped to capture such a ship from the Ta'Akar. But that task proved beyond our means, and the effort was abandoned. The base, however, remains available. Once inside, your ship would be invisible to all scans. And as far as anyone else knew, it would be just another mining camp operating inside an asteroid."

"I'm a bit confused, Tug," Nathan stated. "If this place is such a good hiding place, why didn't Jalea tell us to go there instead of Korak, or Haven for that matter?" Nathan suspected he already knew the answer. He also suspected that the answer he was about to receive would not be the truth.

"Simple, Captain. Neither she nor Marak knew of its existence. The project had been completed by my cell, under my supervision. The other cells knew of the project, vaguely, but not of its location."

"Who else knows about this *hideout*?" Jessica asked.

"My entire cell was killed during our attempt to capture a Ta'Akar warship. I am the only one left alive who knows that this *hideout*, as you put it, is still available and is located in the Darvano system."

Nathan wasn't sure he believed Tug's explanation. While it did explain a few things, and it lined up nicely with what they already knew about the rebels, it seemed convenient.

"What about patrols?" Jessica asked. "Are there any Ta'Akar ships stationed in the system?"

"The Ta'Akar are down to only about twenty warships. But only three of them are the large capital ships. There were once four of them, until you arrived." Tug smiled respectfully.

"And the others?" Jessica asked.

"About six of them are the heavier cruisers, like the one that is probably still sitting in the Haven system. The rest are smaller patrol frigates, like the ones you encountered in the Korak system."

"How are they deployed?"

"The capital ships stay closer in. There are usually two of them in the vicinity of the Takara system, in order to protect the capital. They are normally accompanied by a few of the heavy cruisers as well as several patrol ships. The third will tend to wander amongst the other three systems, making unscheduled visits in order to maintain a visible presence. She generally drags one or two patrol ships along with her. The rest regularly patrol the borders of the cluster, occasionally sticking their noses back into territories that they once directly controlled, just to ensure they are not forgotten."

"The patrol ships don't worry me, Captain," Jessica explained. "But the heavy cruisers are a handful, even if we were at full strength. The capital ships? Forget about it. If we hadn't jumped in so close to the first one by accident, we wouldn't have gotten anywhere near it without being vaporized from a hundred thousand kilometers away."

"Yeah, and without even breaking a sweat," Nathan added, remembering the pounding they had taken during their first engagement with the Ta'Akar.

"You are quite correct," Tug said. "That is exactly why we were never able to capture any of the larger ships. Their reach and their fire rates are too great. We could never get anywhere near them."

"So you think this base, the one inside the asteroid—this will be a good place for us to hide?"

"Yes, Captain. I do. It was designed to accommodate the repair and retrofitting of spacecraft of at least your size."

Nathan looked at Cameron. "What do you think, Commander?"

"I'm not crazy about the idea of flying the Aurora into a cave," she stated emphatically. "What happens if they find us? We'd be sitting ducks inside that rock. How would we even know if anyone were out there when it came time to leave?"

"The base was equipped with external sensors to monitor the area, as well as external communications equipment."

"They could see that, couldn't they?" Cameron said. "A rock with sensors and comm towers on it has got to look suspicious."

"Unless yours is not the only rock that has such equipment," Tug pointed out with a smile. "Commander, there are at least a hundred active mining camps located inside such rocks. All of them are similarly equipped. It would look no more suspicious to the Ta'Akar than would the comm-array on your ship."

"Hiding in plain sight," Jessica commented, "one of the oldest techniques in the spy game." She looked at Nathan. "There's no better way to gather intel than to park your butt right in the middle of the enemy's backyard."

"I'm sure you're right, Jess," Nathan agreed, "but I have to side with Commander Taylor on this one. The idea of a Ta'Akar ship trolling around the belt while we're hiding inside an asteroid... well that makes me just a bit nervous."

"The Ta'Akar ships do not *patrol* the area in the sense that you mean. When they enter the system, they usually just enter orbit over the most populated world in the system, sit there for a few days, and then depart. These days, they spend more time patrolling the borders of Ta'Akar space than the interiors."

"What's the payoff?" Nathan asked. "Other than the cool hideout, what does this system have to offer us?"

"You should be able to find anything you need," Jalea told him. "Food, medicine, parts, raw materials. You can even hire additional skilled labor, if desired, to help you with your repairs. Corinair is not Haven. It is a highly advanced, fully developed, industrialized world with more than a billion inhabitants. There are even small shipyards located within the asteroid belt itself, to service the smaller ships that ply the belt."

"I see," Nathan said, leaning back in his chair. "Then what exactly are you proposing we do?" The question was directed at Tug. Rather than jousting back and forth, Nathan preferred to let Tug explain his vision of a plan and then decide how it fit with their own goals.

"I'm not sure I understand, Captain."

"Assume for a moment that we have agreed to join forces with you to help you defeat the Ta'Akar, in exchange for which you would provide us with a working version of this zero-point energy device. What would your *plan* be?"

Tug looked at Nathan, then Jalea, then Jessica and Cameron. He had not expected such a question and felt ill-prepared. "Well, from what you've told me so far, your ship is not only in need of repair, but its construction is also incomplete. The asteroid base I spoke of would be ideal for this task, as it is already equipped with power generation, living quarters, a medical bay, and even modest fabrication shops. Also, and please take no offense at this, it would appear that your technology is somewhat behind our own—maybe not in all areas, but in most. We might be able to improve some of your existing systems, or even add some of our technology to them to give you greater capabilities. In fact, if we could capture even one small patrol frigate, we might be able to install many of their systems on board your vessel. Combined with the tactical advantage of your jump drive, we could quickly defeat many of their ships—maybe even strike at the heart of the Ta'Akar capital—cutting off the head of the dragon, so to speak."

"Whoa, let's not get ahead of ourselves, there, Tug," Nathan exclaimed. "Helping you take out a few ships, maybe even capture one or two of them to give you a fighting chance—that's one thing. Jumping into the middle of the primary system and attacking their leader? That's quite another."

"If you want access to the zero-point energy device, that's where you have to go. To Takara."

"We're not interested in helping you overthrow the entire regime, Tug."

"No one is asking you to do so. But if you want the device, you have to go to Takara. If you wait for them to install it on one of their ships in the hopes of trying to capture that ship, it will be too late."

Nathan sighed, wondering how they had managed to get in so deeply in such a short period of time. All he had been doing since they had arrived was trying to find a way home.

"Doctor Sorenson," Nathan asked, "how long

would it take us to multi-jump all the way home?"

"Assuming that we restrict ourselves to jumps of eight light years, for safety's sake, and that we spend ten hours at each stop to recharge and perform service and diagnostics—about fifty-two days. Throw in down time for maintenance along the way, and I'd revise that estimate to at least two months. And that's assuming the drive can make that many jumps without any catastrophic failures."

"And what are the chances that we could significantly reduce the transit time utilizing the zero-point energy device?"

"If it works, then we could be home in a single jump."

"That's a pretty big guess, isn't it?" Cameron challenged.

"No, I don't believe so," Abby defended. "Look, we got here in one jump, so we know that it can be done. And the math supports the theory of unlimited range. It's simply a matter of available power. We use these energy banks because we don't have the ability to generate that much power all at once. According to the math, a zero-point energy device just might provide the power that we need." She looked around the room, noticing all the doubting expressions. "At the very least, it could reduce the number of jumps needed to get home to a dozen or so. We could be home in a week."

"And the Earth would have not only a jump drive, but also a zero-point energy device," Jessica added. "That sure would help in their defense against the Jung."

"Yes, it would," Nathan admitted.

"As would any of our technology that could be added to your ship, Captain," Tug reminded them.

"Nathan," Cameron pleaded, "so far, we've not been the aggressor, but you're talking about going on the offensive."

"I'm not so sure that the Ta'Akar would see it that way," Nathan said. "After all, we jumped into the middle of the battle and put four torpedoes into a capital ship. I'd call that aggressive."

"But that was only because we were being fired upon."

"Maybe so," he admitted, "but the Earth needs our jump drive to defend herself. And while helping the Karuzari in exchange for technology might not get us home any faster, turning tail and running home may take longer than the Earth can afford to wait. And if that is the case, then a few more days in the Pentaurus cluster won't change that. And it might even make us better equipped to make that journey home, should we decide to do things your way."

Jessica looked at Nathan out of the corner of her eye, as she knew what was coming, just as Cameron did.

"Tug, I would like you and Jessica to work out a plan on how we might best achieve both our goals in short order. I'm not saying that I'm committing to the idea, but I would like to see some ideas on the matter before I decide."

Tug looked at Jalea and then Jessica, before turning his eyes back to Nathan. "As you wish, Captain."

"Dismissed."

There was a slight pause before everyone stood and began to make their way out of the room.

"Doctor, a word?" Nathan asked. Abby sat back down as Nathan waited for the room to clear.

Satisfied that they were alone, he spoke. "What I'm about to discuss is classified, for our ears only. Is that understood?"

"Of course."

"You still have the suicide implant?"

"Yes."

"I need you to rig a booby trap on the jump drive."

"Excuse me?"

"Something that will not only fry the thing, but also wipe all data from your system's main frame. Program an authorization code with a thirty second delay to execution. Set it up so that only you or I can activate it. Can that be done?"

"Yes, sir. It shouldn't be difficult. But why..."

"There's one more thing I need from you, Abby." Nathan leaned forward and looked her dead in the eyes. "You are the only person alive who understands this technology. Am I right?"

"Yes, sir. The project was highly compartmentalized for just that reason."

"That's what I figured. If one of us scuttles the jump drive, I'm afraid you'll also have to activate your suicide implant. It's the only way to ensure that this technology does not fall into the wrong hands."

Abby stared at Nathan for what seemed like an eternity. She had contemplated the possibility of having to take her own life to protect her world since the day the suicide implant was placed into her tooth. But suddenly, the likelihood of that moment actually coming to be was a distinct possibility. "I understand, sir." Her answer was more instinctive than cognitive. After another long moment, she spoke again. "May I ask, why now?"

"Let's just say that I'm not sure who to trust."

"Do you think we're walking into a trap?"

"The thought has crossed my mind," he admitted.

* * *

As he walked into the mess hall, Nathan immediately noticed something was different. Not only were there more diners there, but the place was actually clean. The chaos of the last week, combined with a drastic lack of crew, had resulted in an eating environment that had been in dire lack of attention. It wasn't that the crewmen were slobs, it was simply that no one had the time.

Apparently, the stranded workers from the harvesting team had the time and had taken it upon themselves to give the room a thorough cleaning after they had finished prepping all the molo. Nearly all of the surviving workers were sitting down to eat, as were nearly a dozen of the crew. In fact, Nathan couldn't remember the last time he had seen so many of his crew in one place, other than in the main treatment room in the Medical section.

The room smelled inviting as well, with the smell of what had to be a molo-based dish of some type wafting from the galley to the left of the mess hall. Nathan made his way over to the service window, nodding at diners as he passed.

"Good evening, Captain," a Volonese woman said to him from behind the serving counter. "Would you like some stew?"

"Yes, please." Nathan watched as she dished up a hefty bowl of steaming hot stew. There were big chunks of what he recognized as molo, along with a few other vegetables that Tug had provided. It was all swimming in a dark brown broth that smelled quite pungent as she handed the bowl to him.

"Kala bread?"

"Huh?"

"Would you like some Kala bread?"

"We have bread?"

"Of course," she said, a smile on her face. "You can't have stew without bread," she told him as she handed him a roll bigger than his fist.

"Thank you," he said, placing the warm roll on his tray.

"Nathan." Vladimir stepped up next to him at the service counter. "I heard our guests were cooking something," he exclaimed as the woman handed him a bowl of stew and a roll. Vladimir took a long sniff of his stew. "Oh, I tell you, after eating the food on Haven, I was not looking forward to eating more escape pod food."

Nathan and Vladimir left the service counter and made their way across the room toward an empty table in the corner of the mess hall.

"So, how are the repairs going?" Nathan asked.

"Fine. Not too much was damaged during the last battle. Lost some more rail guns, got more holes in the outer hull. The inertial dampeners are still not up to full power. But all main systems are working. Propulsion, power, life support, maneuvering: they are all good."

"I'd really like to get the torpedo systems working again."

"Nathan, you only have two torpedoes left. We can manually load them into the two undamaged tubes and fire them manually if need be. There are more important things to work on."

"Such as?"

"Most of my people are working for Doctor

Sorenson, making sure the jump drive is working properly. She is most concerned with telemetry from the emitters. She claims that having to make jumps without knowing how many emitters are working is giving her gray hairs. The rest are working with Allet to get all rail guns working at better-than-original specifications, thanks to Allet's improvements."

"Well, that's good news, at least. We're probably going to need them."

"Why? Where are you taking us now?"

"Someplace called Corinair. It's on the other side of the Pentaurus cluster."

Vladimir continued to devour his food at more than twice the rate of Nathan. "What is there?"

"Apparently, they have some sort of rebel base there. And get this, it's inside an asteroid, no less."

"Inside?"

"Yeah. According to Tug, we can fly right in and park. They have some kind of repair and refit facility there."

"Interesting idea," Vladimir said as he tore off a piece of his roll and popped it into his mouth. "So, you are considering using this facility?"

"Yes. I've got to tell you, though; it makes me a little nervous."

"Why? Because you have to fly into cave?"

"No, because it could be a trap."

"You are being paranoid, Nathan."

"You trust them?"

"Of course not. But if they wanted to capture ship, they could this long ago. This ship is not as secure as everyone seems to think it is."

"Well, that's comforting."

"My point is I do not believe their intention is a hostile takeover."

"I hope you're right. I sure wouldn't mind fixing the hole in the bow. Flying around with a hole in our hull just doesn't sit well with me."

Nathan noticed Tug and Jalea entering the mess hall, along with both of Tug's daughters. "It's got to be hard for them," Nathan commented, gesturing toward Tug and his girls, "losing their mother and their home all in one day."

"Deliza seems to be handling it pretty well," Vladimir said.

"Really?"

"She was following me around engineering, asking me questions for more than an hour. She said she was bored sitting in her cabin. She is very smart young lady. And she is much easier to understand than Allet."

"Maybe you should put her to work," Nathan said, only half joking.

"I just might," Vladimir said in between spoonfuls of molo stew. "I can use all the help I can get down there. And who knows; she might teach me some new tricks, yes?"

Nathan had to smile at the image of his larger-than-life Russian friend taking lessons from a demure sixteen year-old girl on how to fix the ship's systems.

"You know, this molo stew, it is not too bad," Vladimir commented as he finished the last of his serving, sponging up the remaining broth with his roll.

"That's good, because we may be eating a lot of it for awhile."

"More stew, sir?"

"Yes, please," Vladimir exclaimed, his mouth still full of bread as he leaned back to make room for the

Volonese woman. She filled her ladle and deposited its contents into his bowl. Vladimir admired the woman's ample bosom as she deposited a second scoop into his bowl, then looked at Nathan, his eyebrows bouncing up and down twice in rapid succession as a grin formed on his face. Nathan just shook his head slightly, smiling back. Despite all that had happened to them over the last week, Vladimir hadn't changed a bit.

"My compliments to the chef," Vladimir exclaimed. "The stew, it is *Ochen fkusna.*"

"*Spaseeba,*" the woman answered.

Vladimir's mouth dropped, as did his spoon. "You're Russian?" He was as excited as a little boy on his birthday.

"*Nyet,*" she told him.

"But you speak Russian?"

"I speak many languages," she stated proudly. "Sadly, though, my Russian is not very good."

"I will teach you, then," Vladimir promised. He quickly brushed off his hands on his pants before offering it to her. "I am Vladimir. What is your name?"

"Naralena. My friends call me Nara."

"Then I may call you Nara?"

"We shall see," she answered coyly.

"Ah, there is hope," Vladimir exclaimed victoriously.

"You have an interesting accent, Naralena. Where are you from?" Nathan asked.

"Volon, Captain. The same place you pretend your ship is from." She suddenly dropped her accent and started speaking in what Nathan recognized as perfect Angla. "The accent was more for the benefit of your friend. I can use many accents."

"That's an unusual skill."

"I was a translator before I was sent to Haven."

"Really? How many languages do you speak?"

"At last count, I believe it was eight."

Nathan almost choked on his stew. "You speak eight languages?"

"Fluently, yes. But I can also communicate in several others, only not as well."

"That's quite impressive."

"Thank you, Captain. But it is not as impressive as you might think. I was genetically skewed to have a talent for languages."

"I see. Nevertheless, I am still impressed."

The woman smiled politely as she left to check on the next table of diners.

Vladimir leaned forward in order to be discreet and smiled. "I think I'm in love."

"What, again?"

"Captain, Chief," Josh addressed as he and Loki stepped up to the table, their dinner trays in hand, "mind if we join you?"

"Not at all, gentlemen. Have a seat."

"Thought you might like to know; we've got one shuttle all checked out and ready to go," Josh told him as they sat down and prepared to eat. "And between the harvester and the other shuttle, we should have enough used parts to keep the remaining shuttle flying for some time as long as we don't get shot at too much."

"We'll try to keep you out of the line of fire," Nathan promised. He noticed a confused look on Vladimir's face. "Didn't I tell you?" he said to Vladimir. "I hired these guys to be the flight crew for the shuttle. This way, we won't have to depend on strangers for rides."

"And they are not strange?" Vladimir said.

"Well, he is," Loki admitted, pointing at Josh.

Vladimir let out a chortle. "Listen, I've flown with you two. Trust me, you're both insane."

Both Josh and Loki watched the big Russian's facial expression cautiously until they were sure he was kidding.

"Did you say that you can use parts from the harvester for the shuttle?" Nathan asked.

"Sure," Josh answered, as if it were common knowledge.

"They're both made by the same manufacturer," Loki explained. "Many of the systems are identical."

"Makes sense," Nathan said as he scooped up the last of his stew.

"Captain," Josh started, "I was wondering something."

Nathan noticed that Josh looked a little apprehensive, as did Loki. "What is it?" he asked.

"No offense intended, but if this ship is from Earth, and we all originally came from Earth, why is that most of our technology is more advanced than yours?"

Nathan thought for a moment. "Well, you've all heard about the Legend of Origins, right?"

"Sure," Josh said, looking at Loki who nodded as well.

"What does it tell you about what happened on Earth?"

"Just that there was some *terrible evil* that drove humanity *deeper out into the galaxy.*"

"Well, that's a pretty vague description, but fairly accurate."

"So, what really happened?"

"Well, it happened about a thousand years ago.

At that time, there were five more worlds that had been colonized and fully developed. There were also about a dozen or so fringe worlds that had recently been settled. I guess you could say it was similar to the Pentaurus cluster, except a little more spread out, over about a hundred light years, actually. But then there was a plague—the Great Bio-Digital Plague. That's what we call it. This plague started as a computer virus that rapidly spread throughout the various networks on Earth and then eventually out to other worlds."

"The terrible evil was a computer virus?" Josh asked. "How is a computer virus such a threat?"

"Back then, most people regularly used cybernetic implants to link their brains with computer systems. Through these implants, the digital virus would cause chemical reactions in the brain that would create a biological virus—a sort of super-cancer— that would rapidly reconfigure cells in the body and cause them to grow out of control. The result was rapid disfigurement, both internally and externally. It had a mortality rate of over ninety percent. And once it became biological, it was also contagious. To make matters worse, it constantly transformed itself, making it impossible to combat."

"Damn," Loki muttered. "Who would create such a thing?"

"No one ever found out," Nathan told them. "Once the plague started spreading, everything rapidly fell apart. Economies crumbled. Infrastructure fell apart. Governments collapsed. People went crazy with fear, rioting, looting, killing each other in order to survive. In less than a decade, eighty percent of the population of the Earth and the Core Worlds had either died or left. If it weren't for a small percentage of the population that seemed to have a natural immunity, the Earth and the Core Worlds would probably still be abandoned."

"But I still don't get why our tech is more advanced," Josh said.

"With so few people left on Earth, there were not enough people to keep things going. Industry quickly ground to a halt, and within a century, the population of Earth became more tribal and agrarian. They were just trying to survive. Within a few generations, technology became nothing more than useless garbage. And since books had all been converted to digital format centuries earlier, there were no records of what once was. Everything was basically forgotten. What little was remembered was passed down through the generations through stories more than anything else."

"How did you guys rebuild? I mean, obviously you did, or we wouldn't be talking right now."

"Slowly, over many centuries. Most of our technology had to be rediscovered, relearned. We still had some memory of what we had been, but we'd forgotten a lot of the basics. Quite frankly, it was difficult. We lacked the population needed to support rapid industrial and technological advancement. And our health care was also sorely lacking. At the rate we were progressing, it would've taken us at least another five hundred years to get back out into deep space."

"So how did you make the leap?"

"The Data Ark," Nathan said.

Josh and Loki looked at each other. "The what?"

"A hundred years ago, archaeologists uncovered a massive underground complex in northern Europe. It contained all human history, culture, religion, and science for as far back as human history had been recorded. With the knowledge contained in the Data Ark we were able to advance our civilization as much as three hundred years in only a century."

"What about all of us?" Josh asked. "How did we get out here?"

"Well, we're not really clear on that. It seems that only the very beginning of the plague was recorded in the Data Ark. Once it started getting out of control, the facility was sealed for fear of contamination. But what we have been able to piece together is that there were a lot of last minute expeditions carrying refugees trying to escape the plague. At first, they were trying to seek refuge on fringe worlds that had already been settled. But when the plague started showing up on those worlds as well, they started closing their doors to others. So the refugees must've gone farther out into the galaxy. There were quite a number of habitable worlds that had been cataloged and scheduled for exploration at the time. But to my knowledge, none of them were this far out. How your people ended up all the way out here is as much a mystery to me as it is to you."

Josh was deep in thought as he considered what Nathan had just told them. It was an uncharacteristic expression for the young man whose face was usually quite animated. "But our tech is not that much more advanced than yours," Josh observed. "I mean, if we've had a thousand years to build on while you all were back to pooping in the woods, we should be a lot more advanced."

"Most of those expeditions left in a hurry," Nathan told him. "Like I said, the exact details are sketchy, since everything was falling apart as they left. But I would imagine that many expeditions left somewhat woefully equipped. Who knows how much tech, supplies, and equipment your forefathers brought with them? Or how many people were on your expedition as well? Or what happened to your settlements over all those centuries? There's a lot of reasons that your development could have stalled to some degree. The fact that you have all done as well as you have, and this far away from Earth—that alone is amazing."

"I suppose you're right," Josh agreed. "So who are these Jung I keep hearing your crew talk about?"

Nathan was a bit surprised by the sudden change in topic. "What are they saying?"

"We just overhear things, mostly. People talking about how they need to get back to Earth to help protect it against the Jung."

Nathan nodded his understanding.

"So who are they then?"

"Gentlemen, I'm going to have to let the Chief here tell you about that. I've got to get some rest," Nathan announced, stretching his arms as he prepared to depart.

"You cannot use our quarters," Vladimir told him.

"What?" Nathan stopped in mid-stretch. "Why not?"

"It has been commandeered by medical. I've moved into Chief Patel's quarters." Vladimir shrugged sympathetically. "Sorry, roomie. I guess you'll have to move into the captain's quarters."

"Yeah, I was kind of hoping to avoid that as long as possible," Nathan admitted as he rose. "Gentlemen, I leave you in the hands of Chief Kamenetskiy."

Josh and Loki bid the captain goodnight as he departed. A moment later, they eagerly turned their chairs to better face Vladimir.

"So what about these Jung?" Josh repeated.

"Well, we do not know much about them," Vladimir began. "In fact, we only learned of their existence a little over twenty years ago. We had not even gone beyond our own orbit at the time. All that we know, we have learned by monitoring transmissions emanating from other worlds in the core. We know that the Jung have conquered all of the core, except Earth. Alpha Centauri—the closest system to Earth—was the last to fall, not even a month ago."

"What makes you so sure that they will come to Earth?"

"Well, no one can be sure. But their behavior suggests that their eventual goal is to control all human inhabited worlds."

"Sounds familiar," Loki said.

"This ship—and her sister ship, the Celestia— were to be the first ships capable of faster-than-light travel. We were going to try and negotiate a peaceful coexistence with the Jung Dynasty."

"Do you think that would work?" Loki asked.

"Many people hoped so. But at the same time, we were preparing to defend ourselves against invasion. We already have four battleships patrolling our system. They are very powerful and heavily armed. But they are only sub-light ships, and not even very fast ones."

"What about these jump drives? Can't you put them on the other ships as well?"

"Ours is the only one in existence, I'm afraid."

"Then what the hell are you doing out here?" Josh wondered aloud.

"That is also a long story," Vladimir sighed.

"We've got time," Loki assured him. By the rate

that Josh's head was nodding up and down, it was obvious that he had the time to listen as well.

* * *

Nathan pressed the touch panel on the wall alongside the hatchway. In response to his touch, the lights in the room began to glow softly, coming up to half intensity a moment later. The room, although spartan, was much bigger than the tiny two-bunk cabin he had shared with Vladimir.

He closed the hatch behind him and took a few steps deeper inside the main room. It wasn't too big, maybe four meters square. It had a large rectangular view screen running along the back wall over what looked to be a comfortable couch, with a metal coffee table in front of it. The wall directly opposite the couch had another large view screen, presumably for entertainment purposes. To his right, there was a small office area, complete with desk and computer workstation. To his left was the entrance to his private bedroom and bath.

As he slowly walked around the cabin, he couldn't help but feel like he was intruding on the private chambers of the late Captain Roberts. Rumor was the captain had spent very little time in his quarters, coming here only for sleep and showers. He had lived in his ready room for the most part. He had only been in command of the Aurora for a few months before he died. And all but the last day had been spent in port. He had never even taken the time to put up a single picture on the wall or place a memento on the nightstand.

Nathan entered the bedroom, activating the lights in that room as well. The closet was standing open and Nathan could see that his uniforms were already properly hung. No doubt Cameron had seen to it hours ago. His duffel was on the floor of the closet, next to his athletic shoes and extra duty boots.

The bed was large and comfortable, but Nathan couldn't bring himself to lay on it. Instead, he turned off the lights and returned to the living room. He meandered about the room, imagining Captain Roberts sitting at the desk in the corner, hard at work. Despite the fact that he had spent so little time here, Nathan couldn't seem to shake his presence.

Nathan made his way to the small kitchenette area tucked in behind the office. He opened the fridge and pulled out a bottle of water, opening it and taking a long drink as he made his way to the couch. He plopped down unceremoniously, letting out a long sigh before pulling another long drink of water. This morning, he had woken on an alien world and dined on a simple porridge. By lunch he had been under attack by Ta'Akar assault troops. By dinner, he already had his security chief and the leader of the local rebellion drawing up plans for a surgical strike against a potentate who saw himself as a God. It had been a full day.

Nathan noticed a small black box sitting on the coffee table in front of him. He leaned forward and picked it up. He opened the box and found the bloody captain's bars that the late Captain Roberts had given him on his death bed. He recalled the Captain's last words. *Get them home. It's their only hope.*

He carefully placed the small box back on the coffee table, leaving the lid open. After taking another drink from his bottle, he stretched out on the couch to rest. *So much for an easy assignment,* he thought.

CHAPTER FOUR

Nathan had skipped breakfast this morning, partly because he had over slept, and partly because he wasn't really that hungry. He also knew that there wasn't much in the way of traditional breakfast foods available on board, so it was just as well to wait until later. He could always snack on more dried fruit and nuts if he got hungry later.

He had also woken up a little stiff and sore and had considered stopping by medical. But it wasn't exactly on his way, and he also didn't feel like getting a lecture from the doctor about any number of medical protocols he had broken in the last few days. Doctor Chen was taking to her new position rather nicely, and the power was going to her head just slightly.

He convinced himself that his sore back and arm were merely the result of spending the night on the couch in the captain's quarters—or rather his quarters. He still wasn't used to that idea. Regardless, he was sure that the soreness would pass as the day wore on.

"Captain on the bridge," the guard announced as Nathan stepped through the hatchway. The statement caught Nathan a bit by surprise, not only because his presence was being announced but also by the fact that once again there was a guard posted at the entrance to the bridge. Due to the short-staffing, they had discontinued that practice a few days ago.

"Morning, Captain," Jessica said from the tactical console at the back of the bridge.

"Good morning. What's with the guards?" he asked, pointing back over his shoulder.

"With all the *guests* on board, I decided it was best to at least keep the bridge secure."

"What about the other door?"

"Sealed off on the other side of the break room. Port hatch is now the only route in or out of the bridge."

"Where's Commander Taylor?"

"In your ready room, sir."

"Call Abby to the bridge, and then you two join us."

"Yes, sir."

Nathan looked at the forward view screen. The image was just a collection of nondescript stars, none of which he recognized, except for the slightly brighter amber one in the middle of the screen. "I won't miss that place," he said, pointing at the amber star on the screen as he turned to head to his ready room.

Cameron sat at the desk in the captain's ready room. Having always been an early riser, she had come on duty at zero four hundred hours. She had given Jessica, who had taken the first watch on the bridge, a few hours off to get some rack time before the morning pre-jump briefing. Jessica also was not much of a sleeper and had been fine with just a three hour nap and a hot shower. Having had her fill of molo while on the surface of Haven, she too had opted for dried fruit and nuts.

Cameron, on the other hand, had decided to brave another selection from the escape pod meal kits. Some type of scrambled eggs and sausage that she wished she could've passed on, but since the idea to use the escape pod meal kits was her idea, she had to set an example for the crew. It hadn't been that bad, and she was sure that, if stuck on an escape pod for weeks on end, it would be just fine. But at this point, even the molo, despite Jessica's less than favorable reviews, seemed more desirable.

Cameron liked sitting in this office. It felt right to her. Ever since she was old enough to enlist, her dream had always been to command a starship. Although the history file stored in the Data Ark showed many women had commanded such ships in the distant past, no women had commanded a ship of any kind since the great plague. Women had been too valuable for the repopulation of the Earth to risk them on such hazardous assignments. But since the discovery of the Data Ark, the infant mortality rate had dramatically decreased, and the human life span had doubled to well over one hundred years. Most people were continuing to work well into their eighties and nineties. Only a century ago, humans on Earth rarely lived past seventy.

It wasn't that she wanted to be the first, since obviously that distinction was technically assigned more than a millennium ago. But she wouldn't mind being the first since their return to space. And she sure wouldn't mind being the youngest. Perhaps that had been why she had been so disappointed when Nathan had been made helmsman and promoted over her. She knew she could do the job. Sure, Nathan had a natural instinct—a *gift* as Captain Roberts had referred to it—for flying, but there was a lot more to being a pilot, and even more so a captain, than *instinct*.

So she had spent many hours in this very chair, wondering how she might have handled the events that had transpired over the last week. She was certain she would've done most things differently. And she was pretty confident that the outcome could have been better. But she wasn't positive, and that fact alone caused her some concern.

"Good morning, Commander," Nathan greeted as he entered the ready room. Cameron immediately began to rise to relinquish her seat to its rightful owner. "As you were," Nathan insisted. He had never been one for the protocols of rank. And considering what they had been through together, it seemed just plain silly, especially when they were the only ones in the room. "How's everything?"

"Repairs are on schedule," she began. "Three rail guns were brought back online, and Allet is upgrading the system to increase their rail launch velocities. He also thinks he can increase their fire rate and accuracy by rewriting the software, making it more efficient."

"That's great, Cam. But I meant, how are *you* doing?"

"I'm fine, sir."

Nathan eyed her for a moment, looking for a chink in her armor. "You're fine? I'm beat to hell, even with a full night's sleep. And knowing you, I'm sure you only got in four or five hours at best."

"Well, you were down on the surface getting shot at from every direction."

"While you were up here, fighting off a Ta'Akar boarding party *and* one of their warships, which you did quite well, by the way."

She knew he was just trying to be nice, to be a good friend, but she had never been too comfortable confiding in others about her feelings. She had grown up in a house full of boys—five of them, to be exact. That had forced her to be tougher than most. Then, enlisting in the Fleet straight out of college hadn't helped matters. Despite the rapid change in social mores brought about by the discovery of the Data Ark, most military organizations on Earth were still dominated by men.

Still, there was a part of her that wanted to trust Nathan, to be able to speak with him as a friend. But her duty as his executive officer came first, and she just couldn't see them as anything other than mutually exclusive.

"Nathan," she said in a less official tone than usual, "I'm fine, really." Nathan stared at her for a moment. "Really," she repeated, standing to leave. "Now, if you don't mind, I need to take a quick break before our pre-jump briefing."

"Okay," Nathan answered, holding both hands up in resignation. He had made the offer, and that was all he could do for now.

Cameron moved out from behind the desk and exited the room just as Jessica and Abby entered.

"Where's she going?" Jessica asked. "I thought we had a meeting."

Nathan got up and moved around behind the desk, leaving room for Abby to take a seat in front of the desk, while Jessica took her usual position sprawled out on the couch.

"She'll be back shortly," he stated as he took his seat. "Abby, I assume you already have a plot calculated for a jump to the Darvano system?"

"Yes, sir. I also have a tentative escape jump

ready, just in case we jump into another... situation."

"Considering our history so far, that's not a bad idea. In fact, perhaps we ought to make that standard procedure—jump to just outside a system and take a peek before jumping all the way in."

"Kind of like testing the temperature of the water before diving in?" Abby stated as a comparison.

"I've always been more of a *jump-right-in* kind of girl, myself," Jessica said.

Nathan smiled. "Now why do I find *that* so easy to believe?"

"Actually, Captain, once I'm able to verify the accuracy of these new star charts, I should be able to pre-plot many jumps. In fact, it might be useful to create a network of pre-defined jump points."

"How would that help us?"

"Rather than having to plot a jump from a point in space that you expect to be at when you execute the jump, you simply fly to that point, executing the jump at the precise moment that you cross the threshold."

"Maybe I'm missing something, but that doesn't sound much different to me."

"The difference is that currently, we have to plot the jumps on the fly, which our systems were never really meant to do. And we usually don't have time to verify the plots, which I shouldn't have to remind you is incredibly risky. Predefined jump points would already be verified, therefore the risk would be minimized."

"Interesting idea, Doctor," Nathan admitted, "but I'm hoping we won't be around this area long enough to need such a network."

"As do we all," she agreed. "However, the idea could also be applied to short-range hops as well. For example, the parameters required to make a jump of say, one light hour, are the same regardless of departure and arrival points. It is only the departure and arrival points that differ from jump to jump."

"You're talking about making some jump plot templates, right?"

"Yes, in a manner of speaking."

"Are you sure it's worth the effort?" Nathan asked. "You yourself said that we needed to refrain from using the jump drive if possible. You said that you couldn't guarantee how long it would continue to function."

"I may have been a bit conservative in my concerns."

"What made you change your mind?"

"Your engineering staff and my team managed to get the rest of the emitters' telemetry feeds re-established. After analyzing the data from the emitters collected over the last few jumps, we were able to make a few adjustments to the field generators. I believe that it may last considerably longer than I anticipated."

"So you think it could make all one hundred and twenty five jumps to get us home?" Cameron asked as she entered the room. She had heard Abby's last statement from the hatch as she entered.

"It's too soon to promise that many jumps from the system, but I do feel better about our chances today than I did yesterday."

"That's good news, Doctor. Thank you," Nathan said as Cameron took her seat next to Abby.

Nathan took a deep breath to bolster his confidence. He knew that what he was about to say might not be well received, especially by Cameron. He wasn't sure Doctor Sorenson would like it either, but she was not the type to argue in front of others. And from their conversation after yesterday's briefing, he was pretty sure she understood the bigger picture better than most.

"I've decide to take the ship back into the Pentaurus cluster." Nathan held up his hand to prevent Cameron from objecting before he finished his opening statement. "I believe the possible benefits of the zero-point energy device justify the additional risk for two reasons. First, it might give us the power we need to get home in a fraction of the time. And second, the device could also be of significant assistance in the defense of Earth— maybe even more so than the jump drive itself."

Nathan could feel resistance boiling up from inside Cameron, and she looked like she could explode at any moment. "Now I understand that some of you may be opposed to this idea. But let me point out a few other factors that heavily influenced my decision." Nathan leaned back in his chair, looking at each of them in much the same way that Captain Roberts had done. "Did it ever occur to anyone that the odds of running into not one, but two Jung patrol ships, just beyond the Oort cloud, might be too high to even calculate?" Nathan looked to Jessica. Being special operations trained made her naturally suspicious. If anyone would understand his line of thinking, it would be her.

"They either knew we would be there," Jessica said, her mind racing, "or they were already preparing to invade."

"Our detection grid doesn't reach that far out," Cameron added, "at least not accurately enough to pick out ships against any other objects in the Oort. Especially if they were matching the speeds and trajectories of other objects."

"And if either one of those two possibilities are true, it would be suicide to return in our present condition."

"If they were prepping for an invasion," Jessica said, "don't you think they would've had something bigger than a couple of patrol ships out there?"

"Maybe," Nathan admitted, "but the Oort is an awfully big place. They might have only put patrol ships out there to be sure that we didn't spot them too quickly and jump away again."

"It could also have just been dumb luck," Cameron reminded him.

"Yes, it could have been. But I'm not willing to take that gamble, at least not until we're in a better state of readiness. If we returned home now, we could be jumping into a whole new hornet's nest. If we stay here, at least for awhile, we can not only get our ship fixed up, but we might even pick up some cool new tech to show the folks back home," Nathan said with a smile. "To that end, I think it best we continue to ally ourselves with the Karuzari. At least until we determine the validity of this power source."

"If what you're saying is true," Cameron argued, "then the Jung could be invading Earth at this very moment, while we're sitting here talking about joining some local rebellion."

"Even if we had started jumping our way back home from day one," Jessica interrupted, "we'd still be a couple of months out from Earth."

"But if it was just a coincidence that we ran into those two Jung patrol ships, the invasion may not have happened yet."

"And if that's the case, then a few more days out

here getting ourselves repaired won't make much difference, will it?" Nathan said.

"Listen up," Jessica barked, trying to take command of the argument. She could tell that Nathan and Cameron could spend the entire day hashing this out if they were allowed. She was a bit shocked, as it was no way for a captain and his XO to behave, especially in front of command staff. But she also knew that their already tenuous working relationship had been severely strained not only by Nathan's sudden advancement to captain, but also by the fact that Cameron disagreed with most of his decisions.

Nathan and Cameron both fell silent, turning to look at Jessica, who now had a bit of a sheepish look on her face as she realized that she too had just overstepped her bounds.

"If I may," she began, looking to each of them for their silent approval. "Assume for a moment the worst-case scenario. At the time we ran into those two patrol ships, the Jung already had Sol surrounded and were about to strike. If true, it's already happened, the Earth is fucked, and there's not a damned thing we can do about it, at least not in our present state. Do we agree on that much?"

Again she looked to them both, getting grudging agreements. "Now, assume the best case scenario. It was just a co-winky-dink. The Jung are still cleaning up and reinforcing after their invasion of Alpha Centauri. Our best intel puts their top speed at ten times light. So even if the Jung had left the Centauri system the day after the invasion, it'll still be another five months before their forces reach Earth." Jessica turned her attention to Abby. "Doctor, if we were in port, how long would it take to outfit another ship with another jump drive?"

"I don't know. It took us years to build the prototype."

"Best guess, assuming that every man, woman, and child was working on the project."

"One year, maybe."

"So that's not an option. Captain, again, if we were in port, how long to make us fully up to specs?"

"A few months, I suspect."

"Okay, possible, but even then, it's still just one ship against God knows how many. And we're not heavily armed, even if we had all of our squadrons on board."

"But the jump drive does give us a huge tactical advantage," Cameron reminded her, hoping to prop up her point of view on the matter.

"True, but it's also an advantage that can be taken away with a few lucky shots. Or worse yet, captured and used against us."

"So, are you saying we should or shouldn't go back?" Cameron asked. She was beginning to get confused, as Jessica was showing support for either case.

"I'm saying that we have time to decide. Making snap decisions isn't going to make our or the Earth's situation any better. And if the captain's right, and we can pick up some advanced tech, that might make all the difference in the world. Or in our case, the Sol system."

"It only makes sense to stay here for awhile and see what develops," Nathan concluded.

Cameron wasn't convinced. "I just don't know, Nathan. All I can think about is the people back home. It just feels like we shouldn't be risking our necks out here. We should be doing it back home."

"But we are risking our necks out here for the people back home. Just because they are so far away doesn't make it any less so." Nathan looked at Cameron. He could see the doubt in her eyes. It wasn't her usual stubborn streak this time, and she wasn't scared; he knew better. Cameron had already proven herself in battle as much as, if not more so than, any of them. She was scared that they were making the wrong decision—that they were putting the Earth in further jeopardy. "Look, Cameron, we all know that I can make it an order. But I don't want to have to do that, especially not in this case. I really want your support on this." Nathan flashed her a smile, that same one that had always gotten him out of trouble with his mother as a boy. "You know I'm not smart enough to pull this off without you."

Cameron looked at Nathan and his goofy smile. "Well, at least you understand that much," she said, leaning back in her chair in resignation. "All right then, I'm with you."

Jessica clapped her hands. "Great! What's the plan, skipper?"

Nathan's smile faded for a moment as he turned to Jessica. "Would you stop calling me *skipper*?" Jessica shrugged apologetically, holding both hands up with her palms forward, a goofy grin on her face. Nathan returned his attention to the group. "We make two jumps to get to a position just outside the Darvano system, say about one light day."

"Why two jumps?" Cameron asked. "Darvano is only nine point five light years away."

"Two reasons. First, the good Doctor suggests we don't push the limits of the drive unless we have to, at least until she has more time to review the performance data collected over the jumps to date. Second, I'd prefer to arrive at any destination with enough power in the drive to do a quick escape jump, in case we jump into yet another bad situation."

"Makes sense," Cameron agreed.

"Once we get there, we locate the hideout Tug spoke of and plot a jump to get as close as possible so that we can sneak in undetected."

"That might require more than one jump, Captain," Abby warned. Nathan looked at her quizzically, forcing her to better explain. "It would take hours—maybe even days depending on how erratic the trajectories of the objects in the asteroid belt are—to gather enough data to make a close in jump. It might be better to jump in next to a planetary body, or a moon—something with a bit more stable and predictable orbit. From there, we can get a more accurate and more up-to-date trajectory mapping of the belt before plotting a jump deeper into the belt itself."

"Makes sense. But I want to get the ship into that hideout as soon as possible. The longer we're sitting out in the open, the more chances there are of being spotted."

"Captain," Jessica interrupted, "I'm not too crazy about the idea of flying this ship into some kind of cave without checking it out first."

"You think it might be a trap?" Cameron asked.

"The thought has crossed my mind," Jessica said.

"Yeah, mine too," Nathan admitted. "Suggestions?"

"We could send that hotshot Josh in first," Cameron suggested with a wry smile. "Put him and his copilot into the shuttle and let them recon it."

"Not a bad idea, Commander. Jess, maybe you should go along with them."

"Sounds like a hoot," she exclaimed.

Nathan smiled. "Wear your flight restraints... Trust me."

"Will do, skip— Sorry, Captain."

"Okay. So they do a fly-through inspection first, then we follow them in. Once the ship is secured inside the hideout, we'll send a team over to power everything up so that we can get busy repairing the ship. I especially want to get the hull patched up so we can have access to our forward sections again. More than seventy percent of our living quarters are in there and between the wounded and the extra guests, we're running out of space."

"What about supplies?" Cameron asked. "If Corinair is as advanced a world as Tug says, we might be able to get some decent supplies this time."

"Yeah, like something besides molo," Jessica complained.

"We still have credits to spend and a bunch of raw ore that we can sell," Cameron added.

"I was thinking about that," Nathan said. "As much as I know you like to gather intel in the field, Jessica, I don't think it's a good idea for any of us to go down to the surface on this trip. I think we'd stand out too much this time. Besides, according to Tug, you cannot get past the Port Authority without proper ident-chips."

"I guess I can sit this one out," she said with a wave of her hand. "Besides, I've been thinking; if this secret base of theirs has comm gear, maybe we could do some signals intelligence gathering."

"Good idea. Meanwhile, we'll send Tug and Jalea down to the surface in the shuttle. They can sell off the rest of our ore and buy us some supplies. We'll leave them on the surface for at least a day or two so they can also make contact with any rebels that may be hiding out on Corinair."

"And what, bring them back here?" Jessica objected.

"Hey, we need all the help we can get at this point. I'm hoping that some of them might also help with repairs as well. So far, they all seem to be pretty good with tech."

"Let's just be sure we don't end up outnumbered on our own ship," Jessica warned.

"From Jalea's estimates, I don't think that many of them survived. I'd be surprised if they find more than a handful of them."

"How long do we plan to stay in the Darvano system?" Cameron asked.

"No longer than necessary, of course. But hopefully long enough to at least get all the major repairs done. We'll have to play it by ear." Nathan looked around the room. "Any more questions? All right. Let's get ready to make our first jump—in say, thirty minutes?"

Abby nodded in agreement, as did the others.

"Great. Dismissed," he announced. As they got up to leave, Nathan activated the comm-panel on his desk to hail the comm-officer on the bridge. "Can you send Josh and Loki to my ready room?"

* * *

Twenty minutes later, Josh and Loki arrived at the entrance to the bridge. Having been forewarned of their arrival, the guard at the hatchway escorted them the few meters down the short corridor that led into the aft port side of the bridge.

"Whoa," Loki muttered as he gazed upon the

bridge and the main view screen that wrapped around the entire front half the room and up over the helm and navigation consoles.

"This is nice," Josh whispered back to Loki. Despite the fact that most of the Aurora's technology was less advanced than that found on even the older ships used on Haven, the layout of the bridge left him in awe. "I'd love to get my hands on the flight controls of this baby, eh, mate?" he added, jabbing Loki in the side with his elbow.

"This way, gentlemen," the guard stated, reminding them of why they were here. Josh and Loki turned to see the guard standing behind them, his arm outstretched to point toward the door to the captain's ready room, just inboard from the entrance they had just passed through. "The captain's expecting you."

Josh and Loki followed the guard, looking back over their shoulders to catch a last glimpse of the bridge on their way out. The guard swung the hatch open and they stepped inside the ready room.

"Gentlemen," Nathan greeted them nonchalantly, "what took you so long?"

"Sorry, Captain," Loki began, "but we had just pulled the computer core from the harvester when you called. Once pulled, you only have ten minutes to get it hooked back up to power or you lose all its base programming."

"That's understandable. Have a seat," he said, gesturing to the two chairs in front of his desk.

Josh felt a bit uncomfortable. His flying technique had gotten him and Loki into hot water on more than one occasion. Right now, it felt similar to the time they had been called into the Haven Port Authority Flight Controller's office. They had gotten scolded for nearly an hour that day, and had just about lost their flight status. "Have we done something wrong, Captain?"

"No, not at all. I have a couple of missions I wanted to discuss with you; that's all."

Josh started to relax a little, as did Loki.

"*Missions*?" Loki asked, not quite sure what the term meant.

"You know, flights. What do you call them?"

"Flights, I guess," Loki answered with a shrug.

"What kind of *missions* did you have in mind, Captain?" Josh asked.

"The Karuzari have a base of some type inside a hollowed out asteroid. We would like to use it as a place to hide while we conduct repairs."

Josh's eyes lit up. "This place must be pretty big, if you can fit your whole ship inside it."

"Apparently, it's an entire facility of some sort."

"Captain," Loki asked, "why do you need us to fly in?"

"We need someone to recon the entrance, the main port, and the exits before we take the ship inside."

Josh could see that his friend was getting suspicious. "You expecting trouble?" he asked the captain.

"I wouldn't say *expecting*," Nathan said. "Let's just say we're being overly cautious and leave it at that."

"Say no more, Captain," Josh told him. "We quite understand. Never trusted the Karuzari much myself, either."

"It's not so much a matter of trust at this point," Nathan corrected. "As I said before, it's more a matter of caution. We have too much at stake to risk it all haphazardly."

"Yeah," Josh agreed, changing to a more somber tone, "the chief told us all about the Jung and such. You blokes certainly have your plates full."

Nathan smiled at the expression. "Yes, we do at that."

"Captain," Loki interrupted, "you said missions," he added, emphasizing the plural.

"Yes. Later, we'll also need you to make a couple of runs to the planet surface. First to deliver Tug and Jalea, along with most of the ore your team collected. And then to bring them and a load of supplies back to the ship a day or two after."

"The surface? The surface of what? We're not going back to Haven, are we?"

"No. We'll be going to the Darvano system."

"Darvano? But that's nearly ten light years away. That'll take weeks," Loki exclaimed.

"Not for us, remember?" Nathan reminded him.

"You're gonna jump?" Josh asked, unable to hide his excitement.

"Yes."

"Oh, I wouldn't mind seeing that. I don't mind tellin' ya," Josh stated. Although not as easily excited as his friend, it was obvious that Loki was also excited.

"We're going to jump in about five minutes," Nathan told them. "Would you like to hang around and watch?"

"Oh, you bet," Josh stated, Loki's head nodding rapidly up and down.

"Very well, then. Follow me," Nathan said as he rose from his desk.

Josh and Loki followed Nathan out of the ready room and back out onto the bridge.

"You guys just stand back here," Nathan told them, pointing to the back of the room in front of the burnt-out comm station that had been offline since they had first encountered the Ta'Akar.

Nathan moved down from the upper platform that held the tactical station in the center, the jump control console on the right, and the new temporary comm station on the left. "Are we ready to jump?"

"Jump drive is fully charged and ready. Our first jump is plotted and verified," Abby reported.

"Where will the first jump take us?"

"Exactly five light years from here, to a point pretty much in the middle of nowhere, sir. But definitely deep within the Pentaurus cluster."

"Helm ready?" Nathan asked as Cameron stepped down from the upper level and moved in front of him to sit at the helm console.

"Helm is ready, sir."

"Are we gonna feel anything?" Josh asked Jessica, who was standing at the tactical console directly in front of him.

"No," she said, turning her head slightly to cast a disapproving look at his question.

Nathan heard Josh's question. "Commander, you know, maybe we should always warn the crew and passengers when we are about to jump. I mean, there is no sensation involved—not like when we're accelerating or decelerating. It might be better for the crew to be aware of any abrupt change in location."

"It might at that," she agreed.

"Jess, any problems with that?"

"None that I can think of, sir."

"All right then. From now on, procedure will be to announce a jump at least one minute before, then give a five-second count down. Afterward, we should announce that the jump is complete and specify our new location."

"Is all that really necessary?" Cameron asked.

"Too much?"

"It does seem a bit dramatic. But then again, you may be right about the psychological effect on the crew. What good is it to have served aboard a starship if you never even knew where you went?"

"Great. You might want to add that to the manual, Commander," Nathan announced with satisfaction.

"Might I also suggest that we rig some sort of auto-adjustment of the viewer to take place just before and after a jump, instead of shutting it down and then back up. It takes a few seconds for the system to reboot when it's shut completely off, and those few seconds could be crucial upon arrival."

"That's an excellent idea. Add that one to the book as well."

"Captain," Jessica began, "who makes the announcement?"

"Well, as long as Abby is controlling the jump, then she can make the actual jump announcements. Comms can make the initial ship-wide, and then announce our new location when we arrive." Nathan turned to the comm-officer. "Ensign."

"Attention all hands. Stand by to jump in one minute."

Nathan took a seat in his command chair, located on the middle level between the tactical console and the flight consoles.

"Why one minute?" Cameron asked as she turned around from the helm to face him.

"I don't know. Because it sounded good?"

"We can fine tune the procedures later," she said with a raised eyebrow, as she turned back around to face the helm console and the main view screen.

Josh and Loki watched as the bridge staff calmly pressed buttons, checked readouts, and made adjustments to various systems as they waited for the jump to occur.

"Captain," Abby said. "I've taken the liberty of adding a small subroutine to the jump sequencer that will dim the brightness and contrast of the main viewing system as soon as the jump is initiated. It will restore the original settings immediately after the jump is complete."

"Excellent."

"Ten seconds to jump," Abby announced.

Nathan looked over his left shoulder toward the comm-officer, gesturing to him. "Patch the doctor ship-wide."

Abby's voice echoed throughout the ship as she announced the jump sequence. "Jumping in five..."

Abby turned the key to arm the jumping system.

"Four..."

She flipped open the two clear covers that protected the jump field generators from being activated accidently, and flipped both rocker switches.

"Three..."

Josh and Loki both looked nervous as they swallowed hard.

"Two..."

Abby flipped open the cover over the large red button that a technician had wired into the console to serve as the main jump initiation button.

"One..."

The main view screen suddenly dimmed.

"Jumping."

Abby pressed the button and initiated the jump.

Josh and Loki watched through the dimmed viewer as a pale blue wave of light quickly spread out from the emitters on the hull. Within a split second, each wave of light had connected with its neighbor and their brilliance increased rapidly into a blinding flash of white light, subdued only by the lowered display settings on the main view screen. A second later, the flash subsided, revealing that the stars had shifted ever so slightly.

"Jump complete," Abby announced calmly.

"Verify position," Nathan ordered.

After a few seconds, Cameron responded. "Position confirmed. We are now halfway between Takara and Darvano, approximately four point five light years from the Darvano system and about twenty light hours outside of the known shipping lanes. We are now deep in the middle of the Pentaurus cluster."

"Any contacts?" Nathan asked.

"Negative, sir," Kaylah responded.

Sensing that the jump was over, Josh could no longer control himself. "Oh that was just the greatest thing I've ever seen!" Loki said nothing, only standing there with his mouth hanging open.

"Let's do it again," Josh exclaimed.

"We will," Nathan promised, "in about five hours."

"Great! That should be just enough time to teach us how to fly this thing," Josh exclaimed, as he started advancing toward the front of the bridge.

"Easy there, fella," Jessica warned him, stepping in his path.

"No, wait a minute," Nathan said, much to everyone's surprise. "That might not be such a bad idea."

"What? Are you crazy?" Cameron responded.

"Well not right away, of course. But why don't we

put them in the simulator and see how they do? I mean, they can't crash the simulator."

"I'm not so sure of that," Cameron spouted. "Have you seen him fly?"

"I was riding with him, remember? Seriously, Cam. You've been on duty pretty much nonstop for days now, with no more than a few hours of sleep here and there. It might not be a bad idea to have a backup pilot and navigator."

"Nathan, get serious. These guys don't know the first thing about this ship."

"Let's just throw them in the sim and see what happens. You never know. And it might keep them out of trouble."

"Yeah, come on, love. Give us a shot," Josh called out from the back of the bridge.

Cameron rolled her eyes, letting out an exasperated sigh.

"I'll cancel your debt," Josh added.

"What?"

"You still owe me two dinner dates, remember?"

"Fine, they can play in the simulator. But there is no way they're flying this ship unless they do better in the sims than any of us ever did."

Nathan smiled. "Jess, would you mind getting them started?"

"What the hell," she said. "We're not going anywhere for awhile anyway." She turned around to head out. "Come on, boys. I'll show you the arcade."

As Jessica led the two pilots into the corridor, they met Vladimir and Tug's oldest daughter, Deliza, coming from the opposite direction.

"Good morning, Jessica," Vladimir greeted.

"Hey, Vlad. Hi, Deliza," Jessica said. "What'cha up to?"

"Deliza has been a very big help in engineering. I thought I would reward her by showing her the bridge."

As Vladimir was talking, Deliza was stealing shy glances at Josh and Loki, who were only a few years older than her. Noticing her glances, Josh instantly turned on the charm.

"Hi, I'm Josh. You probably don't recognize me. Last time I saw you I was wearing my flight helmet. I'm the pilot that saved you from Haven."

"We're the pilots that saved you from Haven," Loki corrected, stepping up next to Josh, vying for Deliza's attention.

"Enough boys," Jessica scolded. "Eyes forward and keep going."

Vladimir looked confused. "Where are you taking them?"

"Captain wants to toss them into the flight simulator, see how they fair at flying this ship."

"Really? Why does this not surprise me?"

"Nothing Nathan does these days surprises me," she agreed as she followed them off down the corridor.

Vladimir turned back toward the entrance to the bridge. He spied Nathan through the hatch. "Nathan!" he called. He turned to Deliza. "Wait right here," he instructed before stepping through the hatch onto the bridge. "Nathan, I was wondering if I could show Deliza the bridge."

"Today seems to be the day for tours. Why?"

"She seems to have a knack for identifying inefficiencies, especially with computer systems. And I think she is interested in the jump drive. I thought perhaps she might be of assistance if and when we get our hands on the zero-point device."

121

"But she's only sixteen."

"This is true. But I get this feeling that she understands our technology better than we do."

Nathan looked at his friend. "You're serious?"

"Da."

Nathan peeked past Vladimir at Deliza standing in the corridor on the other side of the hatchway. "What the hell. I just sent a pair of nineteen year-olds to learn how to fly this ship. I guess I might as well let a sixteen year-old try to fix it."

Vladimir turned to motion Deliza to enter. "Deliza, you remember Nathan?"

"Yes, sir. Thank you for allowing me on the bridge."

"No problem. Vladimir tells me you understand our system quite well. I imagine they must seem antiquated to you."

"No, of course not," she said, not wanting to offend him. "Your ship is very interesting. It is true, that the systems are... different. And in many cases some of your systems use a design that we abandoned long ago. But that doesn't necessarily mean they are not as good. Some of them I find to be far more robust and dependable. Advancement for the sake of advancement is not always a good thing."

"A very wise observation," Nathan agreed.

"My grandfather used to say, '*A flame will provide enough light, without running up bill.*'"

Nathan and Deliza both looked at Vladimir.

"Okay, my grandfather was a little crazy."

"I am most interested in this jump drive that you use for interstellar movement. I understand that it utilizes some combination of expanding and collapsing energy fields to initiate..."

"Whoa, you're already flying way over my head, there," Nathan admitted. "Perhaps you should introduce her to Doctor Sorenson," he recommended, pointing toward Abby.

Vladimir led Deliza the few steps over to the jump control console, where Abby was busy processing the calculations for the next jump plot. "Doctor Sorenson, if I may bother you for a moment?"

Abby turned to face Vladimir, expecting to have another confrontation with the stubborn engineer. Their working relationship had been trying since day one. Though things had improved due to the nature of their situation, both of them still approached one another cautiously.

When she saw Deliza standing next to Vladimir, she was a bit surprised. The last person she expected to see standing next to the arrogant Russian was a demure sixteen year-old girl. Suddenly, her maternal instinct kicked in, as she was reminded of her own daughter back on Earth. She was still far younger than the girl that stood before her, but there was the same innocence in her eyes.

"Doctor Sorenson, I would like to introduce Deliza Tugwell. She is Tug's oldest daughter."

Abby remembered that the rebel leader's wife, this young woman's mother, had been killed during the battle on Haven not even a full day ago. And yet here this young woman was, standing proudly on the bridge of a foreign ship, meeting complete strangers—and quite at ease.

"This is Doctor Sorenson," Vladimir continued. "She is in charge of the entire jump drive project. She is a very smart woman."

"It is an honor to meet you, ma'am," Deliza said softly, holding out her hand.

"It is my pleasure."

"Deliza is also a very smart young lady, Doctor. She has been helping her father maintain his ship for many years. And she has already helped me in engineering. She is very interested in your jump drive technology. Perhaps she could visit with you for awhile? Ask you some questions?"

Abby looked uncomfortable, and looked over at Nathan by the ready room entrance for approval. Nathan shrugged and held up his hand, putting his thumb and forefinger a few centimeters apart, indicating *just a little*.

"Sure," Abby said, her frown changing into a smile, "a few seconds. But you will have to wait a few minutes. I am running some calculations for the next jump. When they are complete, I will have more time. Maybe five minutes?"

"Of course," Deliza answered, stepping back out of the way to wait.

"I must return to engineering." Deliza waved to Vladimir as he left.

"Hey, Vlad," Nathan said, stopping him on his way out. "If she's so much help to you," he said under his breath, "then why are you leaving her here?"

"She is very smart, yes, *and* very helpful. But she will not stop asking me questions. Why, why, why, all morning long."

Nathan smiled as Vladimir left the bridge. He was about to return to his ready room when the comm-officer called for him.

"Captain, I'm picking up a lot of communications signals."

"What kind of signals?"

"Everything: audio, video, telemetry, even news

broadcasts."

"From where?"

"From everywhere," the comm-officer reported. "My guess is that since we're sitting right smack dab in the middle of the cluster, we're picking up signals from every star around us."

"Don't we always pick up such traffic?"

"Well, yes, but the signal strengths are usually too low to be of any use. But these are all quite strong."

"Start recording them," he instructed, "and call Jessica to my ready room."

"Yes, sir. But Captain, with so much of our core still down, we're going to run out of storage space in about twenty hours if I record everything."

"Understood. I'll let you know."

Deliza stood behind Abby and off to the side, twisting and straining to see the displays on the physicist's console as the numbers danced across the screen, changing every few seconds as the calculations constantly updated. After several minutes, she could no longer control herself. "Are you running those calculations concurrently through the same processing bank, or are you running each stream through a different bank?"

"Excuse me?" Abby asked. She was a bit put off by the child's question, as well as a bit impressed.

"I'm sorry," Deliza apologized. "I shouldn't bother you."

"That's all right," Abby assured her, remembering the poor girl had recently lost both her mother and her home. "They are running through separate processing banks. Why do you ask?"

"It's just that the calculations seem to be running abnormally slow."

"Yes, they are," Abby admitted. "I'm afraid this console wasn't really designed for these types of calculations. Spatial equations can be quite processor-intensive. Normally, we would run them on the main frames, but much of that system was damaged during our first battle."

"The computers in my father's ship could run those equations in one tenth the time," she said enthusiastically, "maybe even less."

"Really?"

"Of course. Even the ones in the shuttles could run them faster. The shuttles are highly automated, and their flight systems use entire arrays of processing banks. They need them to run the auto-piloting systems."

"That's interesting," Abby admitted. "Do you think it's possible to interface them with our systems?"

"I don't see why not. They might lose a bit of performance due to the need to translate languages, but the hit should be negligible. I can help you install them," Deliza offered.

"I'll speak to the captain about it as soon as I finish plotting the next jump."

"The next jump? Where are we now?"

"We're in the middle of the Pentaurus cluster, about halfway between Takara and Darvano."

"That's in the middle of nowhere. Why are we out here?"

"Due to our limitations in power generation, the jump drive only has a range of ten light years. And the captain prefers to jump into a system with enough energy to jump out again in a hurry, in case there is trouble."

"A wise precaution. Then we are waiting to recharge your energy reserves?"

"Yes," Abby answered, surprised that she had come to the correct conclusion with so little information. "You catch on quickly, don't you?"

"My father says I have a gift for science," Deliza admitted. "It's really all I do."

"Don't you have any other interests or hobbies?"

"No, not really. But I do enjoy science, very much in fact."

"You remind me of myself at your age. I couldn't get enough of it. My mother used to tell me to go out and be with my friends, but I preferred to study."

Suddenly, the console beeped. Abby turned to check the status of her calculations. "There we are. All done." She turned back to Deliza. "Now, let's go talk to the captain about those computers."

"You wanted to see me, sir?" Jessica asked as she entered the ready room.

"Yeah, Jess. Remember how you were talking about signals intelligence earlier?"

"Sure," she answered as she plopped down on the couch.

Nathan was amused at the way she always went straight to that couch. "You really like that couch, don't you?"

"Hey, what can I say? I've got a thing for couches."

"Have you moved into your new quarters yet?"

"Naw, why?"

"They're bigger. And they've got couches."

"Great. I guess that's next on my to-do list. So what were you saying about signals intel?"

"Comms reported a lot of civilian signals coming in from all directions. Mostly general broadcasting and communications stuff. Guess since we're sitting in the middle of everything, we're getting it from all over the cluster. I told comms to record everything, but he says with half the main frame still down, he'll run out of storage space in less than a day."

"Well, since we're at least a few years out from any star, everything we pick up is going to be at least a few years old so none of it will be actionable. But it could help give us a feel for the area: its history, customs, popular opinion, and the like. Hell, it could even tell us what the rebellion has been up to over the last few years. That is, if we get lucky and pick up a news broadcast or something."

"Yeah, you're right. But what about the storage issue?"

"Doesn't matter. We're only going to be out here for five hours anyway. After that we'll be sitting much closer in, so the Sig-Int will be fresh. Of course, that presents a whole new problem. How are we going to translate it all?"

"There's a women, one of the workers. She was serving molo stew last night. Nara-something. Naralena, I think. She speaks, like, eight languages fluently. Worked as a translator before."

"Eight languages? How the hell did she end up on Haven?"

"No idea. I wasn't sure it was polite to ask, to be honest. Maybe she can help."

"What the hell. Apparently we're accepting all applicants."

Nathan's eyebrows raised momentarily, acknowledging that her pun had more truth in it than she might have realized. He pressed the call button on the comm-panel on the desk. "Can you hail Naralena to my ready room? She's one of our guests."

"*Yes, sir,*" the comm-officer replied over the comm-set.

"Captain," Abby's voice came from the hatchway, "a moment?"

"Of course, Doctor," Nathan said, gesturing for her to enter. Abby stepped through the hatchway into the ready room with Deliza following. Deliza looked sheepishly into the room, obviously feeling ill at ease in the captain's official office.

Abby waited for Deliza to step up next to her before beginning. "Deliza has informed me that the computers used on the shuttle might be more efficient at processing the multi-spatial calculations used for plotting our jumps. If she is correct, it could speed up the process tenfold. With your permission, I'd like to look into it."

"As long as it doesn't interfere with the operations of the drive, I don't see why not," Nathan answered. "You can probably use the one from the out-of-service shuttle. I believe they were planning on using it for spare parts anyway. I'll let Josh and Loki know that you'll be coming by." Nathan looked directly at Deliza instead of Abby. "Thank you, Deliza."

"You're quite welcome, sir," she answered as they turned to exit.

Jessica shook her head. "And the applicants just keep getting younger."

"According to Vlad, that little girl is smarter than any of us."

A few moments after Abby and Deliza departed, the Volonese woman, Naralena, appeared at the hatchway.

"Excuse me," the woman said. "I was told you wished to speak with me."

"Yes. Naralena, right?"

"Yes," she said as she entered the room.

"This is Jessica Nash, my Chief of Security."

"Pleased," Jessica said. Naralena simply nodded politely.

"I was wondering if you could help us out," Nathan said.

"I'd be happy to help in whatever way that I can, Captain."

"We're collecting a lot of transmissions from neighboring stars and such: communications, broadcasting, all sorts of stuff. But it's all in languages that we don't yet understand. We were hoping that you might be able to translate at least some of it for us."

"I can certainly try. I do speak most of the common languages in this area. Is there anything in particular you are looking for?"

"We're just trying to get a better understanding of the societies and cultures of the area, as well as a bit of recent history."

"Yes, of course. I can see how that would be of use to you. Of course, I'd be more than happy to translate whatever I can."

"Great, I'm going to have you work for Jessica for now. She'll get you set up in one of our auxiliary offices for now, where you should be able to work without interruption."

"It sounds like an interesting assignment," she admitted. After working for the harvesting team on Haven for the last six months, sitting in a climate controlled, clean office translating any number of common languages into ancient Angla was going to be a joy.

Jessica rose to escort Naralena to her new office.

"You know, in Sig-Int, they usually have computer

algorithms that search for keywords and phrases, tagging them for further analysis. Maybe we can rig up something similar."

"Talk to Vlad," Nathan told her. "He might be able to help you out with that."

* * *

Nathan was a bit surprised to see Deliza sitting on the floor, behind and beside the jump control console aft of the starboard side of the bridge. She had several large electronic components arranged around her, one of which was connected to an external battery of some type. The side panel to the aft end of the jump control console was open, and Deliza appeared to be peering into the opening, comparing what she saw inside the console to the array of connectors she had splayed out across the deck in front of her. As she checked each connector, she entered information into her data pad, apparently double-checking and triple-checking everything.

"What's she doing?" Nathan whispered to Jessica at the tactical station.

"I think she's figuring out how to connect that computer core from the shuttle with the one in Abby's console."

"That's not going to interfere with anything, is it?"

"Not according to Abby. But I advised that she wait until after we reach the hideout before she started connecting anything. For now, the little brainiac is just figuring out how she's going to do it. I'm pretty sure I heard Abby talking about running some simulations on the shuttle core first, though."

"How are we looking, Doctor?" Nathan asked

131

Abby.

"Jump drive is fully charged. The last jump to just outside the Darvano system is plotted and ready, and an escape jump from Darvano is also ready."

"Very well. Stand by for a jump."

"Standing by," Abby said. She leaned down toward Deliza. "You might want to see this." Deliza grinned and immediately stood up, moving into position to better view the event.

Nathan looked around. "Where's Cam?"

"Getting some rack time," Jessica told him.

"We can do this without her, can't we?"

"You're the captain. What are you asking me for?"

"Right. Let her sleep. Give a ship-wide jump warning—except for Cam's cabin."

Jessica pressed a few keys, telling the computer to exclude Cameron's cabin from the broadcast. "All hands, one minute to jump. Repeat, one minute to jump."

"Kaylah. Any contacts in the area?"

"No, sir. The scope is clear."

Nathan leaned back to whisper to Jessica again. "You know, this used to give me the heebie-jeebies. But now that I'm getting used to the idea, I'm starting to kind of like it. It feels really powerful to be able to give the order, and just like that, we're suddenly light years away."

Jessica looked at Nathan's boyish grin. "You're kind of weird, sir."

"Ten seconds to jump," Abby announced. She switched on her headset, which was now preprogrammed to broadcast ship-wide during a jump. She counted down from five to one and jumped the ship yet again.

Deliza watched the main viewer as it darkened just enough to prevent the sudden explosion of blue-white light from blinding all those looking directly at it. As fast as it had come, it was gone, and the stars shifted again.

"Jump complete," Abby announced. "In position just outside of the Darvano system, thirty-three point four light hours out from Corinair."

"Contacts?" Nathan immediately asked.

"No contacts," Kaylah announced after a moment's pause. "The scope is clear."

Abby turned around just enough to see Deliza's face.

"That was amazing!" she exclaimed.

"Yes, it was," Abby agreed. She could see the wonder in the child's eyes. But she could also see the mind of a genius as she calculated the scientific implications that such a device carried. It was the same dancing eyes she had seen on her father when they had accidentally discovered a way to jump vast distances in space during their testing of advanced energy shielding. The accident that had revealed this miracle of science and physics to them had been so discreet that the effect on the test vehicle's position had almost gone completely unnoticed. In fact, it had for several months. And it would still be a mystery had her father not noticed the discrepancy. *And he might still be alive*, she thought.

"How often do you guys do that?" Deliza asked.

"Oh, a few times a week, at least," Nathan bragged.

"You *are* weird," Jessica mumbled.

Nathan just sneered at her. "Kaylah, scan everything you can, and compare it to the star charts that were translated from Tug's fighter. I want to know everything possible about this system before we try to sneak into it."

"Yes, sir."

"Doctor, how long until we can enter the system?" Nathan asked.

"Four and a half hours to be fully charged," Abby answered. "But there is more than enough power to jump in now and still have enough for a short escape jump, if you prefer not to wait."

"I can wait," Nathan insisted. "I prefer to enter with as much jump juice left over as possible. We'll have a pre-jump briefing in four hours: command staff, shuttle crew, and Tug and Jalea," he said as he turned to head back to his ready room. "You have the conn, Jess."

"Aye, sir," Jessica responded. She slowly turned her head to face Abby, waiting for Nathan to leave the room. "Jump juice?"

Abby just shook her head at the euphemism.

CHAPTER FIVE

In the four hours since arriving on the outer edges of the Darvano system, Nathan had managed to eat, study the details of the system from Tug's star charts, and had even gotten up the nerve to visit medical for his post away-mission checkup. As expected, he had received an earful from Doctor Chen regarding not only his tardiness, but also the trauma inflicted on the prisoner. Despite his repeated apologies, he doubted she would be forgiving him any time soon.

Fortunately, the prisoner had not been seriously injured. His facial lacerations were already on the mend, as was his fractured nose, no doubt the result of Jessica's well-placed boot heel. He had also had a pretty decent neck injury due to the initial blow that Jalea had delivered. Jessica had later explained to Nathan that Jalea's first blow to the prisoner's neck had been intended to kill. Had it not been for the prisoner's quick reactions, she probably would've succeeded.

That knowledge of intent troubled Nathan, as this was quite probably the second time he had witnessed the brutal warrior side of Jalea's personality. The woman was usually so cold and dispassionate in day-to-day conversation. Even when they had been under fire on the surface of Haven, she had still remained cold and calculating the entire time. In fact, that episode in the brig was the first time he had seen her snap emotionally. And it made him wonder exactly how much anger was still trapped inside of her.

Nathan wandered down the corridors surrounding the flight decks, looking for the squadron briefing room that Jessica had advised him to use for this pre-jump briefing. With a total of twelve people in attendance, the command briefing room would be too small, yet the main briefing room would be too large. The squadron briefing room accommodated up to thirty-two pilots and was equipped with all the audio-visual displays they would need. Nathan had been too embarrassed at the time to admit that he didn't exactly know where this particular briefing room was located. Now, he only hoped that by the time he found it he would only appear *fashionably late.*

"How many times are you going to pass this corridor before you realize it's the one you're looking for?"

Nathan turned and saw Cameron leaning against the bulkhead a few meters down the corridor, her arms crossed and a look of disbelief adorning her face.

"Really, Nathan. You're the captain of the ship, for Christ's sake."

"Ssh," he said, putting his forefinger to his lips. "Don't tell anyone," he pleaded as he turned down the corridor towards her.

"Am I going to have to put *study ship's layout* on your to-do list?" she teased as she turned and led him down the corridor and into the squadron briefing room.

"Captain on deck," she announced as she led him into the room. Vladimir, Jessica, and Enrique—

being the only actual crew members in the room—all jumped to attention. The rest, feeling out of place, started to stand as well.

"Don't," Nathan objected, motioning for them to remain seated. He glanced over at Cameron, who appeared quite pleased with herself. "Very funny," he muttered under his breath. Despite the joke at his expense, he was happy to see the lighter side of Cameron popping up now and then.

"Good afternoon, everyone," Nathan began. Nathan looked about the room. He had been in similar rooms during his small craft flight training back at the academy but this one was considerably nicer. It was darker than most of the spaces on the ship, lending a more serious tone to the room. The seats were all high-backed and overstuffed, and were arranged in four rows of eight, with a center aisle splitting the rows into pairs of four. Each row was slightly more elevated than the one in front of it, ensuring that everyone in attendance had a clear view of both the speaker at the podium and the three large display screens along the wall directly behind him. The lighting was subdued but adequate, with tiny spotlights shining down onto each seat from above. Nathan could easily imagine the room full of swaggering fighter jocks, ready to jump into their cockpits and catapult out into the blackness to face the enemy. In fact, at that point, Nathan really wished he had both those fighter pilots and their ships at his disposal, as it would make him feel a whole lot safer. Instead, he had this collection of fresh-faced academy graduates, Karuzari rebels, and a few refugees from Haven. Considering his own lack of qualifications and experience, he didn't feel fit to command even this ragtag group. Yet here they all sat, ready to perform whatever task he set them on, and without question no less. That was the most amazing thing about command. They were all aware of his lack of experience—at least those in the Fleet were—yet they were still willing to do his bidding. They placed their faith in his ability to make decisions and protect them from harm as best he could while still carrying out their duties.

"We are about to enter the Darvano system. It is a heavily populated and fully industrialized system with at least three populated worlds. The bulk of the population is on Corinair, the fourth planet out. There are also a few populated moons located in orbit around the sixth planet, which is a gas giant. Our destination is in the asteroid belt which lies between Corinair and the fifth planet, also a gas giant. Asteroids within this belt are mined from the inside out, leaving a relatively empty shell that is later de-orbited so it can be captured by Corinair's gravity to be broken up and harvested later. Apparently, this is all a very lengthy process, resulting in hundreds of hollowed out asteroids waiting for their turn to be de-orbited. Within one of these hollow rocks is a base that was constructed by the Karuzari some years ago for the purpose of servicing captured Ta'Akar warships. Unfortunately, they were never able to make such captures, hence, the base has gone unused since its original construction. Our plan is to use this base as a hideout in which to conduct repairs."

Jessica and Enrique were both sitting together in the back row. Ever mindful of security, Jessica always wanted to be in a position where she could keep an eye on everyone else. "If the belt is constantly mined," Enrique asked, "isn't it possible we'll be spotted?"

"The breadth of the belt and the distance between most objects makes it highly unlikely, unless there just happens to be a ship in the vicinity when we arrive. Tug assures us that once inside the facility, we will be well hidden to even the most active penetrating scans."

Nathan turned on the display behind him. A representation of the layout of the Darvano system showed up on the screen. "We'd prefer to jump into the system as unnoticed as possible, and close to our final destination. Tug, do you have any recommendations?"

Tug, Jalea, and Allet were all sitting in the front row. Allet, having been working pretty much nonstop since he came aboard, looked like he could fall asleep at any moment. Tug and Jalea, although probably no more rested than anyone else, appeared more attentive.

Tug straightened up slightly before speaking "Captain, I would suggest arriving on the far side of the fifth planet. It is a massive gas giant—almost a proto star—that gives off a lot of radiation which will obscure the sensors of most ships. As long as we remain in a relatively low orbit, we should remain undetected."

"Is there no traffic in the area?" Vladimir wondered. "Perhaps the nearby moons?"

"Because of the radiation levels, the gas giant's moons are not hospitable," Tug explained. "And the close proximity to the asteroid belt results in frequent collisions between the existing moons and rogue asteroids captured by the planet's gravity well. For these reasons, this part of the system is not commonly navigated."

"What about the radiation?" Vladimir asked. "Is it safe?"

"As long as we do not linger in orbit for more than a few hours, we should be safe," Tug promised.

"Doctor," Nathan said, looking at Abby who was sitting by herself directly behind the three members of the Karuzari, "will the gas giant's gravity well present any problems?"

"As an arrival point? No. However, you may have to compensate for its gravity rather quickly when we jump in next to it."

"Maybe we should assume a speed equal to the orbital velocity of the altitude we expect to arrive at before we jump." Cameron suggested.

"That would probably help mitigate the sudden change in gravitational forces," Abby agreed. "If done properly, I suspect you will require no more than a minor orbital inclination correction burn."

Nathan looked at his audience for signs of any other questions. Sensing none, he continued. "Okay then, that'll be our entry point. Once we have achieved a stable orbit, we'll launch the shuttle. Josh, you guys will be carrying a team of four into the base. Tug, Jalea, Vladimir, and Jessica will all be going into the base to check it out and make sure it is still operational before we take the ship inside. Now, the place has been powered down for years, so you'll all have to go in full pressure suits."

"Captain," Josh interrupted, "are you saying we're gonna be flying *inside* that asteroid?"

"That's the plan."

"Excellent. I've smashed rocks, captured rocks, and even dodged rocks. But I've never flown *inside* a rock."

"The shuttle doesn't have an airlock, sir," Loki

pointed out.

"Then I guess you'll all be wearing pressure suits."

Josh looked excited about that prospect as well, even if Loki did not.

"Once you get inside, Jess, check the place out and power it up. Once both you and Tug are satisfied that it's safe, we'll break orbit and get inside as quickly as we can to avoid detection."

"And if there's traffic in the area?" Jessica asked.

"If necessary, we'll jump in close. But we'd like to avoid that if possible, as the jump itself creates quite a flash which is highly noticeable if you happen to be looking in the right direction."

"It is highly unlikely that we will encounter any traffic," Tug insisted. "This particular asteroid was chosen due in part to its location. Most of the asteroids in the area have already been mined to their limit, so there should be no interest in that particular region."

"What are you planning on doing once you get inside this rock?" Marcus asked.

"Once inside and securely docked, we should be able to power down many systems and more easily conduct repairs. While we're there, we'll be sending Tug and Jalea to Corinair, along with a load of ore to sell. They should be there for at least a day, during which time they will procure more supplies and attempt to make contact with members of the Karuzari that may be hiding on Corinair." Nathan looked around the room again. "Any questions?"

"Yeah," Marcus grunted. "How long we gonna hideout here?"

"As long as it takes, but no longer than necessary," Nathan said, intending to be vague. "We make that determination on a day-by-day basis. All right, we've got about thirty minutes until we're ready to jump. So you might as well get suited up and ready. Good luck."

Nathan stepped down from the podium and quickly exited the room with Cameron on his heels. "How did I do?"

"Okay," she answered. "Confident, relaxed. Not bad, considering you got lost on your way to the briefing."

"Don't be insubordinate," he told her with a wry smile.

* * *

Nathan stood at the tactical console, reviewing the deep system scan reports that Kaylah had performed over the previous few hours. They had collected more than enough data to confirm the accuracy of the star charts translated from Tug's fighter, and Abby felt confident that her plot into the system was a safe one.

Deliza again stood by Abby's side. Since she had begun working with her on using one of the dead shuttle's computer cores to make jump calculations, the two had become inseparable. Nathan suspected that, whether she was aware of it or not, the physicist had taken on the role of surrogate mother in the wake of the death of Deliza's real mother.

"Bridge, Nash," Jessica's voice came across the comm-set.

"Go ahead," Nathan said over his comm-set.

"We're all suited up and ready to go down here."

"Very well. Have your pilot taxi out onto the flight deck. I want you guys ready to launch the moment we arrive."

"*Copy.*"

Nathan looked down at the console, noting that the shuttle was already moving out of the hangar and into the main transfer airlock. Within minutes, it would be positioned outside the ship, sitting on the flight deck, exposed to space. *They're going to have quite a show,* he thought.

"Helm, put us on an intercept course for the jump in. Match velocity to the orbital velocity of the gas giant."

"Yes, sir," Cameron responded. She had been sitting at the helm since they had returned from the pre-jump mission briefing nearly thirty minutes ago. She had received the navigational data from Abby at least ten minutes ago and had already verified and entered it into the Aurora's nav-com long before Nathan gave her the order to do so. But she knew that he was just going through the motions, making sure he didn't forget anything.

"Attention all hands," Nathan called throughout the ship. "Stand by for jump in one minute. Repeat, we jump in one minute."

As the shuttle rolled out of the transfer airlock and onto the open flight deck, Jessica—who was sitting in a jump seat directly behind the flight crew—couldn't help but notice that neither of the pilots seemed to know exactly where every control was located in their cockpit. "Uh, you guys have flown one of these before, right?"

"Define *flown,*" Loki asked, a bit of uncharacteristic sarcasm in his voice.

"You know, launch, fly around, and then land

again… safely, I might add."

"No worries, love," Josh chimed in with his usual arrogance. "They all fly the same way."

"Yeah, it's just figuring out where all the little buttons and switches are that's the tricky part."

Jessica looked at Loki, then Josh, then back to Loki again. "You guys are messing with me, aren't you?" She leaned back into her seat, either confident in her revelation or just not wanting to know the truth.

Loki glanced back over his shoulder, "Of course we are," he assured her. He shot a guilty look over to Josh, who returned the expression in kind. Loki repositioned his helmet mic and contacted the Aurora. "Aurora, this is Shuttle One. We are in position and ready for departure."

"Copy that, Shuttle One. Stand by. Oh, and guys, don't forget about the flash," Nathan reminded them over the comms. *"We don't need two blind pilots."*

"Copy Aurora," Loki answered as he dropped his darkened visor from the compartment along the top of his helmet down to cover his eyes.

"What's with the Shuttle One?" Josh asked as he dropped his own visor into place.

"What was I supposed to call us, Shuttle Two?"

"Well what do we need a number for? We're the only bleedin' shuttle around."

"In case we get another shuttle later, I guess. What do you care?"

"At least you could've come up with something cool, like Recon Shuttle or something."

"Listen, you just fly this thing. Let me talk on the radio, okay?" Loki insisted.

"Stand by to jump in five," Abby's voice counted down over the comm.

"Don't get all testy," Josh teased. There was nothing he liked more than pushing Loki's buttons.

"Four."

"I'm not getting testy."

"Three."

"Yes, you are. Like a little girl you are," Josh prodded.

"Two."

"Everyone close your eyes," Jessica instructed the passengers.

"One."

"Little girl, am I?" Loki said, beginning to take offense.

"Jump."

Outside the shuttle, the bluish-white light again shot out from the emitters on the hull, quickly connecting them and covering the ship in a light that almost instantly intensified into a brilliant white. Through their polarized visors, Josh and Loki could see the hull of the Aurora outside, a momentary white halo covering and contouring to her hull lines. When the light subsided, the black star field was instantly replaced by the image of the massive, turquoise gas giant that filled the sky in front of them, except for the blackness off to their starboard side.

The sudden arrival of the massive gas giant gave them both a start, causing them to jump slightly in their flight couches.

"Whoa!" Loki screamed.

"Jesus! That's the coolest thing ever!" Josh exclaimed.

"Cool? I just about pissed myself!" Loki admitted.

"Shuttle One, Aurora. You're cleared for launch."

"Copy. Shuttle One taking off," Loki replied as he

lifted his visor.

Josh immediately fired the thrusters, pushing the ship up and away from the flight deck of the Aurora.

"Visor, dumbass," Loki said to Josh, who still hadn't raised his polarized visor.

"What's that smell?" Josh asked, pretending to sniff the air as he raised his visor.

"I said almost," Loki defended.

Josh looked at his displays and glanced out the windows of the shuttle, checking his position relative to the Aurora. "Hang on!" he called out to his passengers as he fired his thrusters again, slid the shuttle sideways, and rolled off over the Aurora's starboard side. He fired his mains at full burn, throwing everyone back into the seats as he drove the shuttle away from the Aurora at a steep angle.

"It's going to take a lot of velocity to break orbit from that big bitch out there," Loki warned.

"Stable orbit achieved," Cameron reported.

"The shuttle's away," Nathan reported, after checking his console displays. "Kaylah, any contacts?"

"Negative, sir. The area is clear. But there is a lot of traffic around Corinair, as well as the asteroid belt itself. It all seems to be avoiding this area."

"I guess Tug was right," Nathan said.

"Let's hope he's right about the hideout as well," Cameron added. As much as she disliked the idea of piloting the ship into a giant cave in space, she preferred it to sitting out in the open in a system that was regularly visited by Ta'Akar warships.

"Abby, are you plotting an escape jump?" Nathan

asked.

"Yes, sir. But we'll have to get some distance from this planet before we can safely jump. Its gravity well is enormous."

"Cam, plot an intercept course to meet with the shuttle halfway, in case we all have to clear out in a hurry. Abby, you can plot your escape jump from anywhere along her intercept course."

"Yes, sir," Abby answered.

"It looks like it will take them at least a couple of hours to get there," Cameron informed him, "even at a full burn."

"I guess all we can do is wait."

* * *

The climb out of the gas giant's gravity well had been long and difficult. The noise of the shuttle's main engines fighting to break free of the planet's hold on them had been deafening. Even closing and sealing their helmets had done little to reduce the ear-splitting whine.

Finally, after what seemed an eternity, the shuttle broke free of the planet's gravity and reached its cruising speed. The whine of the engines suddenly ceased as Josh ended the long, torturous burn. But instead of a much welcomed silence, there was the steady, grating sound of Marcus, the former harvesting crew foreman now turned shuttle crew chief, snoring away.

"For all that's holy," Josh chuckled. "The man is like a plasma drill," he declared as he climbed out of his seat and moved back into the main compartment. When he reached Marcus, he carefully plugged in the life support umbilical from the ship to his suit and gently closed and sealed his helmet. Finally, the snoring was reduced to a tolerable level.

"That's better," Josh decided, taking a seat next to Marcus and across the compartment from Jessica. "The man can sleep through just about anything," he joked.

"You've known him for a while?" Jessica asked. Part of her was curious, and part of her was just making small talk.

"Since I was little. My mom was a worker on his team. She died. Marcus took me in, took care of me as best he could. He's been sort of like a father to me." Josh looked at Marcus as he continued to snore away. "A loud, obnoxious, drunken, bastard of a father," he laughed. "Took good care of me though."

"How did you end up flying?"

"Used to steal his credits when he wasn't looking. Spent them down at the VR game arcades. Nothing but flight games. Didn't care much for the other ones. Got damn good at them too. Finally, Marcus here decided it was cheaper to pay for flight school than to keep losing his money to my thieving hands. Been flying ever since."

"But you're only, what, sixteen?"

Josh appeared shocked. "I'll be twenty next month, I will."

"How old were you when you went to flight school?"

"Graduated right after me sixteenth, I did."

"Four years? That's it? Hell, it takes us that long just to get through the Fleet Academy back on Earth."

"I've racked up nearly fifteen thousand hours since then, love."

"Whattaya live in the cockpit?"

"Ten, twelve hours a day, nearly every day."

"You ever get bored?"

"Nope, flying is the best thing around, far as I can tell."

"What about your pal there?" Jessica asked, pointing toward Loki who was manning the controls while Josh took a break. "How did you two end up flying together?"

Josh removed his helmet, setting it on the bench next to him. "Well, to be honest, I had a hard time keeping copilots. Seems most folk don't care much for my stick style, if you get my meaning," he said, scratching his scraggly mound of dirty blond hair.

"They think you're too reckless, or something?"

"No, nothing like that. They just kept getting sick, tossin' up all over the place. The inertial dampeners in the harvester ain't worth a damn. Jeez, I was spending an hour after every flight just cleaning up the cockpit."

Jessica shook her head. "You're just a bit off, aren't you?"

"That's what Loki keeps telling me."

"How long have you been flying with him?"

"Don't rightly know, maybe six months, maybe more. What about you, then?" Josh asked, trying to change the subject. "Did they train you to be so tough in that Academy of yours?"

"Sort of. I was hoping to be a covert operative."

"What does a covert operative do?"

"They drop you on some alien world, where you try to blend in, gather intelligence on the enemy, maybe even conduct raids and such."

"Sounds dangerous."

"Apparently no more dangerous than flying with you—at least according to Vlad."

Josh nodded. "Ah, the chief. He seems a good bloke."

"Yeah, he's all right. Pretty dependable in a firefight. That's for sure."

"Told us a lot about Earth and all the other night. Interesting stuff." Josh looked over at Tug and Jalea, who were sitting at the far aft end of the compartment, talking amongst themselves in their own language. "What about those two?" Josh asked, his voice a bit more subdued. "He's not exactly what I expected, for a terrorist that is. She is, but he's not."

"What makes you think they're terrorists? Aren't the Ta'Akar worse?"

"Don't get me wrong. I'm no fan of the Ta'Akar, not by a long shot. That Caius fella, he's got a few loose ones upstairs, you know. But some of the stuff you hear about... The things the Karuzari have done... Well, it don't seem much different, really. Just on a smaller scale is all."

"So you don't think they're in the right?"

"Oh, they're in the right. Gettin' rid of the Ta'Akar would be the best thing to ever happen to this part of the galaxy. Just don't know that they're goin' about it in the best way. That's all."

"How so?"

"It's like they're on the outside, trying to get in by beating at the wall with hammers and chisels and the like. They need to find an easy way in to clean house all at once. Get it over and done with. Everyone knows you can't fight a guerrilla war forever. Sooner or later, you're gonna run out of guerrillas."

"Ten minutes out, Josh," Loki called over his shoulder from the cockpit.

"Enough philosophizing," Josh said with a grin.

He reached for his helmet, donning it on his way forward.

"Hell, this ain't nothing," Josh proclaimed as he took his seat in the cockpit. "You could fly a planet between these rocks."

"It's an asteroid belt, Josh, not a ring system," Loki teased.

"You find our rock yet?" Josh asked, ignoring his remark.

"If we come starboard about thirty and down a bit, she should be dead ahead. Gonna have to brake pretty hard to keep from smacking into her, though."

"I believe that's how we always do it," Josh bragged.

"What, the braking hard or the smacking into her?"

"Always with the negativity, Loki." Josh fired the maneuvering thrusters as he applied power to the main propulsion system, changing their vector as he brought the ship onto its new heading.

"Standard braking maneuver, I assume?"

"Yup," Josh said as he prepared his ship for the next maneuver. He looked up and saw that the asteroid was fast filling the windows. "Pitching up." He pulled the nose of the ship up and fired the main landing thrusters. Second only to the main drive in raw thrust, it was the fastest way he knew to slow a ship down in a hurry. He could've approached at a lower velocity, but that would just leave him visible to any ships nearby even longer.

"You know, you didn't have to come in this fast," Jessica commented.

"Just trying to be *covert*," he responded.

A few minutes later, the shuttle matched the asteroids velocity on its orbital path around its parent star, leaving the shuttle holding a position only a few hundred meters away. Josh pitched the nose back down to take a look.

"Aw," he exclaimed with disappointment, "we've gotta be at least a hundred meters away." He turned to look at Loki. "Did you pad the reading again?"

"Shut up. I'm trying to find the entrance."

"It will be on the underside," Tug explained, stepping up behind them. "You'll see a deep crack. Go down into the crack, and you'll see the entrance on the port side. There is an overhang that conceals it from above. You can only see it from within the crack."

"Cool. Now we're flying into a crack?" Josh stated as he pitched the nose down slightly and applied forward thrust.

The asteroid slid up and over them as they slowly approached.

"Aurora, Shuttle One," Loki called. "We're at the asteroid and moving in. We'll be losing comms any moment now."

"Copy that. Good luck," the Aurora's comm-officer called back. His voice was already sounding tinny and broken as their signal degraded.

"Activating terrain scanners," Loki reported. "Recording all scan data."

"Throw some extra light on it, will ya?" Josh asked.

Loki reached up above his left shoulder to the overhead side panel. Running his finger along a row of rocker switches, he found the right one and clicked it on.

Outside the shuttle, several banks of exterior lights burst to life, washing the surface of the asteroid above them in bright, white daylight.

"Dang. Scary looking rock, ain't it?" Josh commented.

"You're going to have to flip over," Tug said, "so you can hover using your thrusters. The asteroid may not be that big, but it is big enough to have some gravity."

"Really?" Josh said using a mock-idiot voice. "It's got gravity?" As quickly as he had turned it on, he turned his mock voice back off again. "Thanks, pops. I think we've got this one."

"The gravity will change as you travel deeper into the heart of the asteroid," Tug continued, ignoring their sarcasm.

"Yeah, we understand. Just take your seat, okay," Loki said. He knew that if he didn't get the old rebel leader off their backs, Josh was going to get them in trouble with another smart remark.

Tug resigned himself to the fact that his life was in the hands of these two young pilots, both of which he highly doubted had ever flown under such conditions. But he had learned many decades ago that his destiny was not always in his own hands.

"Is that going to be a problem for the Aurora?" Jessica asked Tug as he took a seat across from her. "The gravity, I mean."

"Once we are inside and the facility is powered up, there are compensation mechanisms built into the crack and the tunnels that will maintain a zero-gravity environment. The Aurora will not have to compensate as we will."

"Well that's something, anyway," she muttered. She looked at Marcus, who was still sitting on the bench across from her, next to Tug, sound asleep and snoring inside his helmet. She reached out her foot and gave him a kick.

"Wake up!" she hollered.

Marcus shook slightly, opening his eyes with a start. For a moment, he wasn't quite sure where he was. The fact that he was closed up inside a pressure suit also caught him by surprise. It was, in fact, the first time he had worn one, and he didn't care much for the idea.

Scrambling to get the faceplate up, they could hear his muffled curses aimed at Josh for closing his faceplate to begin with.

"There it is," Loki said, pointing at the crack in the asteroid over their heads.

"Lining her up now," Josh announced as he corrected their approach course to line up with the crack above them.

Both Tug and Jessica leaned in toward the center of the shuttle, trying to see forward through the cockpit windows. Despite their best efforts, the view was not very revealing.

Josh began thrusting toward the asteroid to bring them in closer. "Just a touch, to let the asteroid's gravity pull us down," he said. "Rolling over." Josh rolled the shuttle on its longitudinal axis so that its bottom was now facing the asteroid.

"Are there any other windows back here?" Jessica asked. "I'm supposed to be checking the place out and I can't see shit from back here."

"Lock your visors down and go to internal support," Marcus instructed them. Marcus watched as each of them locked down their helmet visors, checked that their internal life support systems were working and then reported such to him with a *thumbs-up* sign.

"Depress the ship," Marcus told Loki.

"Depressurizing."

Slowly, over a few minutes, the sounds inside the shuttle faded away as the oxygen that carried them was sucked out of the cabin. Once they were in silence and could hear nothing other than their own respirations, Marcus moved to the back of the ship and activated the loading ramp. The big ramp, that when closed made up the aft wall of the cabin, lowered away, creating a platform off the back end of the shuttle.

"Did you order a view?" Marcus asked, gesturing toward the open back end of the shuttle.

Jessica walked out onto the platform, activating the magnetic grips in the soles of her boots to keep from falling off. Once at the extreme end, she turned around to face forward. The shuttle was not all the way down in the crack, which was about three hundred meters deep and more than three times that in width. It was a breathtaking view, with the massive turquoise gas giant in the distant black sky. "This is amazing," she exclaimed.

"The entrance is coming up on the port side," Loki reported. "We'll be coming to port in about ten seconds."

Jessica could see the overhang jutting out on the port side for a few seconds before they turned. Moments later, they were inside the massive tunnel. The walls were ragged, but overall they were a lot smoother than she had expected. Every twenty to thirty meters, she saw strategically placed rings that went around the inside of the tunnel's diameter. "What are those rings?"

"Lighting, gravity displacement emitters, sensors, and comm-arrays," Tug explained as he stepped out onto the ramp next to her. "They are located all along the tunnels. It makes the tunnels very easy to navigate when the facility is operational."

"Did you guys do all this yourselves?"

"No. We could never afford this level of construction. The facility was once a mining base. It was abandoned decades ago and has been awaiting de-orbit. We simply took advantage of its availability. We only had to provide the power plant, which we got from a few otherwise inoperable Ta'Akar ships."

"Still, it's pretty impressive."

"You do not have such facilities on Earth?"

"Oh, we're mining our asteroid belt as well, just not from the inside out."

"It takes many generations to fully excavate some of the more massive asteroids. This one is one of the smaller ones. It is only a few kilometers across, but it was perfect for our plans. I only wish we had been given an opportunity to utilize it much earlier."

The tunnel suddenly opened up into a much larger cavern, at least a kilometer in diameter. The walls, floors, and ceilings were craggy and irregular, and there was another tunnel that appeared to be an exit on the opposite side. All along the walls were strange boxes and domes, some joined together by surface tunnels, others seemingly standing alone and disconnected. Along one side of the cavern there was a large framework surrounding what looked like a platform of some type jutting out from the wall. There was an entrance with big double doors that led from the platform into the rock itself.

"Is that the facility?" Jessica asked.

"That's the dock, yes. All of these buildings are the facility."

"But they're all at such varying angles," Jessica commented. "Doesn't it get disorienting?"

"Each building has its own gravity plating. It's

easier than trying to orient every structure to use the asteroid's rather weak gravity. You get used to it after a while."

"Take us down onto the platform to port," Tug instructed the flight crew.

The shuttle turned to port and descended slightly. As it approached the platform, it slowly rotated until its aft end was facing the big double doors on the wall. The shuttle backed over the platform before finally extending its landing gear and setting down.

Marcus lowered the boarding ramp the last meter until it made contact with the platform, allowing Tug, Jalea, and Jessica to step off the ramp and onto the platform.

Jessica turned back to face the shuttle. "Josh, you and Loki stay with the ship. If we're not back in thirty minutes, head back to the Aurora and get help."

"Got it."

"What about me?" Marcus asked, not sure that he wanted to hear the answer.

"Come on, tough guy. You're with me."

"Great."

Jessica and Marcus followed Tug and Jalea across the platform to a small personnel hatch just to the right of the cargo doors. Tug spun the hatch lock and swung the hatch open. There was very little illumination from the shuttle's exterior flood lights making its way into the next room, so Tug and Jalea both turned on their helmet lights as they entered. Following suit, Jessica and Marcus did the same. They stepped into the airlock and closed the hatch behind them, repeating the process to pass through the inner hatch. Once inside, they made their way down a long, dark corridor, the beams from the helmet lights dancing about the walls. After about ten meters, they came to a door marked *"Control."*

The small control room consisted of four consoles on one side of the room and another four opposite them. Within moments, Tug was at the correct control panel and had activated the emergency lighting.

"I have activated the emergency backup power. The external communications array should be active in a few moments. It will have a limited range until the main reactor is online, which will take about an hour. So it can provide communications in the general vicinity of this asteroid only. Once the main reactor is online, we should be fully operational."

"Shuttle, this is Nash."

"Go ahead," Loki answered.

"We're good here. It'll take about an hour to get everything powered up. Meanwhile, take off and get outside. Once you're outside the asteroid, contact the Aurora and tell her she's clear to approach. Transmit your scanner data back to them and then stand by until you hear from me."

"Copy that. Taking off."

"So what do we do now?" Marcus asked. "Sit around and wait?"

"I don't know about you," Jessica said, "but I'm gonna take a look around this place."

* * *

"It should take about an hour to bring the facility fully online," Loki reported over the comms. *"So by the time you get here, it should be fully operational."*

"Copy that," Nathan answered from his command chair on the bridge. "How were the tunnels?"

"Pretty straight, not too long, plenty of room. Shouldn't be a problem. Plus there's an exit tunnel on the opposite side. The toughest part is the initial turn into the tunnel. You have to come down into a crack and then slip under this massive overhang that hides the entrance. The first turn into the tunnel is a little sharp, but after that it's no problem. He had to fight the asteroids gravity the whole time, but Tug says the whole thing is lined with gravity plating, so you'll have a zero-G environment when you get here."

"And the main docking area? How's that?"

"It's huge," Loki exclaimed. *"You could park three of your ships in there."*

"Copy." Nathan turned to Cameron, who had been standing next to him and listening to the conversation the entire time. "What's our ETA there?"

"We can go quite a bit faster than the shuttle, so just under an hour."

"Send us your scan data," Nathan ordered. "We'll be there in just under an hour."

"Copy that. Sending scan data now."

"Whenever you're ready, Commander."

"We're receiving the scan data, Captain," the comm-officer reported.

"Very well. Kaylah, use their scan data to build a 3D navigation map. I think we'd like to get a look at the route before we take the ship in there."

"Yes, sir," Ensign Yosef responded.

Cameron took the seat at the helm console and prepared to break orbit.

"I don't suppose you need my help flying the ship." Nathan offered.

"For a basic transfer orbit?" Cameron said. "Please, I can do this in my sleep."

"Doctor, I assume it's just as pointless to ask if you have escape jumps plotted?"

"Correct, it is," Abby answered, her eyes never leaving her console.

"All right, then. As strange an order as it may seem, take us to the hideout, Commander," Nathan ordered.

* * *

The asteroid now filled most of the main view screen as the Aurora closed in on the massive rock. Lit mostly from behind and to port, the irregular mass was riddled with shadows that were barely softened by the ships external floodlights. Cameron had slowed their closure rate as they approached and they were now nearly matched in their orbital velocities around the parent star.

"I think this place will work fine," Jessica reported over the comms. *"We've been through most of the main compartments, but it's only a fraction of the entire facility. According to Tug, most of it is closed off and powered down since they never really needed it. But there's a full space dock, with gantries and robotic arms and the like. There are also several machine and fabrication facilities. In fact, they have something similar to the 3D component printing technology that we use, only a lot more advanced from the looks of it."*

Cameron looked at Nathan from her seat at the helm, her face showing hope for the first time in days. From what she was hearing in Jessica's initial report, the rebel hideout might be a blessing in disguise.

"Sounds good. We're on approach now, so we

should be docking shortly."

"Yeah, we've got you on our scope here, so we'll be tracking you all the way in. Nash out."

"Captain, Shuttle One has just arrived in our hangar," the comm-officer reported.

"Very well," he answered. "Have them refuel and get the shuttle ready to launch again, just in case." Nathan turned back to Cameron. "Are you ready for this, Commander?"

"Don't worry, Nathan. This will be easy."

"Easy? You're about to pilot a spaceship through a tunnel in an asteroid. I don't remember ever running any simulations on this."

"Not to worry. I used the 3D nav-map that Kaylah assembled to plot a series of maneuvering waypoints that I programmed into the navigation system. The ship will practically fly itself through the tunnels. All I've got to do is get her in the front door and to the first waypoint. The computer will take it from there."

"Very well. Take us in."

"Aye, sir." Cameron pushed the nose of the ship down slightly and applied a bit of forward thrust to move closer and slip down under the asteroid, rolling the ship over as they drew closer. The image of the asteroid on the main view screen moved up and then rotated over, until it was only showing along the bottom quarter of the screen and was slowly rising as they descended towards it.

Nathan moved over into the copilot's seat as he watched the main view screen. Cameron noticed him assuming the navigator's position with some dismay, as she had been pretty much flying the ship solo since they had arrived in this part of the galaxy.

"I've got this, Nathan," she said under her breath.

"I'll be good," he promised quietly. "I'm just going to sit here in case you need me." She shot a quick glance his way, not wanting to take her eyes off the console displays. "Besides," he added, "I feel useless sitting back there." Nathan glanced back at Cameron and noticed a slight smirk forming on her face. "Don't start," he warned.

Cameron slid the ship slightly farther to port in order to line her up with the crack into which they needed to descend. The flight display showed a line drawing of the basic shape of the crevice, as well as both the recommended and their actual flight path. All she really had to do was keep to the recommended flight path until they hit the first waypoint. At that point, she could use the ship's auto-flight system to run them through a series of maneuvers she had already programmed using the data collected by the shuttle. Although she felt confident that she could pilot the ship through the tunnels manually, there was no reason not to let the computers do the work. She was quite sure that, had Nathan been sitting at the helm, he would have chosen to fly through the tunnels on his own. Back at the Academy, she had noticed that most of the male pilots were reluctant to let the computer do any of the piloting. It was just one more thing about the male ego that she failed to understand.

As they came uncomfortably close to the asteroid's surface, she could see Nathan becoming agitated. He kept glancing over at her, checking to see what she was doing. She was sure that he was curious about the fact that her hand never went for the manual control stick, choosing instead to do everything by computer commands.

"Picking up a change in gravity ahead, Commander," Kaylah reported.

"Must be the zero-G corridor they were talking about," Nathan said.

"That's affirmative, sir. I'm now reading zero gravity in the crevice, starting in about five hundred meters."

Nathan looked down at his flight displays. "Wow. You're going to hit your mark perfectly," he admitted, realizing that Cameron had chosen to let the asteroid's weak gravity field pull the ship closer at a rate that would leave them at the perfect altitude when they crossed the threshold into the artificially induced zero gravity in the crevice.

"There's more to piloting a starship than just yanking on a joystick," she quipped.

"I'll have to remember that."

The ship settled in a scant one hundred meters above the floor of the crevice as it crossed into the zero-gravity channel. A small blast from the thrusters made sure that their descent stopped as they continued to crawl forward down the long, deep crack in the massive rock. Although it had appeared to be naturally occurring from orbit, up close it was obvious that much of the surface had been cut away to make the crevice more easily navigable for larger ships. Nathan suspected that the Karuzari had been hoping to capture something as large as one of the Ta'Akar capital ships; although he wasn't quite sure one of them would actually fit into this channel.

"Coming up on the entrance," Nathan muttered before catching himself.

Cameron applied a slight thrust on the braking thrusters to slow the ship even further. The massive cliff faces on either side of them, visible through the main view screen, barely seemed to be moving at this point.

"There it is," Nathan said, pointing to the left

side of the screen.

Cameron didn't react, didn't even look up. Her attention was focused on her console as she prepared to initiate a slight turn to port. A few moments later, she fired the attitude thrusters, yawing the ship and bringing her nose slightly to port. But the ship continued to slide to starboard, still traveling along the same path it had been prior to the yaw maneuver. She simultaneously applied forward thrust as well as even bow and stern starboard thrust, thus changing the ship's flight path to match the direction that its bow now pointed, which was directly into the massive tunnel veering off to the left of the crevice.

Nathan looked up as he watched the overhang of the tunnel entrance pass over them. The sight sent shivers down his spine. He remembered piloting the ship out of the assembly platform in orbit of Earth, watching the trusses pass overhead. Had he collided with them, the resulting damage to the ship would have been minimal. He was quite sure that any collision with this asteroid, even at their minimal velocity, would be far more serious.

"Coming up on primary waypoint," Cameron announced as her fingers danced across her input keys. A few moments later, she tapped the final key, left her hands floating above the console for a moment, and checked that the auto-flight systems had taken over properly.

"We're locked in," she announced proudly. "The auto-flight system will take us the rest of the way into the main cavern. Once inside, all I have to do is slide us into position in order to make hard dock."

"If their system will mate with ours," Nathan reminded her.

"I'm sure if it doesn't, Vladimir will figure out something," Cameron assured him.

CHAPTER SIX

"Any idea what we're waiting for?" Loki asked. They had been sitting at the entrance to the transfer airlock for several minutes, waiting for clearance to depart.

"No clue, mate," Josh answered. "Maybe the door's stuck," he joked.

Loki looked out the port window and saw Jessica approaching, wearing a pair of heavy, padded headsets that ground crew might normally wear in the noisy operating environment of the hangar bay. "I think we're about to find out," he said, pointing to Jessica as she approached.

Jessica walked up to the nose of the ship, opened a small access panel and plugged in her headset.

"What the hell is she doing?" Josh asked, sitting up as tall as possible to try and see her.

Jessica pointed to her headset then held up three fingers.

"I think she wants to talk to us on channel three," Loki said, switching their headsets to the appropriate channel on the side console. "We're here," Loki stated over the comms.

"Anyone on the line other than you two?" Jessica asked over the comms from outside the shuttle.

"Nope, just us two. You want everyone on?"

"No. Are your passengers within earshot?"

"Uh, no," Loki answered. "They're at the back,

with all the ore between us and them. Marcus is back there with them."

"Can you put Marcus on the same line without them?"

"Yeah. Stand by."

Josh switched Marcus's headset to the same channel, making sure that Tug and Jalea remained on the primary channel. "Don't say anything, Marcus," Josh told him in a hushed tone. "We don't want them to know we're talking to you."

"Cough once if you understand," Jessica told him. A moment later they heard Marcus cough.

"What's going on?" Josh asked. "Why all the cloak and dagger?"

"I don't much like the idea of sending those two down to Corinair unescorted. There's no telling what they're up to. So you guys keep your eyes open. Got it?"

"No worries, love," Josh promised.

"And one more thing. We already got jumped once by a shuttle full of bad guys. We don't want it to happen again. So if you're coming in under duress, you need to give us some kind of signal."

"Like what? You want me to flash my running lights or something?"

"No, something vocal. Something you wouldn't normally say, yet still seems appropriate."

"How about if Josh talks like a real pilot?" Loki teased.

"Yeah, and Loki doesn't. Oh, I know, he can start talking like me."

"Oh, using love and mate every other word?"

"And let's not forget, no worries, eh?"

"Yeah, that'll work fine. What about for Marcus?"

"Oh, how about if he just stops swearing?" Loki

suggested.

"I don't think he can," Josh joked.

Suddenly, several loud, hacking coughs came from Marcus.

"I think he just did," Loki laughed.

"I know," Josh interrupted. "He can just use the word please. That'll make you do a double take, eh?"

"Fine," Jessica said, just wanting to shut the two clowns up. "Please it is. Does that work for you, Marcus?" A single cough confirmed his understanding. "Have a good flight, guys," she said as she unplugged her headset.

"I believe we're both going to get our heads firmly thumped later," Josh declared.

As Loki reached down to change their comms back to the primary channel, a single cough came across the comms to confirm Josh's declaration.

* * *

Nathan poked his head into the auxiliary systems support room just down the corridor from the bridge. The room had been converted into a makeshift signals intelligence office. Naralena, Enrique, and a few of the other refugees from the harvesting crew were busy poring over audio and video recordings that had been gathered over the last few hours.

As he entered the room, he noticed stacks of a few dozen data cores on one of the tables. There were at least four separate workstations setup, as well as a large, wall-mounted view screen on the wall.

"What are you watching?" Nathan asked as he entered the room.

"Nothing too interesting, sir," Enrique explained

as he kept skipping ahead in the video as if looking for something. "Just skimming through news broadcasts and marking anything that looks promising for translation."

"Is this stuff live?"

"Naw, this is all the stuff we collected before we jumped into the system. It's all at least a day old. We picked up stuff that was just a few hours old while we were orbiting the gas giant though. For now we're dark."

"Why is that?"

"We can't pick anything up while we're inside this rock. At least not until they patch us into the facilities external comm-array. Vlad's people are working on it with Allet, but until he gets the boarding ramp to secure properly to the ship, the only way over there is by EVA, so it's slow going."

"When does he expect to be finished?"

"Vlad's working on the boarding ramp while Allet works on the comm-array. Last I heard, a few hours at least."

"What's with the data modules?" Nathan asked, pointing at the stacks of the black and silver components.

"Vlad pulled them from the damaged mainframe cores. Since they're not being used, we've been swapping them out when one of ours gets full. Gives us a bit more storage capacity."

Nathan nodded. "Good idea. If you want, I can scan through some of this stuff as well... if you could use the help, that is."

"Sure. Take as many as you want. Just mark the file and location of anything that looks promising."

"Okay. Carry on," he ordered as he picked up a few data modules on his way out.

* * *

Josh and Loki gazed out the windows at the city below. It stretched out in all directions as far as they could see: tall buildings, most of which came to points up high in the sky, surrounded by lush green parks and crystal white walkways. There were overhead monorail systems running on what seemed like impossibly thin rails. Even the more congested parts of the city appeared pristine by Haven standards.

"I don't much care for this auto-landing crap," Josh complained.

"They probably already heard how you fly and are just playing it safe. Just relax and enjoy the scenery," Loki told him.

"Listen to you two," Marcus teased over the comms from the rear of the shuttle. "You sound like you've never been to a core world before."

"I ain't been off Haven since I was what, four or something?" Josh reminded him.

"I've been a few places besides Haven," Loki admitted, "but never any place like this."

"How many people do you suppose live here?" Josh wondered.

"Over four billion was the last estimate," Tug reported over the comms. "Most of them are clustered on the main island nations in the upper and lower oceans."

"How much of this planet is covered with water?" Loki asked.

"More than ninety percent," Tug explained. "Most of their exports are water-based commodities."

"How come nobody lives in the equatorial

regions?" Loki asked.

"This planet has no axial tilt, and its orbit is nearly a perfect circle; hence, it has almost no seasonal changes. The equatorial regions are just too dry to support life."

"How can any place on a planet that's ninety percent water be too dry?" Josh wondered aloud.

The shuttle continued on its gradual descent over the city as it approached the local spaceport. The closer they came to the port, the more ships they saw coming and going. There was an incredible amount of air traffic, ships of every conceivable shape, size, and purpose.

"Jesus, no wonder they require ships to use the auto-landing system. Look at this!" Loki exclaimed.

"It reminds me of when you go into the kitchen at night, and turn on the lights, and all the bugs go running for cover," Josh commented.

Outside, another larger shuttle appeared to be coming straight at them. "Uh, Loki," Josh said, a slight bit of concern in his voice, "is that guy coming right at us?"

Loki looked down at his scanner display. "I'm not sure."

"Whattaya mean you're not sure?" Josh's concern was beginning to show signs of panic as well.

"There are so many tracks on here; I can't make out who's who."

"Well, are any of them coming right at us or not?"

"They all look like they're coming right at us, Josh!"

Josh began frantically trying to disengage the auto-flight system. "How the hell do you shut off this crap?!" Josh was really starting to panic as the approaching ship drew nearer at an alarming rate.

"We're going to collide!" Josh yelled as he ducked down, holding his arms up over his head to protect himself.

The massive shuttle skimmed over the top of them, missing by no more than a few meters. The jet wash from the larger ship's engines shook the smaller shuttle for several seconds after passing overhead. By the time the roar of the passing ship's engines subsided, all that remained was the sound of Loki's laughter.

"What are you laughing at?" Josh demanded.

"I thought you never flinched?"

"Real funny, that was. Real funny."

Ten minutes later, the shuttle was on the ground and had rolled to a stop at one of the countless cargo terminals. Tug and Jalea came down the boarding ramp almost before it had completely deployed.

"We'll secure a transport for the ore and return," Tug advised Marcus as they walked away.

Marcus watched as the two Karuzari walked across the tarmac until they reached the terminal building, where Tug went to the left toward the transportation office and Jalea went into the terminal building. Jessica had told him to keep an eye on the two of them. He didn't know why she didn't trust them, but as trusting people wasn't in his nature any more than it seemed to be in hers, he had no problem obliging her request.

Jalea took a moment to let her eyes adjust to the interior lighting after coming in from the harsh afternoon sun of Corinair. After looking around to get her bearings, she spotted a communications service counter and headed toward it.

"Can I help you, miss?" the clerk at the counter asked in the local language of Corinairi.

"I need to purchase five comm-units, please."

"Of course. Will those be local, global, or interplanetary?"

"Two local, one global, and two interplanetary units."

"No problem. Just give me a few minutes to activate them for you."

Jalea waited calmly as the clerk activated each unit. After paying for the comm-sets, the clerk placed them all into a clear plastic bag and handed it to her.

Jalea left without delay, heading for the exit. She stopped short of the doors, pausing to take the global comm-set out of the bag and put it into her jacket pocket before heading through the doors.

As she stepped out, Tug pulled up in a large, flatbed cargo skimmer. Jalea stepped into the open cab and took a seat next to him, the skimmer sinking slightly lower to the ground temporarily as it adjusted to the additional weight of another passenger. Tug immediately sped off across the tarmac on his way back to the shuttle.

"What do you suppose she was doing in there?" Marcus wondered aloud.

"Using the bathroom?" Josh offered.

Marcus just glared at him. He continued watching their skimmer as it hurtled across the tarmac, adjusting its speed and course to avoid ships and other skimmers sharing the tarmac with them. After a few minutes, the skimmer finally arrived and Tug backed it into position as close to the rear of the shuttle as possible.

As the skimmer backed up, Marcus raised the ramp so it was level with the tarmac. Tug adjusted the hover height of the skimmer until it was level with the shuttle's boarding ramp and backed it up until it was flush with the boarding ramps leading edge. A moment later, four legs extended from the skimmer and made contact with the tarmac below, after which Tug shut the skimmer down.

Marcus wheeled the crates of ore out of the back of the shuttle and onto the bed of the cargo skimmer, carefully positioning the crates in order to fit all of them onto the vehicle. The entire off-load took only fifteen minutes.

Jalea climbed down out of the skimmer's cab and walked over to Marcus. "You may use this to contact us should the need arise. It will work anywhere within the Darvano system, even inside the asteroid base."

"This thing will work inside a rock?" Marcus challenged.

"The external comm-array will relay the signal to the interior of the facility. It will work just fine. Unless instructed otherwise, you may meet us here tomorrow morning, between nine and ten, local time."

"And what will you two be doing while we're gone?" Marcus asked, trying, but failing, to not appear abnormally inquisitive.

"Our instructions were to sell the ore and use the money to purchase supplies for the Aurora, which you will haul back to the ship tomorrow."

"That shouldn't take too long. Maybe we should just wait around."

"That will not be necessary. We are also going

to attempt to locate any *friends* on this world that might lend assistance."

"Uh huh. What kind of friends?"

"I do not believe that is any of your concern," she said as she turned and walked away.

Marcus looked down at the comm-set she had handed him and then back at her as she climbed into the cab of the skimmer. Tug climbed in the other side of the cab, powered the vehicle back up, and retracted the legs before pulling away.

"That is one icy bitch," Marcus muttered.

"So, time to blast off?" Josh asked.

"Soon," Marcus told him. "First, let's go and get us some real food." A big grin came across his face. "I'm buying."

* * *

It had been relatively easy to dispose of the Aurora's shipment of raw ore as Tug had asked for a price that left the buyer with plenty of room for profit. Now that they had concluded the first task of their visit to Corinair, they were more than ready to depart the dirty, industrial part of the capital city.

"We must go to the market and purchase supplies," Tug announced.

"Perhaps it would be more efficient if we were to separate. You go to the market and procure the supplies the captain requested. I will secure us lodging for the night and place discreet ads on the net that only our friends will recognize. This will provide additional time for them to contact us."

Tug did not like the idea of separating. Not only was the capital city a large and heavily populated city,it also had its dangerous side. He had no doubt that Jalea could handle herself and would not take any undue risks, but he was yet unsure how much he could trust her. Jalea had normally been a master at self-control and emotional discipline, despite some of the more passionate moments they had shared in the distant past, long before his third marriage to Ranni. But her recent behavior, including her sudden violent outburst in the Aurora's interrogation room, had him a bit concerned—not only for her well being, but also as to her true intentions.

"Are you sure?" He did not want to come right out and announce his misgivings. "There is yet sufficient time."

"I will be fine," she assured him. "It is not my first time on this world. Besides, I wish to seek counsel from a member of the Order."

"You still cling to such superstitions, even in the light of our new reality?"

"It still provides me strength," she told him. "Do not judge..."

"Of course. But we must first purchase comm-units," he insisted, "so that we may stay in contact."

"I have already taken the liberty," she informed him, pulling one of the local comm-units from her shoulder bag.

Tug tried unsuccessfully to hide his surprise. "How did you pay for these?" he asked, worried that she might have left a financial marker that a watchful Ta'Akar intelligence operative might notice.

"Do not concern yourself. I used standard universal credits. And I reprogrammed my ident-chip prior to departure, as I am sure you did as well." Jalea smiled to reassure him. "You forget that I am not new to subterfuge. I also purchased a pair of interplanetary comm-units and gave one to the

Havenite in case we need to communicate with him later. We can also list one of the numbers as the contact in our advertisement, in case one of our friends tries to contact us after we return to the ship."

"Ah, Jalea. You have always been good at thinking on your feet," he commended.

"You trained me well," she told him, touching his arm. "Call me once you have secured our cargo at the spaceport and I will let you know of our lodging arrangements."

Tug watched her walk away. She seemed as normal as ever, but there was still something about her demeanor that bothered him. But there was little he could do about it at the moment, and he had business to conclude before the day ended on Corinair.

* * *

Nathan sat in his ready room behind his desk, skimming through video footage on the large view screen on the forward bulkhead over the couch.

"Captain?" Cameron asked as she stuck her head in the open hatchway.

"How many times do I have to tell you, Cam?"

"Sorry, Nathan." She stepped over the hatchway threshold into the ready room, looking at the images on the view screen as she approached his desk. "What are you doing?"

"Skimming through video recordings from Corinair."

"What for?"

"Just marking anything that looks important enough to warrant the time of our only translator."

"You don't have anything better to do?"

"Not really. Apparently, being in command of a broken-down starship with a skeleton crew hiding out inside an asteroid doesn't require much effort," he joked. "Besides, our Sig-Int team can use the help."

"Okay."

"You know," he said, as he stopped to make a note of the file and location of the current finding, "you can actually learn a lot about a civilization by watching this stuff."

"But you don't even understand what they're saying," Cameron pointed out.

"Hell, I don't even have the sound on. But the images themselves tell you a lot. Like I can already tell that Tug and Jalea's claims about the brutality of the regime of Caius are not exaggerations."

"That's unfortunate."

"You're telling me. I was hoping they were just blowing smoke up our butts. It would've made it a lot easier to jump the hell out of here after we got ourselves patched up."

"What?" Cameron was confused.

"You didn't really think I wanted to stick around and fight someone else's war, did you?"

"Well, actually, I guess I did."

"Jesus, Cam. Do you really think I'm that stupid?"

"Do you really want me to answer that?"

"Look, don't get me wrong. If it turns out to be better for the Earth for us to stay here and help these people with their little rebellion, then that's what we'll do. But until I'm one hundred percent convinced of that, my plan is to start jumping home just as soon as the time is right."

"But after that meeting, I was sure that you..."

"That was a negotiation, Cam. And all negotiations are basically just staged performances. That's something I learned from my father. The best way to motivate someone to do what you want them to do is to make them think they have a chance of getting what they want."

"It seems a bit dishonest."

"There's nothing dishonest about it, unless you never have any intention of giving them what they want, which in this instance is not the case. That decision is yet to be rendered. I'm simply allowing them to believe that I'm more inclined to *help* them than to *not* help them."

"I had no idea you could be this devious," she admitted.

"Sorry to disappoint you."

"I'm not disappointed. Relieved, yes, but not disappointed."

Nathan continued skipping through the images on the view screen. "So why did you come by?"

"Oh, yes. I wanted to let you know that Vladimir finally got the boarding tube to mate up and seal properly. We now have a direct pressurized passageway to the rebel base."

"Well that's good news."

"Yeah. I've already got two teams exploring the facility. We should have a better idea of its capabilities within a few hours."

"Great work."

"Thanks," she said as she rose to exit.

"Hey, how are Josh and Loki doing in the flight simulator?"

"Better than I expected," she admitted. "Loki is actually a pretty good navigator as well. Josh, on the other hand... Well, if he can learn to take his hand off the stick once in awhile, he might make an adequate pilot someday. And I emphasize the word *someday*." Cameron turned to exit, when a thought suddenly occurred to her. "Wait a minute. Before, when you were saying that you didn't want to stay and fight someone else's war, were you saying that just to make me believe that *you* were actually on *my* side?"

"Dismissed, Commander," Nathan ordered with a smile. It was rare that he got the last word with his XO in private.

* * *

Jalea walked the crowded pedestrian paths that ran between the tall buildings of the downtown quarter of the city. As she had been taught, she regularly found ways to check behind her for any undue attention without being obvious about her intent. Looking perfectly innocent when one was far from it was a skill that required very little effort. One only had to pretend that one was innocent of any ill intent, and one's actions would belie that belief to all onlookers. It was a common adage among the Karuzari that had served her well for many years.

Although fully trained in the art of combat, Jalea had spent most of her time with the Karuzari as an intelligence operative. So much so that she felt she was able to blend in to just about any situation and to seek out any advantage available at a moment's notice. More than once, her talents had not only saved her own life, but had turned events in the Karuzari's favor. However, no amount of subterfuge had been able to overcome the dying rebellion's waning support, the result of years of brutal and aggressive counterterrorism tactics used by the current commanders of the Ta'Akar military. But the recent string of failures at turning the tides of war had not discouraged her to the point of surrender. Not yet.

Jalea turned and entered a small cafe on the corner of one of the smaller buildings. The inside of the shop was warm and smelled of freshly baked pastries. There were a dozen or so small tables scattered about, with several stools at each of the counters running along the two main windows.

"Good afternoon. What can I get you?" the young man behind the counter inquired.

"Hot spiced tea and a sweet roll, please," she told him, pulling out her small coin purse. A few moments later, the young man returned with her order and collected her payment. "Do you have any terminals?" she asked, holding up her comm-unit.

"They're built into the window counters," the man instructed. "Just drop your unit into the slot and the display will sync up to the net."

"Thank you," she said, flashing a smile at the young man. She moved to the counter on her right and took the seat at the far end, making sure she was as removed from any of the other patrons as possible. It was mid afternoon on Corinair, and as expected, the cafe was not busy. So there were few prying eyes to be concerned about.

Jalea placed her tea and pastry on the glass counter as she took her seat. She pulled the interplanetary comm-unit from her bag and dropped it into the small slot just as the man behind the counter had instructed. The section of the glass counter directly in front of her lit up, displaying the logo of the Corinair data and communications network. She moved her tea and pastry aside in order to have a clear view of her screen.

She spent the next ten minutes casually sipping her tea and dining on her sweet roll in much the same manner as any other patron might have done on an afternoon break. Her fingers danced and drew lines across the glass counter as she manipulated the display underneath. She checked on the local weather forecast, caught up on the news, and even spent time checking for local dining sites and local taverns. After writing down on a napkin the address of a nearby tavern of interest, she removed the comm-unit and returned it to her bag.

After discretely checking for any undue attention, she pulled one of the local comm-unit from her jacket pocket and dropped it into the same slot. Again, the display lit up. She immediately called up the appropriate interface and composed a brief message that simply read, *'Karuzari leader currently hiding on Corinair along with mysterious disappearing warship.'* and signed it *'TM.'* She addressed the message to the Ta'Akar Office of Military Intelligence on Corinair, encrypted it, and sent it off.

As quickly as possible, but without attracting attention to herself, she wiped her fingerprints off the glass counter, pulled her comm-unit out of the slot, wiped it down and place it into her jacket pocket, still wrapped in the napkin, as she picked up her bag and walked out of the cafe.

Once back on the pedestrian walkway, she quickly made her way to the nearest monorail station and ascended the stairs to the boarding platform. She waited patiently for the next car to arrive, which took no more than a few minutes. Stepping onto the crowded car, she moved into position, pulled the comm-unit from her jacket pocket, and immediately bumped into an older gentleman in a business suit carrying a shopping bag. As she bumped into him, she dropped the comm-unit into his bag.

"Oh, please excuse me," she said, pretending to be embarrassed.

The gentleman turned toward her, prepared to reprimand her for her clumsiness, but immediately found his irritation diffused by Jalea's beguiling green eyes and olive complexion.

"That's quite all right," he assured her.

She moved away and slipped out the next exit and back onto the platform just before the doors closed and the car sped away. Within moments she was back downstairs on the pedestrian walkway, moving along with the foot traffic at a pace and manner equal to everyone else.

* * *

"How can you be tired of this already?" Vladimir asked.

"This is my fourth meal made of molo in two days," Nathan argued, "as is yours. Are you telling me you're not tired of molo yet?"

"Do you want to eat escape pod meal kits again?"

"Not really; at least not yet."

"You know what your problem is? You always worry. You worry too much, Nathan."

"I'm the captain, remember? I'm pretty sure it's in my job description."

"My grandfather always said, 'Worry only about things you can change; let someone else worry about things you cannot change.' He was very wise man."

Nathan stared at him, trying to decipher the

deeper meaning of the phrase. After a few moments, he decided there was none and continued eating. "So what was it like over there?"

"It is quite impressive. I mean, it is obviously slapped together with bits and pieces from many different places, but they have created quite a facility in the process. Machine shops, fabrication shops, component printers: I believe we can fix nearly everything here."

"I'll be happy if we just patch up the hole in the hull," Nathan admitted.

"This we can definitely do here. We just need some material for the fabricators."

"What else do they have?" Nathan wondered.

"Living quarters, agricultural rooms for growing food. They even have small hospital."

"Does Doctor Chen know about this?"

"Yes, she is going over there tomorrow to see if this facility can be of any use to us."

"How is Deliza doing with the computers for Abby?"

"They are running simulations to verify that the shuttle's computers can process our machine code. So far, everything seems to be going fine."

"That's good news. Between you and I, the jump drive worries me the most. If that thing breaks down, we're pretty much screwed."

"Do not worry, Nathan. My people have been checking all of her circuits and controls. So far, everything looks good."

"Do you think... I mean, if we manage to get our hands on that zero-point device, do you think we could make it work with our jump drive?"

"It should be possible. The power lines and emitters will need to be beefed up in order to handle additional power loads. It would be helpful if we could find better conductor for power distribution, something with less resistance, perhaps. Yes, that would help a lot, I believe."

"I sure hope you're right."

"See? Again, you worry. Listen, Nathan. I admit that I do not understand how the jump drive works. But from what I have seen, she was not kidding when she said they overbuilt system. It is very robust. And believe me, Russians know robust. Everything we build is robust."

Nathan sat there picking at his food as he watched Vladimir clean his plate and signal for seconds. He only hoped that his friend's assessment of the jump drive was correct. He had still not quite gotten used to the idea of instantly jumping up to ten light years. Jumping hundreds or even thousands of light years? He didn't think he'd ever get his mind to wrap around that one.

* * *

Jalea knew the moment she entered the tavern that she had chosen the correct establishment. It had all the telltale signs of a front for the Order of Origin. One only had to know what those signs were.

As she entered the poorly lit establishment, she unzipped her jacket and pulled the collar of her shirt open farther to reveal more of her cleavage. She knew from experience that it was an effective way to get men to honor her requests. As she took a seat at the bar, she could tell by the look on the bartender's face that this man was no exception to the rule.

"Can I get you something to drink?" the bartender

asked.

"A light ale, cold," she said. The bartender returned a moment later with a crystal mug of a pale, yellowish liquid with a slight bit of white foam on top.

"Four credits," he announced, setting her drink on the bar in front of her. She placed a one hundred credit chip on the bar and slid it toward him.

The bartender looked down at the significant overpayment, and with one eyebrow raised he asked, "Is that the smallest you've got?"

"Consider it a tip," she said with a smile.

"For what?" he asked, his eyebrow still raised.

"I seek only counsel, to get my affairs in order."

The bartender looked her over, lingering longer than necessary on her cleavage before responding. "I'll see what I can do." He picked up the credit chip and left the bar, disappearing through a doorway at one end.

Jalea picked up her mug of ale and took a sip. She had never truly acquired a taste for such intoxicants but had learned to tolerate it as operations often called for their use. She was sure that the bartender had gone to confer with others who were probably watching her through a hidden video monitoring device at this very moment.

A few minutes later, the bartender returned, placing her change on the counter. He leaned forward and whispered in her ear. "Down the hall, third door, downstairs. Now, slap me like I just propositioned you."

Without hesitation, Jalea leaned back and slapped him hard with her open hand, followed by tossing the remainder of her ale in his face. "Pig!" she yelled as she rose from her barstool and stormed off down the hallway.

The bartender laughed in the face of the onlookers. "Worth it," he chuckled.

Jalea strode indignantly into the hallway, going right past both the men's and then the women's restrooms, instead entering the third door just as instructed. The room was dark, lit only by a bit of light coming through a crack in the curtain that covered the small, high window. She found a light control by the door and activated the overhead light panel. The room was small with many storage shelves on one wall and a large wash basin on the other. She felt around the storage shelves until she found what she was looking for. On the side of the shelving unit was a small catch. She grabbed it and pulled, causing the shelving unit to swing forward slightly. She pulled harder and swung the unit open to reveal a staircase that led down to a lower level.

Jalea carefully stepped into the dim staircase, pulling the shelving unit back behind her until she felt it lock back into place. She descended the staircase slowly, her footsteps echoing down the long corridor at the bottom of the stairs.

Once at the bottom of the stairs, she followed the long hallway. She was sure it was going under the pedestrian walkway outside, possibly even over to another building on the opposite side. At the end of the hall, she reached a door, which she opened.

The next room was only a few meters square and was decorated with tapestries depicting the Legend of Origins. She had seen such artworks many times as a child, her father having served as a priest of the Order. His service to the Order had been the inadvertent cause of her mother's death when she was still young, and it had been the direct cause of his own death much later. But despite these tragic memories, she had made herself remember all the trappings and rituals involved in the Order, knowing that the knowledge would someday come in handy.

To her left, there was a table full of candles and artifacts. In front of the table was a kneeling pillow. She stepped up to the pillow and knelt down. She picked up one of the unlit candles and held the tip to the flame of the main candle in the middle of the table. Once lit, she placed her burning candle on the table at the end of the row of already burning candles that had been placed by previous visitors that day. She crossed her hands in front of her chest, bowed her head down, and began to mumble an almost inaudible prayer. When she was finished, she drew a cross over her chest and rose. To her right were two small doors, each decorated in much the same fashion, although the symbols on the doors were obviously different. There was another door in the wall behind her directly adjacent to the table full of candles, but she already knew that the purpose of that door held no interest for her.

She entered one of the two doors and stepped into a small confessional booth. After closing the door, she turned, sat down, and waited for someone to come. After waiting for several minutes, a bright blue beam of light washed across her, traveling from her head to her toes in less than a minute. She knew instantly that she had been scanned. It was not an uncommon precaution, considering how deep into the Ta'Akar-controlled Pentaurus cluster the Darvano system was located. The Legend of Origins was still a forbidden practice under the order of Caius, and all caught in its practice were summarily executed.

Once the scan completed, she heard the sound of the third door in the room as it opened and closed, followed by the sounds of footsteps as someone—a man by the weight of his footfalls—made his way across the small outer room, opened the door to the adjacent booth, and closed it behind him.

A moment later, the opaque screen on the wall between them began to glow, the silhouette of the occupant in the next booth showing on its surface.

"Why do you seek counsel?" a benevolent male voice came from the adjacent booth. The screen was nothing more than a piece of cloth casting a shadow of the occupant; hence, the man's voice came through quite clearly.

"I've had a dream," she began.

"We all have dreams, child."

"Perhaps *dream* is not the right word."

"What word might better describe what you experienced?"

Jalea paused for a moment, feigning hesitation for an unknown emotional reason. "I'm not sure," she lied.

"Are you unsure, or unwilling to admit the truth?" the man prompted.

"A bit of both, I suppose."

"Do not worry, for you are not judged, at least not by me."

"It was not a dream, really. I want to call it... a vision, but I've never had such and have no way to tell if that description might be any more accurate."

"What makes you think it was not a dream?"

"I was not asleep at the time," she admitted softly.

"I see," the man said. "Perhaps, if you tell me of this experience, I might be better able to help you identify it, to understand its meaning."

"It was a voice," she told him, "a man's voice. An old man, I believe. I'm not sure."

"And what did this voice say to you?"

"He told me to look to the sky on this night. To the level of the first moon, but a quarter rotation to the north. At twenty-eight thirty, *on this night*," she told him. Jalea was pouring all her emotion into her performance, playing the tortured and confused soul for all she could muster.

"What is it that you are supposed to see?" the man asked.

Jalea could tell that the priest's curiosity was piqued. "He said a sign would be given. And that on the next day, a gift would be bestowed upon us all, a gift that would save us all from evil," she told him, almost in tears. "Oh, Father, do you think me insane?"

"Of course not, child."

"But, Father. I think the voice... I think it was God, Father." There was no response from the man after that, and for a moment, Jalea feared she had overplayed her hand.

"I'm curious," the man asked. Jalea could hear the doubt in his voice. She was probably not the first person to tell him that God had spoken to them. "Why do you tell this to me?"

"I do not wish this burden," Jalea told him as she sniffed. "I am not a strong woman. I am a nobody. I fear persecution. Someone else must deliver the message."

"Deliver it to whom?"

Jalea pretended to think for a moment, as if she had not considered that possible question until now. "I'm not sure," she told him, making it sound like an admission. "Other believers, maybe? People

189

who believe in the Legend of Origins?"

"And to what end?" he challenged.

"If something bad is about to happen, or something good for that matter, shouldn't the people know?"

"Perhaps," he agreed.

After another moment of silence, interrupted only by her occasional sniffle, Jalea spoke up once more. "Father, do you think me insane?"

The man felt pity for the woman. If she was telling the truth, she was obviously upset by this revelation. Perhaps it challenged her beliefs, or perhaps it confirmed them, even after she had long suppressed them out of fear of reprisals by the Ta'Akar. If she was lying, then he simply pitied her for her foolishness.

"Who is to say that God does not speak to people such as you and me?" he told her.

"Thank you," she sniffled one last time before she quickly exited the booth and ran out of the room.

The man sat in his booth for several minutes after she had left. He had counseled many during his service to the order, and many had claimed to have visions, to have received messages from their Savior. They were almost always simply the tortured souls of ordinary people that were seeking some sort of forgiveness, some sort of redemption, at least in their own minds. He had never begrudged any of them that which they sought. But none of those that had made such claims before had spoken of impending signs, and never of signs that were to occur at such an exact time and in such a precise location. It gave him cause for thought.

CHAPTER SEVEN

Nathan lay stretched out on the couch in his quarters as he continued to skim through the video recording collected by the signals intelligence team. But unlike his previous sessions, he wasn't really looking for anything in particular; he was just looking.

The door buzzer sounded. Nathan paused the video feed, rose, and went to the hatch to open it.

"Hi," Cameron said. "Got a minute?"

"Sure, come on in," he invited, returning to the couch.

"You still watching that stuff?"

"Yeah. You know, it's kind of amazing, really."

"How so?"

"Well, their society. They've got music, sports, movies, and news. They've got families, schools, hospitals, celebrities. Hell, they've even got politics. It's just like on Earth. I mean, it's not; it's very different. But then again, it isn't. Does that make any sense to you?"

"Yes, actually, it does. I noticed the same thing back on Earth. I grew up on the European continent. We had all these little countries, and each one of them was very different: different languages, different foods, different music. But they were still basically all the same. Why should it be any different out here?"

"Come on, Cam. Not only are we a thousand light years away, but a thousand years have passed since these people left Earth."

"They're still human beings, Nathan, just like us."

Nathan sat quietly in the dark room, the light of the flickering video monitor dancing across the room.

"Listen, I hate to ruin your viewing pleasure, but I thought you should see this," she said, handing him a new data module. "Vlad and Allet got the base's comm-array linked into our systems. This is one of the first signals we collected."

Nathan took the module, got up, walked over to the control unit, and swapped it with the current module. It immediately began playing. The camera work was shaky and it was difficult to watch. It was obviously made up of clips from many different sources. Some of it was obviously done by amateurs and other bits were from news cameras on the scene, but both showed the same death and destruction. It was destruction on a massive scale. There was footage of huge streaks of red-orange balls of energy raining down from the sky and flattening buildings. There were bodies everywhere. Some of them had been torn apart by shock waves and debris, while others were burned beyond recognition. There were even some mounds of red, maroon, and black goo that Nathan later realized were people that had literally melted from the sudden intense heat of the energy blasts. Then, suddenly, the view cut to the weapons cameras of what Nathan assumed were either Ta'Akar fighters or rebel ships. They showed intermittent shots of the battle in orbit above the world that was being decimated. And it showed the

Ta'Akar ship—the same one that he had rammed only minutes after accidentally arriving in the middle of the raging battle. It showed that very same ship raining the deadly balls of energy onto the helpless planet below.

Suddenly, Nathan felt great satisfaction that they had somehow managed to destroy that ship. "Is this what I think it is?" he asked quietly.

"Yes. This is footage from the attack on the last rebel base, the attack we jumped into the middle of. It was broadcast on the news networks on Corinair less than an hour ago."

Nathan looked at Cameron. She had never seen such incredible guilt in anyone's eyes. "Did we..." He had to stop for a moment to get control of himself. "Did I cause this?"

"No, Nathan. We didn't cause this. These images are from before we arrived. If anything, we stopped it."

"But why? Why would they glass the planet? Surely they knew they were slaughtering far more innocents than rebels."

"They don't care. As best I can tell, it's their way of making sure that no one dares oppose them again."

"How are the people on Corinair reacting? Surely something like this has to enrage them."

"Surprisingly, they're not reacting much at all. The few comments we've seen are supporting the action."

"What? Are you kidding me?"

"Personally, I think they're too scared to speak out. I mean, come on. After seeing that, wouldn't you be afraid as well?"

Nathan continued to watch the recording, which

by now was showing the aftermath of the devastating attacks. After a few minutes he had to ask. "So what happened to these people? Did anyone send them any aid?"

"No," she answered flatly. "The entire world has been quarantined. If they're going to recover, they're going to have to do so on their own."

No more words were exchanged between them over the next few minutes as they both watched in fascination and disgust.

"Anyway, I just thought you should know," she told him as she rose to exit.

"Why? To scare me into running away or to make me want to stay and help them seek retribution?"

"I wasn't *trying* to make you do anything, Nathan. I was just giving you the facts. You do what you think is right with them. That's your job as captain of this ship."

Nathan stared at her for a moment, not knowing whether to thank her for trying to help, or curse her for forever searing the ghastly images into his mind. He finally decided she was just doing her job.

"Thanks, Cam."

Cameron looked at him. His expression was as dour as she had ever seen it. "Goodnight, Nathan," she said softly, after which she departed.

* * *

The priest of the Order of Origin was still troubled hours after his last counseling session. In fact, he had been so disturbed by that session that he had closed that day and gone home to spend time with his family. Later that evening when he saw the news broadcast about the Ta'Akar attack against the last remaining Karuzari base, his concern grew deeper. He had always avoided choosing sides. He knew that the Doctrine of Origins was a complete falsehood. He knew it in his very soul. He risked his life every day in his role serving the Order, but it was a calling like no other. He was preserving a belief that had lasted for thousands of years across the galaxy, and no one man could dissuade him or his fellow worshipers of their belief.

Now that he had seen the footage of the near biblical destruction at the hands of the forces of Caius Ta'Akar, he well understood the evil of which the unknown woman had spoken. The evil was Caius the Great, as he liked to call himself. But even more so, the evil was in any one man being able to tell others how they *must* believe. The one truth he knew above all else was that faith had no power unless it was chosen freely.

All that evening he wrestled with his thoughts, with his conscience, and with his beliefs. His wife knew that something was troubling him. Normally a hearty eater, he had barely touched his dinner. And when queried about his thoughts, he simply assured her it was nothing of concern—which usually guaranteed the exact opposite was the case. But she also knew that during such times, it was best to let him sort it all out on his own. As always, in time, he would share with her what troubled him. What she couldn't figure out was why he kept checking the time.

Around twenty-seven thirty, his conscience overcame his disbelief, and he locked himself in his study. He immediately began making calls to others he knew in the Order, instructing them to watch the sky around twenty-eight thirty this night, as well as the quadrant to monitor. He even contacted one of his worshipers who worked at a local observatory and convinced him to not only monitor that area of the night sky, but to record everything around the appointed time. By twenty-eight fifteen, he had more eyes and devices monitoring the quadrant in question than he could count, and each of them in turn had promised to contact others. And contact others they had. By twenty-eight twenty, the net was already abuzz about the upcoming event. A new net frenzy had been created before the event had even happened.

One thing was certain. If there were to be a sign this night, he would not be its only witness. By the night's end, in the eyes of his world, he would either be a prophet or a fool.

* * *

"Yes, sir. I have already locked all sensors on the target area," the equipment operator assured his boss over the comm-unit. "Yes, I have sent out verification requests to any and all observatories with a clear line of sight to that area to monitor for any and all anomalies as well... Yes, they have. At least twelve on Corinair alone... Sir, might I ask what it is that we're looking for?... Well, can I at least inquire as to why you think something is going to happen? It just seems odd to be looking in that exact location at that exact time... No, sir. I don't mean to question your... Sir?"

The equipment operator looked at his comm-panel in disbelief when he realized that his supervisor had hung up on him. He still had no idea why he had been instructed at the last moment to train all sensors on a small area in the northern sky at twenty-eight thirty hours. At this point, he only hoped that nothing would show up. At least then he might have a chance of keeping his job, despite his having questioned the director of the facility.

He looked up a digital readout of the local time. Twenty-eight twenty-nine. On his network monitor, requests were coming in from other observatories all over the planet wanting to know more details about the strange confirmation request he had been forced to send out earlier. He quickly composed a response and prepared to send it in bulk to everyone currently online. It read 'Never mind.' He was confident that in just a few minutes, he would be able to send it out and the evening's circus would be over and done.

He looked back at the time readout. Twenty-eight thirty exactly. He stared at the screen for a full minute, the smile of satisfaction on his face growing wider with each passing second. Once the time readout changed to twenty-eight thirty-one, he reached over to click 'send' but his hand instinctively withdrew when he heard an event alarm beeping at him. His eyes quickly drew to the display from the visible light telescope. There was a sudden, bright, bluish-white flash of light. It was at least four times bigger than the biggest star in the night sky, and it was gone as quickly as it had come.

His satisfied smirk having fallen off his face, he reached over and changed his message to read, 'Did anyone else see that?' and then clicked 'send.' It was going to be a long night.

Within an hour, the event had been verified by at least ten of the twelve Corinairan observatories that had been monitoring the target coordinates as requested. All had described it as a sudden flash of blue-white light. Sensors had shown it to be a massive burst of pure energy that, like the visible light, had come and gone in only an instant. One of the science stations on one of the moons of an outer planet had already dispatched an automated probe to the location of the event. But it would take days for the probe to reach the location, and even then it was doubtful that anything of consequence would be found.

But thanks to the work of the Priest of the Order that had originally contacted his worshiper who just happened to be the director of one of the most prestigious observatories on the planet, the word was already spreading like wildfire across the net. And if this Prophet Priest was correct, a gift sent to deliver them from evil would arrive within a day.

CHAPTER EIGHT

Since the Aurora was tucked away, safely moored to the Karuzari base deep inside the asteroid, the bridge was not fully staffed. Other than the comm-officer and the marine at the entrance, the only other people on the bridge were Abby and Deliza, both of whom were busy working out the bugs in the new jump plotting system.

"Good morning, sir," the comm-officer greeted as Nathan entered the bridge.

"Good morning. Any news?"

"Shuttle is on its way back to Corinair. They should be landing shortly. Other than that, nothing."

"Where's Kaylah?" he asked, noticing her absence. Of the few bridge staff he actually had, Kaylah had been the most dependable. She had been at her station every waking hour since the crisis began. Cameron had commented that Kaylah was perhaps the one person on the ship that slept even less than she did. Nathan hoped the ensign's long hours hadn't finally caught up to her.

"She's crashed out in the break room. She was up most of the night tying in her console with the asteroid's external sensor array."

"Did she get it working?"

"Yes, but it's only a passive system. I guess the Karuzari don't want to advertise their position. I've got her primary display up on my auxiliary here," the comm-officer added, pointing to one of his smaller side screens. "I'm supposed to wake her if we pick up anything out of the ordinary. Would you like me to wake her?"

"No, let her sleep awhile. She's earned the rest, I'm sure."

"Yes, sir."

"Who's the duty officer?" he wondered, not seeing any command staff nearby.

"Ensign Nash, sir. She's in your ready room." The comm-officer made a face indicating that she too was probably sleeping.

Nathan nodded his understanding as he turned his attention to the tactical station in front of him. He stood for a moment looking over the displays. The same passive sensor readings that were currently displayed on the comm-officer's side screen were also displayed on one of the tactical screens. There was plenty of traffic being tracked. But it was all standard civilian traffic, and it was all at a considerable distance from them without a single track bound anywhere near them. All in all, Nathan felt safer than he had in days. If a suspicious ship were to suddenly appear in the vicinity, unless they had sensors that could penetrate several kilometers of solid rock, their asteroid would appear to be just another abandoned mining camp, one of hundreds floating in the belt of the Darvano system. And should something go horribly wrong, he was confident they could exit the underground base, clear the belt, and jump away, all before sustaining any significant damage.

Satisfied that everything was in order, he turned his attention to the upgrade project being conducted by Abby and Deliza. "How's it going, ladies?"

Deliza quickly stood, youthful exuberance and excitement in their little project evident in her demeanor. "Very well, Captain," she announced proudly. "The shuttle's computer core is much more powerful than the ones in this console."

"That's great news," Nathan said, sensing that Deliza needed some confirmation. He looked to Abby for some sort of confirmation as to the young girl's claims.

"She's not exaggerating, sir," Abby assured him. "Not only will this computer greatly decrease the time necessary to calculate a jump plot, but it will also significantly increase the accuracy of the jump as well."

"How so?" Nathan asked. He didn't for a moment expect to understand any of what he was sure she was about to tell him, but he was feeling unusually optimistic this morning.

"The calculations are far more precise than our own computer's. Ours have a fixed number of digits available to either side of the decimal point. Granted, there are many. And in almost all cases they are more than adequate. But their computers use a floating point system that can accommodate a nearly infinite number size." She could see that he did not understand what she was talking about. "The gist of it is that we can calculate most jumps in less than a minute. And the increased accuracy means that we can arrive as close as a few hundred meters without fear of merging with a nearby object."

"Merging?" Nathan shuddered. "That doesn't sound like something we would want to do."

"No," she agreed, "it does not. However, I should point out that we have no idea what the effects of such a 'close-in-arrival' would be, to us or to any nearby objects."

"Don't worry, Doctor. I have no intention of finding out," he assured her as he turned to go to his ready room.

* * *

The skies of Corinair were thick with air traffic, as ships of every possible size and design darted back and forth between the surface and her orbital platforms.

"Is it just me, or does it seem like there's a lot more traffic than there was yesterday?" Loki observed.

"Yeah there is," Josh agreed. "I'm actually glad they use auto-landing systems today. I'd hate to have to try and navigate through all of this."

"Yeah, and most of it is outbound," Loki added. "In fact, nearly all of it is outbound."

"I don't like the looks of this," Marcus commented from behind them. He had been looking between their seats out the front windows for the last few minutes.

Josh looked over his shoulder. Despite the old-timer's many failings, he had grown to trust the man's instincts about such matters. "You think something is bugger?"

"When this many people react the same way, it's usually only one of two things," Marcus said, "something really good, or something really bad." Loki also turned to look at Marcus. "My money's always on bad."

* * *

"Yes?" Jalea answered into her comm-unit.

"Jalea," Loki called through the unit, *"is that you?"*

"Yes, go ahead."

"We're in the upper atmosphere now. Should be touching down in about half an hour."

"The supplies are already there waiting for you. We'll be there by the time you finish loading."

"Copy that. You got any idea what the hell's going on down there?"

"What do you mean?"

"Ships are leaving the surface in swarms! But not many are returning by the looks of it."

"I do not know, but I will attempt to discern the cause."

"Just be sure you get to the port quickly. I have a feeling that we don't want to be hanging around when whatever is about to happen actually happens."

"Agreed," she said, as she unceremoniously ended the call and placed the comm-unit into her jacket pocket.

"What was that all about?" Tug asked.

"We need to hasten our departure from Corinair," she told him, trying not to appear overly concerned.

"Why? What has happened?"

"I do not know. But I suspect we will soon find out," she told him as she quickly gathered her few things.

* * *

Nathan stepped quietly into the ready room. As the comm-officer had guessed, Jessica was asleep on the couch. Between her, Cameron, and himself, that couch was going to wear out in a hurry. He moved silently over to his desk and sat, after which he activated the small monitor on the corner of the desk itself.

First he checked the reports. As usual, the most thorough and informative reports were the ones submitted by Cameron. As suspected, she had turned out to be a fine executive officer, always staying on top of every detail of the ship's operation. From her reports, he knew that all of the rail guns were not only operational, but their rate of fire and rail velocities had also been improved. However, with the increased rates of fire, their ammunition levels were more dangerously low than before. The commander's estimates showed that, given the average length of each engagement thus far, they only had enough point-defense rounds for one engagement, maybe two if they were relatively short. This reality greatly troubled Nathan, since it meant that they could not maintain a toe-to-toe slug out for long. The good news was that, as far as solid kinetic rounds went, they had plenty. In addition, their relatively simple design meant they could manufacture additional rounds in respectable quantity if needed. Nathan suspected that the raw ores left over from their harvesting operation in the Haven system would provide the materials needed.

The bad news was that, although two of the four torpedo launch tubes were again operational, there were no more torpedoes left for them to shoot. Despite the rather adaptable design of the tubes, they were unlikely to acquire ordnance to launch from them.

With no shields, no long-range standoff weapons, and little more than kinetic rounds for the rail guns, Nathan didn't see how they could ever hope to take on anything more powerful than a patrol frigate.

And even then, only if they were lucky. The only trick he had up his sleeve was the jump drive, and that trick might get old really fast.

Nathan just didn't see how he could justify involving the Aurora in the fight against the Ta'Akar, despite the potential benefits to Earth should the Karuzari actually win the war. Even worse was that he didn't know how he was going to break the news to Tug. He could tell that the old warrior was counting on him to at least give them a fighting chance once again. Although they had not yet talked about it, Nathan felt sure that using the Aurora's jump drive to capture a Ta'Akar vessel of at least the size and firepower of a frigate had to be the rebel leader's first objective.

Nathan also suspected that he would not have to tell Tug. The man was a seasoned veteran of armed conflict. In fact, he had considerably more experience than Nathan, as did everyone else for that matter. He wondered if Tug would even ask him to do such a thing, considering the reality.

Looking at Jessica asleep on his couch, he also wondered how the only true *one-night stand* he had ever had ended up to be one of his most trusted officers, and friends. The young ensign was probably the toughest woman he had ever known. In fact, she was one of the toughest *people* he had ever known. She had in fact saved his ass, as well as the ship, on more than one occasion.

Having her on his side definitely made him feel better as he finished reading the status reports and started skimming through the video files collected by Sig-Int once again.

* * *

Tug and Jalea found the walkways more crowded than expected. There were groups of people standing around talking energetically. Some were even arguing. There were people huddled together, crying. And there were more than a few people carrying large makeshift signs, with phrases like *'The Legend Has Come True'* or *'The End Is Upon Us.'*

Tug grabbed Jalea's hand and led her through the crowds, weaving between the different groups of people. As they made their way, they were nearly pulled into a melee between a group of followers of the Order and a gang of young men, all of which were supporters of the Doctrine. They managed to pull away and escape just in time to avoid being swept up in a mass arrest as armed riot police began to descend upon the crowd from troop carriers hovering overhead.

After much difficulty, they managed to make their way up the stairs to the monorail platform. Once at the top, they could see that there was little hope of getting through the crowd of people waiting to get on the next car headed toward the spaceport.

As the next car approached the platform, Jalea, who was pushed up against the side railing, pulled out her small handgun, pointed it in the air and fired off three quick shots, sending energy blasts across the heads of the crowd. Before anyone could see where the shots were coming from, she dropped the weapon over the side, letting it fall into the bushes below.

The crowd panicked, making a mad dash for the exit. By the time the car arrived, most of the crowd had fled the platform for the ground below. Tug and Jalea quickly made their way onto the car, along with the few members of the crowd that had not fled in panic. Even with most of the crowd pouring down the exit stairs, those remaining quickly filled the car to standing room only by the time the doors closed and the car sped away.

"Stay near the exit," Tug warned her. "Do not let them force you off until we reach the spaceport." Jalea nodded agreement. Luckily, the car operator understood the dangers of the crowded platforms and only opened the doors on the left side of the car, which opened to the exit side of the platform where there were no crowds. It was a pointless exercise, however, as it appeared that no one planned to get off the car until it reached at least the outskirts of the city.

One stop at a time, the operator let people off but did not take on any more passengers. Jalea quickly realized that, due to the rioting and numerous public demonstrations, the operator was planning on getting the car back to the station and then finding her way to the safety of her own home. Jalea soon learned, however, that she was only partially correct. The car operator was not planning on continuing her duties, but neither was she planning on taking the car all the way to the end station first. At the next platform, she too disembarked with a few of the others, moving away from the platform and stripping off her uniform jacket as she ran away, headed toward a residential area that must have been where she lived.

Jalea immediately moved forward, pushing her way past the confused passengers still on the car and stepping into the open operator's compartment. Tug followed her, already surmising her intent.

"We're taking this car all the way to the spaceport!"

Tug announced to the remaining passengers. "If you do not wish to go to the spaceport, you have ten seconds to get off this car."

"Who the hell are you to..." a male passenger began as he moved toward Tug.

"I'm the crazy old man with a gun," Tug said as he pulled out his weapon, "that is currently pointed at your head." Tug smiled. "Eight seconds."

The man that had spoken up now backed away, immediately disembarking along with a few others. Several people remained seated, however, and Tug wasn't sure why.

"Are you going to shoot us?" an elderly woman asked.

"Do you plan on trying to stop us?" Tug asked, only half serious. The old woman shook her head. "Then of course not, ma'am. Sit back and relax, everyone. We'll arrive at the spaceport in a few minutes." Tug put away his gun as he turned back toward Jalea in the operator's compartment. "Best speed to the spaceport, if you please."

Jalea activated the controls, and the monorail car began moving slowly away from the platform, picking up speed with each passing second until it reached its maximum safe cruising speed.

"You weren't planning to stop at any of the platforms along the way, were you?" Tug asked. Jalea just shot him a dubious glance. "Just checking."

* * *

The comm-panel beeped twice, announcing an incoming call. Nathan quickly activated the comm, mentally admonishing himself for not muting the system to avoid waking Jessica from her catnap on his couch. But the damage was already done, and Jessica was beginning to stir.

"Go ahead," Nathan said into the comm, trying to keep his volume down.

"Captain, Mendez. I'm down in Sig-Int, and we're picking up a lot of strange broadcasts from Corinair."

"What kind of broadcasts?"

"News broadcasts, sir. There are riots going on— something to do with the Legend of Origins. They're saying there was some kind of sign. They're talking like it's the end of the world or something."

"Can you send it to the viewer in my ready room?"

"Yes, sir, but it won't be translated. I've got Nara working on the translation now."

"That's fine, just send me the video for now. I'll check out the translation later, after you finish it."

"Yes, sir. I'm sending you the live feed now."

The main view screen in the ready room came to life and began displaying a broadcast feed from one of the local news stations in the capital city of the planet Corinair. The broadcast was split into four views, each showing different events happening simultaneously. The image in the upper left corner showed a map of the city, with dozen of icons on it, each representing the location of an event. At random intervals, one of the icons would expand to fill one of the other three views, replacing what had been showing previously.

"What's going on?" Jessica asked, opening her eyes slightly but not yet sitting up.

"Something is happening on Corinair. There are riots and stuff. Sig-Int says the people on Corinair are talking about the end of the world."

"Oh, is that all?" Jessica said, stretching.

The comm beeped again. *"Captain,*

communications. Urgent inbound message, sir."

"From who?"

"*From a Ta'Akar warship, sir. Their captain is asking to speak with the captain of the disappearing ship.*"

Jessica immediately sat up right, her eyes wide. Nathan's eyes were also wide. "I think he's talking about us."

"Uh, put him through, I guess."

"*The signal includes video, sir. Shall we match it?*"

Nathan looked to Jessica.

"Why not? Let's see what the asshole looks like."

"All right. Pipe the video in here as well."

The images from the Corinairan news broadcasts were instantly replaced by a stately looking man, probably in his mid-fifties, with graying temples and a perfectly groomed mustache. His uniform was clean and well pressed, and it boasted numerous ribbons and commendations. Nathan couldn't help but wonder if the man expected to appear in a parade later in the day. He also wondered how this man would consider Nathan's own appearance. No doubt, his scruffy whiskers, unkempt hair, and simple duty uniform carried nowhere near the same impact.

"Hello, Captain," the man on the screen said. His tone was cheerful, although not overtly so. His manner was well rehearsed, no doubt through years of service in his position. Nathan couldn't help but notice that the man seemed somewhat surprised by not only Nathan's disheveled appearance, but also by the obvious difference in their ages. "Allow me to introduce myself. I am Sir Augustine de Winter, captain of the warship Yamaro. To whom do I have the pleasure of speaking?"

"My name is Nathan Scott, captain of the Aurora."

"A pleasure, sir."

Nathan was about to introduce Jessica as well, if only out of instinct. Her emphatic gestures indicating that Captain de Winter should not know that she was there stopped Nathan from doing so.

"To what do I owe the honor, Captain de Winter?"

"I have been authorized by my government to offer you amnesty and safe passage out of Ta'Akar space."

Nathan could tell that the task did not sit well with the officer. It was obvious that he held himself in high esteem, and Nathan got the distinct impression that he did not feel he had been accorded the same level of respect from his peers that he felt he deserved. Being forced to serve as a messenger foremost obviously bruised this man's ego.

"Interesting. However, I wasn't aware that our flight plans required your government's approval."

Jessica smiled. She already liked the position Nathan was taking with this guy. She was able to lean forward just enough to be able to turn her head and see the man's image on the viewer without her image being picked up by the viewer's camera and transmitted back to the Yamaro. As best they could tell, the pompous captain wasn't even aware that she was in the room.

"Yes, well, your recent activities have earned you some degree of notoriety among those of us tasked with maintaining order out here amongst the stars. To put it bluntly, sir, there is a price on your head, as well as the heads of the Karuzari you harbor. Command would prefer that your ship be taken intact." The man thought for a moment. "However, they made no such specification regarding you or your crew."

Nathan didn't care much for threats, veiled or otherwise. His father had always said that threats were a sign of weakness or fear. This man, however, did not appear to be displaying either emotion.

"Let's cut to the chase," Nathan told him. His use of the phrase was met with a puzzled look. "What is it you require from me in return for safe passage?"

"Nothing much. Simply turn over all members of the Karuzari currently on board your vessel, as well as any information you have about the whereabouts of any other members you might possess."

"And that's it?"

"We also require all information regarding the technology you use to so effortlessly jump between the stars. It's really quite an impressive feat, I must say."

"And if we refuse?"

"Then you will be captured and executed. Either way, we shall have the secret of your miraculous method of interstellar travel."

"Captain, I'm curious about one thing. What gives you the right to make such demands?"

"You have fired on and destroyed ships of the Ta'Akar. This, sir, makes you an enemy of the Ta'Akar. As well, you have entered our domain without permission, with the obvious intent of aggression."

"We entered your domain by accident, sir, and without any intent. In fact, we didn't even know anyone's domain was out here. And for the record, your ships fired on us. We merely defended ourselves."

"Furthermore, Captain Scott, you have provided

aid and support to the Karuzari, who are also sworn enemies of the Ta'Akar."

Nathan made no immediate response to Captain de Winter's last accusation, preferring to consider it before responding. His careful consideration before speaking surprised Jessica, as it was not a trait for which he was known.

"I'm afraid your facts are in error," Nathan began. "The people you speak of came aboard our ship while we were helplessly adrift after the mistaken engagement with one of your warships. They offered to help and we accepted. At the time, we did not know of their political agenda or of their conflict with your people. And, I might add, we had little choice in the matter, as more of your ships were on their way."

"While that may be the case, Captain, at this point it is irrelevant. In the eyes of my government, you are guilty as charged. Your only option is to abandon your Karuzari friends and ally yourself with us. Then together we can swiftly end this annoying rebellion and restore order to the galaxy." The captain was getting a bit irritated at Nathan's unwillingness to cooperate, forcing him to take pause to regain his composure. "Captain, do you truly know who you have allied yourself with?"

"I'm sure you're about to explain it to me," Nathan quipped.

The captain of the Yamaro ignored his sarcasm. "The Karuzari are terrorists, Captain. Nothing more, nothing less."

"They claim to be freedom fighters."

"What they are is responsible for the needless deaths of hundreds of thousands over more than two decades."

"That's a pretty big claim, Captain. But it's my understanding that the Ta'Akar are responsible for just as many deaths, if not more."

"The Ta'Akar do what must be done in order to prevent the support of these terrorists. We do what must be done to end this unrest once and for all. We do what must be done to maintain order!"

Nathan was pretty sure he struck a nerve. He decided to push a little harder. "You do what must be done in order to force your population to worship your leader as a God. And you have the arrogance to pretend that you are justified in your actions."

Unfortunately, Nathan's plan did not work. Captain de Winter had not taken the bait. Instead, he was again recomposing himself. "Captain, do, do you really think that people of nobility and rank, such as myself, actually believe that our king is a God? Those of us who serve the crown do so in order to establish our own power and position, not as a result of some religious idealism."

"And this is how you justify the atrocities committed by your commanders?"

"Of course not," the captain answered with a sigh. "But at times, a seemingly unforgivable atrocity must be committed in order to avoid committing an even greater one. It is unfortunate, but nevertheless true, that sometimes the only way to fight terrible evil is to become just as evil."

"Is that what you were doing when you tried to glass the planet that the Karuzari were hiding on?" Nathan stood, wanting to appear strong and resolute. He waited several seconds for a response that he was already sure would not come. "We shall not be accepting your offer, Captain."

"You do realize what will happen if you do not?"

"Yes. We'll simply jump away before you even get within firing range."

"Then I suppose we'll have to chase you all the way back to Earth, won't we?"

"Don't be ridiculous, Captain. Even your comm-drones would take at least a decade to reach Earth. And your ships are nowhere near as fast."

"Not yet, but soon. Of course, meanwhile, as punishment for welcoming you into their system, Corinair will have to be obliterated. A pity, really. It is a lovely planet after all."

Try as he might, Nathan could not hide his shock at the man's threat. "Those people don't even know we are here," Nathan argued. "You couldn't possibly..."

"I can and I will. Make no mistake..."

"You're bluffing."

"Bluffing?" the Captain asked with that same puzzled look as before. "I'm afraid I'm not familiar with that term."

The view screen suddenly switched back to the news broadcast from Corinair being fed to him by the Sig-Int staff. Nathan immediately activated his comm-panel. "Comms! What happened to the connection to the Ta'Akar ship?"

"The signal transmission was discontinued by the Ta'Akar, sir."

* * *

As Tug and Jalea made their way along the raised walkway from the monorail platform to the main terminal at the spaceport, they could see numerous pillars of angry, black smoke rising from the city in the distance. The fires were obviously the result of the riots and other general panic that was taking place on the streets and pathways of the city. Although she did not say as much to Tug, she knew that the panic had been set into motion by the words spoken to the priest of the Order yesterday afternoon. She did not feel guilty, despite the fact that many people may have already suffered or even died as a direct result of her actions. Things were going exactly as she had hoped.

"Jesus," Marcus exclaimed as he wheeled the crates full of supplies on board the shuttle. "Do you think they bought enough food?"

"Stop complaining," Josh told him. "At least we won't be eating any more molo."

Just as they were loading the last of the supplies, Tug and Jalea came running across the tarmac.

"We must...depart...immediately," Tug ordered, out of breath.

"What's going on?" Loki asked.

"Yeah, what are all those fires we saw coming in?" Josh asked.

"Religious zealots," Tug explained between breaths. "Fools rambling on about salvation and the end of the world."

"Bunch of idiots," Marcus exclaimed. "I mean, who cares where we're from? We're here now. That's all that matters."

"We must go!" Jalea urged. Josh and Loki went back into the shuttle, climbing over the mounds of supplies filling their cargo bay in order to get to the cockpit. Tug and Jalea climbed up the ramp and took their seats near the massive aft hatch that doubled as a cargo ramp.

"Hey!" Marcus called out toward the cockpit as he ascended the ramp. "Whattaya think they'd all say if they knew the ship we're crewing on is actually from Earth?" At the top of the ramp he took his seat on the opposite side from Tug and Jalea and put on his headset. "Let's get the hell off this rock!" he called to Josh as he hit the button and start retracting the boarding ramp to close up over the rear opening.

"Light up the mains," Josh ordered as he dropped into his seat.

"I'm on it," Loki answered. He reached up over his head and started flipping switches in preparation to start the engines, but nothing was happening. "What the hell?"

"What's wrong?" Josh asked.

"The mains are cycling over. I can't get the turbines to light up."

"Did you prime them first?"

"Of course I primed them first!"

"Oh shit," Josh exclaimed as he noticed the flashing red display on the center data display console. "We're locked out."

"What? Why would we be..."

"Attention all vessels," the voice came over the surface traffic control frequency. *"This facility is on full operational lock down, by order of the Ta'Akar warship Yamaro. All flight crews will shut down their systems, disembark, and stand beside their ships."*

Loki looked at Josh as the message repeated. "Oh, we're in so much trouble."

CHAPTER NINE

"Get this ship in the air!" Marcus shouted over the comms from the back of the shuttle.

"We can't," Josh responded. "We're locked out. The whole facility is on lock down."

"Then bypass the auto-flight system, you idiots!"

"You can't bypass the auto-flight system, Marcus!" Loki argued. "It's hardwired into the ship's flight systems."

"Not if someone un-hardwired it! Just flip the damn bypass switch, under the starboard console, all the way to the outboard edge. It's a lockset switch. Just pull the toggle down and then flip it forward."

Josh felt along the underside of his console, running his hand until he felt the switch. He pulled the toggle switch down, disengaging the toggle's locking mechanism, and then flipped the switch forward. The flashing red display stopped flashing and suddenly changed to 'Auto-flight Disengaged.'

"That's it! It worked!"

"Of course it worked," Marcus muttered.

"How the hell did you know about that?" Loki asked as he fired up the engines.

"Who the hell do you think un-hardwired the damn thing?" Marcus bragged. "Now get us in the air!"

Moments later, the shuttle began to roll forward on its way to the flight line.

"What are you, idiots?" Marcus hollered. "Just take off from here!"

Josh felt pretty stupid for not thinking of that himself. After all, if they were going against a lockdown order, breaking the rules by taking off from the loading area instead of the flight line was the least of their worries.

The shuttle's engines screamed as Josh applied full thrust, causing the ship to suddenly leap into the air. The cargo shuttle wasn't pretty, but it was made to haul several tons of heavy rock and ore, so a few dozen crates of food and a handful of passengers were no trouble at all.

Nathan stormed onto the bridge from his ready room with Jessica hot on his heels.

"Contact!" Kaylah reported as he entered. "Just came up on passive. Transferring to tactical."

Jessica stepped up to the tactical console along with Nathan. "It's on the outer rim of the system," she reported. "It's decelerating. Based on its speed I'd say it dropped out of FTL at least five or ten minutes ago."

"Got an ID?" Nathan asked, although he already knew the answer.

"Not yet. He's too far out to ID using passive. And if we go active, we'll give away our location."

"Well I'm pretty sure we know who it is." Nathan took in a deep breath and sighed. "General quarters," he ordered calmly. "All hands to battle stations and prepare to get underway."

"General quarters. Aye, sir."

"I'm pretty sure we're going to need an escape jump pretty soon, Doctor," he said to Abby as he moved to the helm to start prepping the ship for departure.

"Captain, we just finished hooking up the shuttle's computer core to our jump system. We haven't even run any simulations yet."

"How long will it take you to unhook it?" he asked as he worked the helm console.

Abby looked at Deliza, who had done most of the work installing the new, improved computer core.

"An hour? But we'd still have to recalibrate your original core after that, so maybe ninety minutes?"

Abby turned to look at Nathan as he shot her a glance.

Nathan felt his heart sink. The jump drive was the one thing they had going in their favor in this part of the galaxy. Now there was a possibility that it wouldn't work when he needed it most. But there was nothing he could do about it now. If he had them disconnect it, he wouldn't be able to jump for over an hour. He seriously doubted they could remain hidden that long. Even if they did, Captain de Winter might become impatient and start laying waste to the surface of Corinair. He briefly considered getting the enemy warship to chase him, possibly buying time until they could jump. But he didn't have linear FTL capabilities, which meant he couldn't outrun the Ta'Akar warship for more than a few minutes. Once again, their fate was left to luck.

"Guess you're gonna have to test it on the fly again, Doc."

Abby felt as if she were turning pale as a cold shiver went through her body. "I'm really getting tired of this," she mumbled to herself as she began calculating an escape plot on the new system.

"Shuttle two-four-one-eight, you are in violation of a lockdown order. Land immediately or interceptors will be dispatched and you will be shot down."

"Help!" Josh cried over the comms. "They've got a gun!" he added, right before he started clicking the talk button over and over. "They're forcing me to take......em......moon......help..." Josh ended the fake broadcast, turning to Loki looking very pleased with himself. "You think they bought it?"

"Oh, sure," Loki said.

"Maybe they're already too busy, what with all the riots and stuff," Josh said hopefully.

"Don't think so," Loki muttered. "We've got company coming up real fast."

Josh looked over at Loki's display. Besides the multitude of outbound contacts, there was a red flashing triangle coming up behind them.

"Hang on back there," Loki called over the comms. "We've got company."

"Who is it?" Marcus asked. Suddenly, the shuttle jumped as something exploded in the air just outside their starboard side. Marcus was nearly thrown out of his seat. "Never mind."

Marcus stood up and pulled a long safety strap from the ceiling, connecting it to his harness. "You two buckled in?" he asked Tug and Jalea.

"Yes!" Tug answered. "Why?"

Marcus grinned and slapped the big red button along the side of the rear cargo hatch. The massive cargo door hissed as it began to open, starting its slow lowering into its ramp position. The sudden change in cabin pressure was immediately felt by all as the wind rushed in around the widening crack between the door and the frame.

"Shuttle two-four-one-eight, you are in violation of a lockdown order. Land immediately or we will fire on you."

"What the hell are you doing, you crazy old fart?" Josh yelled over the comms from the cockpit.

"Just try to keep this thing low enough so we don't all suffocate while I shed this bugger from our ass!" Marcus declared.

The rear hatch continued to lower until Marcus stopped it at its standard platform position, parallel to the deck.

"Give me a hand!" he shouted at Tug.

"With what?"

"We gotta start tossin' some of this stuff," he declared as he picked up the first crate and tossed it out the back of the ship. The crate bounced off the end of the ramp, broke open, and sent vegetables flying towards the local police interceptor that was rapidly closing on them.

Tug's eyes widened. "You don't really think you're gonna stop that interceptor by throwing produce at him, do you?"

"Whattaya think I am, stupid? I need room for my new toy!"

His explanation didn't inspire any confidence in Tug, who rose to help nevertheless. After securing himself to the ceiling in similar fashion, Tug also began tossing boxes of food out the back of the shuttle. Somewhat to Marcus's amusement, the tumbling produce did cause the compact interceptor to dodge back and forth wildly, trying to avoid messing up his windshield.

After a few minutes, they had tossed nearly a third of the boxes out of the back. "That's enough!" Marcus yelled as he started to cycle the hatch closed again. Now Tug was even more confused.

"I'm pretty sure he's lost it," Loki decided.

"What the hell are you doing, Marcus?" Josh cried out.

"Just hold'er steady for a few minutes while I get set up," Marcus told him while he inserted a heavy stand into a socket in the middle of the aft section of the cargo deck, less than a meter from the rear hatch which was now fully closed.

"Gimme a hand with this thing!" Marcus ordered. Tug crossed over to the other side of the cargo bay as Marcus opened a long compartment and started pulling out what looked like one of the energy cannons off Tug's fighter.

"Is this what I think it is?" Tug asked as they wrestled the heavy weapon from the locker and carried over to the post they had set up a moment ago.

"You bet!"

"Where did you get it?" Tug asked as they plopped it down onto the mount at the top of the meter high post.

Marcus uncoiled the power cable from the weapon, flipped open a port on the deck, and plugged the weapon in. "I took it from your little ship!"

"Who said you could..."

Marcus hit the door control to start cycling the rear hatch open again. "You can thank me later!"

"Jesus," Josh exclaimed as air once again began rushing in from the rear of the ship. "Can you override his door controls or something?"

"Shuttle two-four-one-eight, this is your final warning. Land immediately or we will destroy you."

Another burst went off outside, this time to port and even closer. The rear of the ship lurched upward, launching Marcus upward and Tug back over onto the now disorganized pile of supplies. As the door swung open down and away from the shuttle, Marcus swung the business end of the energy cannon outward, another grin forming on his face.

"We've gotta do something," Loki exclaimed.

"Like what?" Josh defended.

"I don't know! Do some of that crazy pilot shit you always do!"

"Crazy pilot shit? I'm just trying to keep from slamming into any of the other thousands of ships flyin' all about us right now!"

Loki turned his head to look over his shoulder toward the rear of the shuttle to see what Marcus was doing. When his eyes caught sight of the weapon mounted in the middle of the deck, he nearly spun around in his seat, his eyes going wide. "Oh fuck!"

Cameron's fingers danced across her console as she entered commands into the helm. The series of waypoints she had programmed into the auto-flight system had carried them out of the cavern and through the exit tunnel with flawless precision. Although she did not state the fact to Nathan, she was sure that navigating the tunnels in this fashion had saved them several minutes over flying through them manually.

"Coming up on the exit," she announced.

"Let me know the moment you have our sensors back up," Nathan told Kaylah. From the moment they had disconnected their umbilical from the base inside the asteroid, they had been blind to the outside world. Had there been someone to stay behind and man the hidden base, they could have at least monitored their own sensors and relayed information to them on their way out. Nathan decided that if they were ever to use such a facility again, he would have to make sure that they had a wireless telemetry feed for such data.

"Yes, sir," Ensign Yosef answered.

"Try to contact the shuttle once we're clear," Nathan told the acting comm-officer. "Let them know we're coming to get them."

"Crossing the exit threshold now," Cameron announced. The rocky ceiling passed over them and was replaced by the black star field. The exit tunnel dumped directly into another long trench that eventually widened and became shallower until it was level with the primary surface, disappearing altogether.

"Where are they, Kaylah?"

"I'm not seeing them, sir," she admitted, double-checking her display to make sure she hadn't missed anything.

"They've got to be out there somewhere."

"The gas giant might be between us and them," Jessica suggested. "Based on their last course and rate of deceleration, it is possible."

"They can't be that dumb," Nathan said. "Even I'm not that dumb."

"I've got them," Kaylah announced with relief. "They just came out from the far side of the seventh planet."

"He's definitely not stupid," Jessica commented. "He had to have picked up speed to make it that far over in such a short time. He did not want to be anywhere near where we thought he would be."

"Should I change course to bring the gas giant

between us?" Cameron asked.

"No, keep on a straight bearing to Corinair, best possible speed, no finesse." Cameron looked at him quizzically. "During our conversation, I got the impression he was surprised by my age. He probably thinks I'm young and dumb."

"Well, he's half right," Cameron said under her breath. Nathan didn't take the bait, but he did like that his XO was starting to become more relaxed under pressure, as it helped keep him in the same mood.

"Let's not give him any reasons to think otherwise," Nathan added. "And remember, no finesse," he added as he turned to go to tactical.

"So, just fly like you then?" she said to herself.

"Comms, any luck with the shuttle?"

"Not yet, sir. But there's a lot of traffic coming from Corinair."

"He's right, sir," Kaylah agreed. "There are at least twenty large transports in orbit, and I'm seeing at least a hundred shuttles coming from the surface of Corinair. And that's not counting the ones that are still in the lower atmosphere, which we can't see from here without going active."

"What, are they evacuating?" Nathan wondered aloud as he stepped up next to the tactical console.

"Could be," Jessica said, "if they know about that warship. After what was showing on their news the other night, wouldn't you?"

Marcus looked out over the top of his makeshift gun emplacement along its double barrels. He could feel the humming of the power cells as he watched and waited for the rear hatch to lower enough to give him a clear line of sight on his target. But as the door nearly reached its platform position, the small police interceptor was nowhere to be seen. Before Tug could react, the interceptor suddenly jumped back up into sight from below them, and Marcus let go a double-shot of bright red balls of destructive energy that leapt from the ends of his barrels out toward the interceptor. "Surprise!"

The interceptor dropped back down slightly, avoiding Marcus's first shot. The interceptor changed its angle to return fire, but as he did so, the rear hatch dropped down into its boarding ramp position, putting its trailing edge into the shuttle's airflow.

The sudden disruption of the airflow under the shuttle's tail caused its back end to jump sharply upward, causing the interceptor's volley to pass just under their tail.

"What the hell!" Josh cried out as he fought to compensate for the sudden change in the shuttle's flight characteristics.

Josh's over compensation for the sudden upward movement of the shuttle's tail caused it to dip back down sharply below their flight path. Fortunately, the motion put the little police interceptor right in the middle of Marcus's view. Marcus again squeezed the trigger, letting out another pair of red balls of energy.

The police interceptor snap-rolled to try and avoid the incoming fire, but one of the red balls of energy caught its wing, clipping off its outer half. The little interceptor immediately began to yaw to the right. A few seconds later, the canopy shot up off the interceptor and the pilot's rocket-powered ejection seat fired, sending the pilot well above his now tumbling ship.

"Oh yeah!" Marcus screamed as he watched the pilot's chute open. He reached over and started cycling the hatch closed again. "Get us the fuck outta here!"

"You got it, pops!" Josh declared as he started to climb again.

Marcus looked over at Tug and Jalea, both of whom were still in disbelief. "Not bad, huh?"

The bridge rumbled as the ship decelerated sharply on its approach to Corinair.

"Captain, I'm getting multiple hails from Corinair's militia demanding identification and intent."

"Ignore them," Nathan ordered. "I doubt they can spare anyone to deal with us right now, considering the chaos on their world. Besides, once they see us change course and veer away, they'll likely lose interest."

"If not, then they surely will when that Ta'Akar warship unloads on them," Jessica said under her breath.

"You don't think he was bluffing?" Nathan asked.

"You saw the video," Jessica reminded him.

"Yeah, but we still don't know for sure who was responsible for that, the Ta'Akar or the Karuzari."

Jessica looked up from her console to look Nathan in the eyes. "Nathan, at some point you're gonna have to decide once and for all who you can trust."

Her words hung in the air for what might have been an eternity, had his thoughts not been immediately interrupted a moment later.

"Captain, I have the shuttle," the comm-officer

reported.

"Loki!" Nathan called over his comm-set. "Did you pick them up? Are you on your way?"

"Yes, but we almost didn't make it, Captain. It's a mad house down there. The entire spaceport is locked down. We had to bust our way out!"

"Cam, can you send them an intercept heading and speed?"

"Heading, yes. Speed? Tell them to go as fast as possible."

"Jessica, how are we looking?"

"It's going to be close," she admitted. "If I had a more exact idea of their weapons range..."

"Abby, adjust your plot to start from a few hundred thousand kilometers downrange of the intercept point that Cam is calculating."

"Got it," Cam announced. "Sending course data to Abby and the shuttle."

"Loki. We're sending you a course heading. Taking that heading at full speed."

"Uh, okay."

"You're going to have to land at full speed. We'll try to slow down to match you as best we can. But we've got bad guys on our tail."

"Yeah. I'm starting to notice that you guys kind of attract them."

"We're three minutes from intercept," Cameron announced.

"Jess?"

"Four, maybe five until they can get missiles on us."

"Holy crap, I can't believe we're doing this," Loki exclaimed as he stared out the forward view ports.

They were approaching the Aurora at full speed, more than ten times their usual landing speed. Loki knew that it was all relative; all that was important was the difference in velocity between the two ships. Still, both ships were traveling incredibly fast. And the fact that they only had a minute or two to land before the warship that was chasing them both got close enough to fire didn't help calm his nerves.

"Relax, Loki. I've got this," Josh assured him.

"Incoming!" Jessica announced from the tactical station. "She's launched four missiles. Impact in two minutes."

"Prepare to fire all rail guns, point-defense mode, aft," Nathan ordered.

"The shuttle is still in the line of fire," Jessica warned.

Nathan snapped his fingers at the comm-officer. "Get me the shuttle." A moment later the comm-officer turned his head back toward the captain and nodded. "Josh, I need you on the deck now. We've got incoming and you guys are blocking my point-defense systems."

"Working on it."

"How long?"

"One minute, max."

Nathan looked at Jessica.

"It takes at least thirty seconds to spin up a point-defense field."

"Damn!"

The shuttle drifted over the Aurora's main propulsion section as it continued on its way forward toward the flight deck.

"Can't you move this thing any faster?" Loki begged.

"A minute ago you were complaining that we were going too fast. Now we're too slow?"

"Just get us down."

The shuttle finally cleared the propulsion section and began rapidly descending toward the flight deck.

"Our firing solution is clear," Jessica announced.

"Fire all rail guns," Nathan ordered.

Having already been deployed and aimed, the rail guns immediately began to open fire just as the shuttle touched down gently on the flight deck.

"We're down!" Loki announced.

"Abby," Nathan asked, "how quickly can you plot a jump to just out of their weapons range?"

"How far?"

"I don't care. Whatever is quickest. Just get us out of the range of those missiles!"

"Give me a minute. Cameron, send me your new course."

Cameron stood slightly and stretched over to her left to reach the middle of the unmanned navigator's station on the other side of the center pedestal that separated the helm and the navigation consoles in order to transfer the course data to Abby.

"Oh shit," Jessica exclaimed suddenly. "One got through. Brace for impact!"

As the shuttle began to roll off the landing apron and into the hangar bay, a missile streaked overhead, no more than twenty meters above their heads just to the left of them.

Josh and Loki looked at each other. "Uh oh."

The missile passed over most of the ship, skimming along until it struck the upper portion of the hull just forward of the primary bulkhead line. The force of the explosion was immense, sending pieces of the outer hull flying in all directions.

The bridge shook violently as the missile exploded. The entire room suddenly shifted to the right, taking the floor out from under anyone standing, as well as sliding the chairs right out from under anyone sitting. Everyone on the starboard side of the bridge immediately found themselves on the floor. Nathan and Jessica, who had been standing at the tactical station, found themselves in a pile just to the left of where they had been standing. Kaylah and the acting communications officer, both of whose consoles were on the port side of the bridge, found themselves slamming into their consoles face first. Cameron, who was partially standing and stretching to her left to try and reach the navigation console went toppling over the center console and into the navigator's chair, ending up in a pile on the far side of the entire flight console.

The lights went dark. Only the illumination from the main view screen lit the bridge. A few systems shorted and sparked, but the lights quickly came back on, and the crew picked themselves up. All but one.

"Abby!" Nathan called out. "Are you all right?"

"Yes," she answered as she climbed back into her chair.

"Tell me you have a jump ready?"

"Yes, sir. I do."

"Jump! Jump! Jump!"

As Abby initiated the jump, Jessica, who had just gotten back on her feet quickly killed the point-defense fire. The view screen darkened and a moment later the room was bathed by the blue-white flash of the jump.

"Cam, verify our position!" Nathan turned toward the helm, but Cameron wasn't there.

"Sir!" Kaylah cried.

Nathan turned his gaze to the left and saw Kaylah dropping to her knees next to Cameron's motionless body.

"Medical team to the bridge!" Nathan ordered as he rushed over to Cameron's side. "Is she...?" He couldn't bring himself to say the word.

Kaylah felt for a pulse at Cameron's neck. "She's alive, sir. But her breathing is very shallow, and I can barely feel her pulse."

"Stay with her, Kaylah." Nathan rose and immediately sat at the helm to assume the job of flying the ship. "Abby, start plotting another jump out of here, just in case."

Nathan scanned the helm displays as he took control of the ship. They were still on the same course and at the same speed. But they were five light minutes farther away from their last location than they should've been at their present speed. It wasn't very far. In fact, Nathan hadn't even realized that the jump drive could be used over such a short distance. It was, however, just enough to keep them comfortably out of reach of the Yamaro's long-range missiles.

Doctor Chen and two crewmen entered the bridge and immediately went to Cameron's side. Nathan kept looking out of the corner of his eye as the doctor struggled to keep his executive officer alive.

"Her right lung is collapsed, and her pressure is way down. She's got to be bleeding internally," she stated as she finished her scan of Cameron's body with her portable medical scanner. "Finish up that line and get her on oxygen. I've got to get her into surgery before she bleeds out."

"Doctor," Nathan said as he continued piloting the ship, "is she gonna survive?"

"She's in bad shape," the young doctor admitted grimly. "I'll do what I can."

Nathan kept his eyes forward as they loaded her pale, motionless body onto the stretcher. She was a strong-willed, determined young woman, but now she was as limp as a rag doll. It crushed Nathan to see his friend in such a state.

Tug and Jalea entered the bridge in a hurry, obviously having rushed there directly from the hangar deck after they had landed. In their hurry, they nearly ran into the medical team carrying Cameron out on a stretcher. Tug's expression immediately turned somber when he realized what was happening.

"Kaylah," Nathan said calmly, "I need you back on your console."

Kaylah looked at him. "Yes, sir," she answered as she rose and climbed back into her chair.

"I need to know the position of that warship. I

need to know if they're still pursuing us."

"Yes, sir. One moment."

"Captain, I have an escape jump plotted to take us outside the system," Abby reported.

"Engineering, report," Nathan called over his comms.

"*No problems,*" Vladimir reported over the comms. "*All primary systems are functioning.*"

"Abby?"

"We're still good, Captain. Ninety-eight percent charged."

"Jess?"

"Lost a couple rail guns along the port side, just forward of the primary bulkheads. But other than that, we're good."

"How about our point-defense rounds?"

"We can hold a field for maybe a minute before we run out. Still full up on kinetic rounds, and about ten percent of our explosive hull-penetrating rounds." Jessica looked at Nathan. "Not much left to shoot with, I'm afraid."

"Not that it matters much," Nathan admitted. "With her missiles we'd never get close enough to be able to hit anything."

"Captain," Kaylah interrupted, "I've found the Ta'Akar warship, sir."

"Is it still after us?"

"Negative sir, they've broken off pursuit. They've assumed a high orbit over Corinair."

Oh God, Nathan thought.

"Captain," Jalea began, "If they're assuming a high orbit..."

"I know," Nathan admitted.

"There are billions of innocent people on Corinair," Jalea said.

"And there are millions of innocent people on my world as well!"

Josh and Loki peeked their heads in through the hatchway to the bridge, unsure if it was safe to enter due to all the shouting.

"Captain!" Kaylah announced. "The Yamaro is opening fire on Corinair, sir!"

"What?!" Josh cried. "Captain! We gotta do something!"

"Yeah, Captain," Loki agreed, "they'll be wiped out!"

"What can we do?" Nathan pleaded. "We're just one ship. We're not even heavily armed."

Nathan looked in the eyes of his guests, and then in the eyes of his crew. Every one of them was scared: scared for the people of Corinair, scared for the people of Earth, and scared for themselves. All except for one. Tug's eyes were sympathetic, as if he understood the pain than Nathan was going through. It was as if he had been through it himself.

Tug stepped forward, placing his hand on Nathan's shoulder. "Nathan," he said softly, "I know that you are young. I know that this responsibility was not yours by choice. And I know that this task seems an impossible one. And you are right; you are but one ship, one small ship. But your ship has a miraculous device, the likes of which has never been seen. I know that you do not know how to use it just yet. But neither do they know how to defend against it. That is your biggest advantage. Trust in me. Trust in yourself, just as we all do. Together, we can do this. We can save them all—both your people and mine."

Nathan was more conflicted than he had ever been in his entire life. No matter which way he decided, he had both tactical and ethical justification. But none of that mattered to him at this moment. He knew that no matter what, he could not bring himself to jump away and leave billions of innocent people to die needlessly, even if it meant risking his own world.

Nathan looked at Jessica. "It seems that fate once again has me in its clutches," he said, a slight smirk forming on the corner of his mouth. He turned toward Josh and Loki. "You two think you're ready to fly this thing?"

"Hell yes," Josh exclaimed, nearly falling over himself to get to the helm, Loki stumbling right behind him.

Jessica stepped up next to Nathan. "Don't get me wrong—I hope Cameron's gonna be all right and all—but it's a good thing she's not here right now, because she'd probably relieve you of command."

"You're right. She would," he admitted. "And what about you?"

"Hey, you know me, skipper. I'm always ready to kick some ass."

Nathan turned back to Tug. "What can you tell me about the Yamaro?"

"She's a heavy cruiser, and she operates several squadrons of short-range attack fighters. She is armed with long-range missiles and short-range energy weapons, of which she has many. But her biggest strength is her shielding. She can project a shield barrier bubble at least two kilometers in all directions. She normally does this to allow maneuvering room for her fighters as they are launched and recovered."

"How do the fighters get past the shields?"

"They can open and close small holes in the

shields to let them in. But the shields are one way. That is, they only keep what is outside from coming in. They do not stop what is inside from getting out."

"Is it possible to knock her shields out?"

"Not from the outside. You would have to be inside her shield perimeter. Then, it would be rather easy. Just take out enough of her emitters. She would not be able to maintain a proper shield and it would completely collapse. But there is no way to get close enough to even try."

"I have an idea about that," Nathan said as he moved closer to Abby and Deliza. "Abby, you said before that the new computer core that Deliza installed makes it possible for you to jump closer more accurately."

"Yes, considerably so."

"Does that mean you can jump closer to another object?"

"Yes, but..."

"How close?"

"I'm not sure."

"Less than, say, two kilometers?"

"Less than one, I would think."

"Could you jump us, to say, five hundred meters off that warship?"

"Yes, I believe so."

"Would that ships energy shields get in the way?"

"Not at all. When we jump, we are traveling in a different dimension. So matter from this dimension would not react with us while we were in transition."

"Okay. I'm not even going to pretend that I understand that. I'm just going to believe you when you say it will work."

"Yes, sir. It will work."

"Great. Plot a jump to take us back to Corinair.

Say, about one light minute out."

"Yes, sir."

Nathan spun around to face the front of the bridge. "Helm, come about. Set course back to Corinair. Reduce speed to one percent light."

"Yes, sir," Josh answered. Josh immediately began executing a slow turn to head back, as Loki began plotting the new course for him. The order to *reduce* speed to one percent of light put a smile on Josh's boyish face. He had never flown anything *faster* than one percent light.

"Captain," Tug interrupted, "you will only get one chance, maybe two if you are quick enough with your second pass. Once he discerns your strategy, he will undoubtedly pull his shields back in close, so as not to give you room."

"Jess..." Nathan said.

"Jump in, shoot, jump out, repeat as needed. Yeah, I got it," she assured him as she began preparing instructions for the fire control computers for the rail guns. "Josh, we'll need to keep our topside facing the target as we pass so I can get all our guns on the target."

"Got it."

"Captain, how many jumps are you planning?" Abby asked.

Nathan turned back to Abby, realizing that she would need to calculate each jump on the fly. "We're gonna jump in to a range of one light minute and then charge in as if we're going to slug it out. Then just after they fire their long range missiles, we jump forward to about five hundred meters ahead and five hundred meters to his side. That should put us inside his shields and give us a clean shot. Then we jump back out to just beyond his range, and repeat as many times as it takes. Or at least for as long as it still works," he admitted. "Can you manage that?"

"Yes, sir. I believe so."

"How long will you need to calculate each jump?"

"At such short distances, maybe thirty seconds each."

"Great. That should be more than quick enough." Nathan straightened up and moved back to the command chair. "Comms, alert both engineering and medical. Let them know we're going into combat."

"Captain," Jessica warned, "she's going to be performing surgery on Cameron in the middle of the battle."

"Yeah," Nathan answered grimly, "I know."

CHAPTER TEN

The blue-white jump flash faded as quickly as it had occurred, the main view screen automatically readjusting its brightness back to normal settings.

"Jump complete," Abby reported.

Nathan looked at the main view screen. "Opticals on the target, insert and zoom in."

Kaylah immediately pointed the ship's long-range optical sensors on the Yamaro and magnified the image. She then put the view in a separate window and placed it in the middle of the main view screen at the front of the bridge for the captain to see.

Nathan turned his head toward Jessica, behind him at the tactical station. "Range to target?"

"Seventeen point nine million kilometers," Jessica reported. "Three thousand kilometers per second closure."

"Tug. What's the max range of their missiles?"

"As you know, Captain, in space, there is no maximum range. However, their effective range is limited by their maximum velocity as well as the amount of energy expended to reach that speed. Generally speaking, you are currently at the extreme limits of their effective range. It is doubtful that any Ta'Akar captain would waste a missile from this range. And even if he did, it would take nearly two full minutes for the weapon to reach you. As you can see, not very effective."

"Very well. Jess, we'll call twenty million kilometers their max missile range from now on."

"Got it."

"Captain," Tug said, "in order to ensure that he extends his shields to their maximum effective radius, you need to get him to launch his fighters. Doing so will require expanding his shields. It is standard procedure for them."

"And how do we do that?"

"You must convince him that you intend to face him head on. It is a matter of pride for a captain to win a battle with as few scars to his ship as possible. If he believes you are about to attack, he will try to preoccupy you with his fighters, allowing him time to move closer and finish you with his main gun batteries."

"So his order of battle is missiles, fighters, guns?"

"Correct."

"So how do we get him to come after us?"

"Simple," Jessica chimed in. "Pick a fight."

* * *

The pristine landscape of Corinair's capital city disintegrated with each blow from the warship orbiting high above the planet. The unprovoked attack which had begun only ten minutes ago had already claimed hundreds of thousands of lives, with ten times as many unaccounted for.

Similar scenes were playing out in cities all over the planet's primary continent. Those that were unlucky enough to lie under the attacker's orbital path were the first to be targeted. Massive balls of red-orange energy streaked down from above, vaporizing everything within a kilometer of impact.

That which was not vaporized was demolished by shock waves that extended several more kilometers beyond.

Aitkenna, the planet's capital, had received the brunt of the initial attack, with most of its suburbs being equally targeted. The bombardment, which seemed to strike every ten seconds, was slowly making its way across the sprawling city as the attacking vessel progressed on its orbit. In a few more minutes the attack on this city would end, at least for now. Eventually, the warship would complete its orbit and once again be over the capital.

In the secret underground churches of the Order, in the homes of those afraid to venture out, and even in the battered streets, people huddled together and prayed as destruction rained down upon them. They prayed for reprieve, for forgiveness, and for rescue. But mostly, they prayed that the sign witnessed the night before was indeed the sign of their salvation.

* * *

"Helm, reduce speed to ten thousand KPH."

"For this ship, that's a crawl," Josh objected.

"A crawl is what we want right now."

"Yes, sir. Reducing speed."

"Ready to broadcast on all frequencies, sir," the comm-officer reported.

Nathan stood up in front of his command chair. After straightening his uniform shirt and running his hands over his hair, he gestured to the comm-officer to begin recording.

"Attention, warship Yamaro. This is Nathan Scott, Captain of the United Earth Ship Aurora. I order you to cease your attack on the planet Corinair and stand down, or we will open fire and destroy your vessel. You have one minute to comply." Nathan froze, staring coldly at the main view screen, trying to look imposing as he waited for the comm-officer to report the transmission was over.

"Transmission ended," the comm-officer reported.

"How was that?" Nathan asked no one in particular.

"Very threatening," Jessica answered, trying unsuccessfully to hide her sarcasm.

Nathan sneered at her. "So what now? We wait a minute and then head towards them?"

"Actually, sir," Kaylah corrected, "you need to wait almost three minutes. We are nearly a full light minute out."

"Of course." Nathan turned and stepped up onto the back upper level of the bridge and moved around to stand by Tug. "How many people will die on Corinair over the next three minutes?" he asked.

"In times such as this, it is better not to dwell on such details," Tug advised.

Nathan contemplated Tug's words, wondering if that were even possible.

* * *

In a desperate attempt to thwart the attack, the leaders of Corinair launched their meager defensive forces. Wave after wave of attack squadrons, once loyal to the Ta'Akar, now targeted their weapons on the powerful vessel laying waste to their world. But the warship's shields were too powerful and their attack squadron's weapons simply exploded harmlessly upon impact. Not a single weapon ever came closer than a kilometer to their target.

As the small ships continued their attack, the warship began picking off the attacking fighters one by one with her guns. Of so little threat were the attacking swarms of combat spacecraft, the warship deemed it unnecessary to use her own fighters to dispatch them. To the captain of the Yamaro, the attacking fighters proved good target practice for his gunners.

As the Corinairan squadrons were rapidly reduced in number, the planet's leaders were forced to launch their defense missiles. Unfortunately, this only angered the captain of the Yamaro, who thus far had chosen a rather languid pace at which to rain destruction down on their world. His intent had never been to destroy the entire planet. He had only hoped to punish them sufficiently while using the attack to draw the Earth ship into a fight that he was confident he would win. But now, these lesser subjects of the great empire which he served were committing the ultimate betrayal. They were attacking a Ta'Akar ship of the line—not only with pesky fighters, but with nuclear weapons as well.

As a result, the pace of the bombardment increased. Strikes began to happen every few seconds, leaving no gaps in destruction, no safe harbors in which to hide. It was apparent to the leaders of Corinair that the warship was now using all its delivery systems in order to quickly finish the job it had started. There was no longer any hope.

Then suddenly the bombardment stopped.

* * *

"Captain, the Yamaro has disengaged and is breaking orbit," Jessica reported.

"You mean it worked?" Nathan said, finding it too good to be true.

"Not unless he's trying to surrender in a hurry. He's headed our way at full power and accelerating fast. I'm pretty sure he's starting an attack run."

"Incoming message," the comm-officer reported.

"Put him up," Nathan ordered.

A moment later, Captain de Winter's image was again on the main screen, displayed in a separate window overlaying the exterior view of space.

"This is Captain de Winter of the warship Yamaro. In the name of Caius the Great, you are hereby ordered to surrender unconditionally. You are to power down all systems and prepare to be boarded. Failure to comply will be dealt with swiftly, surely, and in a manner most unpleasant." The image immediately disappeared.

"I say," Josh began, mocking the captain, "disagreeable chap, isn't he?"

"Quite," Loki responded in similar fashion.

"I guess we got our answer," Nathan concluded.

"Do you wish to answer them, Captain?" the comm-officer asked.

"No. I think he'll understand our answer shortly." Nathan returned to his command chair. "Helm, full speed ahead. We'll take him head on."

"What?" Josh questioned.

"Yeah, what?" Jessica agreed.

"At higher speeds, we're less maneuverable..."

"Yeah, and head on we have fewer guns on the target," Jessica pointed out.

"I want him to continue thinking that I'm young and dumb."

"Well, he'd be half right," Jessica muttered. Nathan rotated his command chair slowly around to look at her, one eyebrow raised. "You are young," she added.

"Hopefully, he'll also think that we either can't or don't want to use our jump drive. The longer he thinks he's in a conventional ship-to-ship engagement, the longer it will take him to start thinking about how to defend against a ship with a jump drive."

Josh increased the main engine's thrust to full power, causing the ship to lurch slightly as it began to accelerate. "Main engines coming up to full thrust."

Nathan turned back to Tug. "Missiles, fighters, guns... right?" Tug nodded agreement.

"Target is also accelerating," Jessica reported. "He'll have missile range on us any moment now."

"How long do you think he'll wait until he fires?" Nathan asked Tug.

"If it were me, I'd wait until my odds of a strike were better. But I tend to be more prudent in my use of ordnance."

"Incoming," Jessica announced. "Four missiles, all conventional, no nukes, accelerating hard. Impact in three minutes."

"I guess he doesn't mind wasting ordnance," Nathan said.

"Curious," Tug observed. "At this range, the missiles are easily defeated using rather simple maneuvers." Tug considered the alternatives for a moment. "He may be hoping to lull you into a false sense of security."

"A curve ball," Nathan said.

"A curve ball?" Tug wondered.

"A slow pitch, looks easy to hit, then it changes direction at the last moment and you miss." Tug still looked puzzled. "Never mind."

"Captain, you want me to evade those missiles?" Josh asked.

"Nope. Hold your course."

Josh looked over his shoulder at the captain, then at Loki.

"Helm, current speed?"

"Uh, twenty thousand KPH."

"Reduce thrust to one percent."

"But Captain, it'll take us forever to accelerate..."

"I don't want to accelerate. In fact, we're going to want to go slower."

Josh was now even more confused but followed his captain's orders nonetheless. "Reducing thrust to one percent."

"Still trying to look stupid?" Jessica quipped.

"Indecisive would be more accurate. Send the missile track to Abby," Nathan ordered. He then turned to Doctor Sorenson at the jump control console. "Abby, calculate your first jump from a point a split second before those missiles hit us, to a point like we talked about—five hundred meters forward and five hundred meters to port of that ship."

"Understood."

"Can you do that in two minutes?"

"Yes, sir."

"Great," Nathan told her. "Josh, just before we jump you're gonna pitch over so we're flying backwards, and you're going to bring the mains back up to full thrust. We need to slow down as much as we can so we get a chance to do some damage before we blow past him."

"Okay," Josh answered, trying not to look nervous. "And that won't screw up our jump?"

Nathan had assumed that it wouldn't matter, as

long as their flight path remained the same. But as he wasn't entirely sure, he looked to Abby.

"It shouldn't be an issue," she promised. "Just don't start your deceleration any sooner than necessary, as an abrupt change in speed could slightly alter our arrival point."

Nathan gestured understandingly at Abby as he continued instructing his new helmsman. "You're also going to have to roll us over just enough to get our topsides facing the target as we slide past her. We need to get as many guns as possible on her."

"No problem," Josh told him. He looked at Loki, who didn't look any more confident than he felt.

"Missile impact in ninety seconds," Jessica reported.

"When do you think he will launch his fighters?" Nathan asked Tug.

"Only when he believes he has severely wounded you... or when he becomes desperate."

"I'm hoping for the second reason, myself," Nathan told him. "Kaylah, what's the current radius of the target's shield bubble?"

"One point five kilometers, sir."

"Excellent, plenty of room," Nathan reassured himself. "Jessica, spin up the rail guns, kinetic rounds only, fastest fire rate they can muster. And point them all straight up."

"Aye, sir. Kinetic rounds, full rate auto-fire. Pre-aiming all batteries straight up."

Nathan noticed a smile on Tug's face.

"I imagine that Captain de Winter is wondering why you are not firing your long-range weapons at him as well."

"Yeah, he must think I'm a real idiot. He doesn't know that I don't have any left," Nathan answered, also smiling.

Tug's expression changed to one of concern.

"Missile impact in sixty seconds," Jessica reported.

"Helm, main propulsion to zero thrust. Abby, prepare to jump."

"Helm answering zero thrust. Speed twenty five thousand KPH."

"*Jessica?*" Vladimir's voice called over Jessica's comm-set.

"Yeah, Vlad, go ahead," she answered through her comm-set.

"*Is everything all right?*"

"Yeah, but we're a little busy up here..."

"*Are you aware we are at zero thrust?*" he asked, his voice curiously concerned.

"Yeah, we're trying to look stupid."

"*Of course,*" Vladimir answered, still confused.

"Don't worry. It's all part of the plan. Gotta run." Jessica switched off her mic and returned her attention to her console. "Missile impact in thirty seconds."

Nathan let out a long, slow exhalation. He was about to take his ship into battle against a vastly superior enemy who had already demonstrated hostile intent not only to his ship, but to his own empire's subjects on Corinair. There was no longer any doubt in Nathan's mind that what they were doing was right. Now all his doubts centered on whether or not his plan would work.

Abby flipped open the safety cover on the jump button to begin her countdown. "Jumping in five..."

"Now, Josh! Pitch over and roll!" Nathan ordered. Josh immediately pushed the Aurora's nose down and her tail up, as hard as he could, starting a slow roll at the same time.

"Four..."

"I hope this works," Nathan muttered to himself.

"Three..."

"Pitch and roll complete," Josh reported gleefully.

"Two..."

"Mains to full power!" Nathan ordered. "Jess! Fire all rail guns!"

"One..."

"Mains at full power," Josh reported.

"Jumping," Abby reported as she pressed the red jump button on her console.

The incoming missiles were met with a sudden flash of blue-white light, after which their target vanished, leaving nothing but an empty hole in space before them. Having lost their target lock, they simply continued forward at break-neck speeds, their acquisition systems automatically changing back to search mode.

A blue-white flash appeared approximately five hundred meters ahead and to port of the Yamaro. When the flash quickly subsided, the Aurora could be seen, her main engines ablaze and her rail guns spewing out projectiles in tight streams as she slid past the surprised Yamaro.

"Jump complete," Abby reported.

"Main viewer to topside!" Nathan ordered.

The image on the main view screen suddenly switched to the view of the topside cameras, looking directly upward. The scene showed a swath of destruction being ripped across the side of the Yamaro as the Aurora's rail guns blasted away at her indiscriminately. The increased rate of fire as well as the increased rail velocities were making a huge difference as the Aurora's guns were now able to inflict twice the damage in the same amount of time. But at the speeds the two ships were traveling, their closure rate on one another was even faster. The first pass gave them only a few seconds of attack at the most. As soon as it had started, they found themselves sliding past the Yamaro and rapidly falling behind her.

"Jesus!" Nathan exclaimed. "Did you see that?"

"Damn, that was nice," Jessica agreed.

"Kaylah, how do his shields look?"

"Weakened, sir. He lost quite a few emitters along his port side, but they're still holding."

"Helm, kill the mains and pitch back over."

"Aye, sir. Pitching over."

Jessica switched the main view screen back to its default view from the forward facing cameras.

Nathan turned to Tug. "Do you think we'll get another pass?"

"If he does not adjust his shields too quickly, then yes. But do not delay your attack."

"Kaylah," Nathan called, "keep your eyes on his shield radius. Let me know if it changes."

"Aye, sir."

"Pitch over complete, Captain," Josh reported.

"Go to full power and come about on a pursuit course. I want to be just a little faster than him on our next pass."

"Yes, sir. Full power," Josh announced as he pushed the throttles forward. "Coming about."

"I'm feeding a pursuit course now," Loki reported.

"Contact is turning to port," Jessica reported. "He's trying to bring his guns to bear."

"Helm, reverse your turn," Nathan ordered, noticing that with the Yamaro now turning to port, they were turning into him instead of with him. "Drop your speed and come about to port as fast as you can. He's got a lot more speed up than we do, so we should be able to turn inside him and set up for another jump pass before he comes around. And we can do more damage if we pass him in the same direction."

"Yes, sir."

The ship immediately began to lean back over to the left, the stars on the view screen rolling slightly in a clockwise direction. The inertial dampeners, still not at full operational strength, only partially compensated for the ship's movement and acceleration. Even though he had been dealing with such sensations for days, it still required conscious effort.

"Abby, we're going to try and get in position behind him for another jump pass. But he's turning, so you're going to have to try and anticipate his position at the time of the jump. This time, preferably just barely inside his shield perimeter. Since he's turning, we may need room to maneuver," he told her.

"Yes, sir," she answered.

"Oh, and put us below and astern of him."

"Yes, sir." Abby began pre-plotting the next jump, trying to use the navigation info currently being fed to her from Loki and Jessica. She knew she could calculate a tentative jump based on the data using her best guess at exactly where both they and their enemy would be at the time of the jump. She could even calculate a small margin within which a jump would be safe even if either target were slightly out of position. At such short jump distances, the timing could be slightly more inexact without the consequences being too dire.

"Good boy," Nathan commended Josh. "You're getting inside his turn."

"Contact is reducing speed, trying to tighten his turn."

"Stay with him, Josh. How are the target's shields, Kaylah?" Nathan asked.

"No change, sir, still at one point five kilometers."

"Set your distance from target to one kilometer, Abby."

"One kilometer, aye."

Nathan smiled slightly, noticing that Abby was beginning to sound more like a bridge officer each day.

"He's launching missiles again," Jessica reported from tactical. "Four more. Still no nukes."

"Time to impact?"

"Four minutes. Looks like he can only launch them forward. They'll take a little longer to reach us. They have to make their turn first."

"That's okay," Nathan said. "In one minute, we won't be on his tail any longer."

"Contact is reversing his turn!" Jessica reported.

"Come back to starboard, Josh. Keep pointed slightly off his starboard side."

"Yes, sir," Josh answered as he reversed his turn to starboard.

"Abby?" Nathan asked, wondering if she was ready to jump.

"Ten more seconds," she pleaded. "I had to update

for his turn."

"Don't bother with a countdown, Abby. The word *jumping* will do."

Abby watched as the progress bar on the transition plot calculations screen passed through ninety-six percent, ninety-seven, ninety-eight. *Come on,* she thought. The progress bar showed complete and the screen displayed the phrase *'Transition Plot Locked.'* "Jumping!" she announced as she hit the button.

The bridge again filled with the flash of the jump.

"Jump complete!" Abby announced, a wave of relief washing over her.

"He's reversed his turn again!" Jessica yelled from tactical.

Nathan looked at the main view screen. They had jumped to a position only slightly astern of the Yamaro and just off her port side. They were considerably closer than one kilometer, and were only a few meters below the enemy warship at best. "Pitch down! Hard to port! Fire all guns!"

"Oh shit," Josh mumbled as he pushed the Aurora's nose down sharply, diving underneath the Yamaro as she moved over them from right to left. As soon as he knew they weren't going to smash into the enemy ship's underside, he leveled off his pitch maneuver and turned hard to port to try and match the Yamaro's turn.

Nathan looked up at the portion of the view screen that was directly overhead. As the Yamaro passed within a few meters of them, he was pretty sure that if he understood their language, he could've read the lettering on one of the access panels on her external hull.

"A bit more roll, Josh," Jessica called out, not bothering to waste time going through Nathan. "I

need a better angle to get the starboard guns on
him."

Josh also didn't wait for Nathan, rolling the
Aurora slightly more to port in response to Jessica's
request.

Their speeds almost equal, the Aurora eased
ahead of the Yamaro ever so slightly. "Watch your
speed, Josh. Let's try to keep our guns on him as
long as possible."

"Yes, sir."

"Abby, tell me you're already plotting an escape
jump," Nathan said.

"From the moment I said, 'jump complete,'" she
assured him.

"When the time comes, we're going to break to
starboard and run," Nathan announced for the
benefit of both Josh and Abby.

They all watched the upper portion of the main
view screen as their rail guns ripped apart the
underside of the Yamaro. As close as they still were,
pieces flying off the enemy's underside occasionally
struck the Aurora as well.

"He's turning tighter than us," Jessica reported.
"He's starting to pull away. Range fifty meters and
increasing."

"Stay with him, Josh," Nathan ordered.

"I'm trying."

"Why isn't he firing back at us?" Nathan asked
Tug. They had already had their guns on them for
over ten seconds, more than three times as long as
on their first pass.

"His guns can't target anything this close. They
never expected a ship to be able to get inside their
shields."

"What about his fighters?"

"He can't launch them while he's maneuvering. It's too dangerous. Besides, as long as you can still go to your maximum sub-light velocity, or jump, his fighters won't be able to catch you. He needs to slow you down first."

"And we won't stay in one place long enough for him to hit us."

"Correct."

For a moment, Nathan felt that he was doing pretty good. But only for a moment.

Suddenly, the Yamaro began losing speed, and she quickly disappeared from the view screens as the warship slid behind them.

"Target is braking hard!" Jessica reported.

Nathan stood suddenly from his command chair. "You're overshooting..."

"Firing braking thrusters," Josh reported.

"Range to contact, one kilometer!"

"Shit, she's moving away too fast," Nathan declared. "Helm hard to starboard, full speed ahead! Abby, emergency jump as soon as you're ready!"

"Range to contact, one point five kilometers!" Jessica updated.

The ship began to vibrate and hum, with several systems shorting out and throwing sparks.

"We're passing out of his shield bubble, sir!" Kaylah added.

The Aurora began to shake violently as the Yamaro's main gun batteries began to pound their hull.

"Josh, zero thrust, pitch over and show them our belly!"

Feeling guilty for having let the enemy ship slip away from them, Josh followed orders without hesitation, even though he didn't really understand why.

"I can't get any guns on him at this angle," Jessica warned.

"I can't afford to show him our tail," Nathan protested. "If he takes out main propulsion, we won't stand a chance."

"Jumping!" Abby yelled. Nathan felt a wave of relief wash over him as the room filled with the light from the jump. The sounds of the explosions that had been rocking the ship were suddenly gone, leaving only the sounds of comm chatter and condition alarms from the various consoles.

"Jump complete," she reported a moment later.

"Damage report," Nathan ordered.

"Lost three of the four aft rail guns. And engineering reports the number four main drive thrust port is damaged and offline. Maximum sub-light velocity is now estimated at half light." Jessica looked up from her console. "Other than that, mostly just outer hull damage."

"A few of the aft emitters aren't answering, Captain," Abby added. "But since we did successfully jump, they are either working but not reporting, or nearby emitters were able to compensate."

"But we can still jump, right?" Nathan asked.

"Yes, I believe so," she answered, "and we still have more than eighty percent charge."

"What's our position?"

"About one light minute out," Jessica reported. "The Yamaro is at our eight o'clock."

"Josh, take the main drive to one percent thrust and come about, slow and easy."

"One percent thrust, coming about."

"Kaylah, his shields?"

"Give me a minute, sir. I've gotta wait for the

light to catch up."

"Medical, bridge," Nathan called over the comms.

"*Medical,*" the voice answered.

"This is the captain. How is Commander Taylor doing?"

"*She's in surgery now, Captain. Would you like me to check on her condition for you?*"

Nathan could hear the sounds of chaos in the background. Although they had only taken a few injuries thus far, medical had already been overflowing with patients.

"No, thank you. Please let us know when there is news."

"*Yes, sir.*"

Nathan clicked off the comm.

"She'll be all right," Jessica softly assured him.

"Yeah."

"Captain," Kaylah called, "the enemy ship has pulled in their shields. They're at one hundred meters now and contoured to his basic hull shape."

"We can't jump inside of that," Nathan said. "That's way too close."

"True," Tug agreed, "but it's also too close for him to launch his fighters."

"Captain, I'm also picking up a fluctuation in his aft shields, along the bottom edge under his main drive section."

"If he is contouring his shields, it would put additional strain on the emitters. If some were damaged, the contouring would make it more difficult for emitters to compensate for neighboring malfunctioning ones. That fluctuation may in fact be a hole in his shields. If it is, you may be able to get a shot through and take out his propulsion plant."

"It would have to be a very good shot."

"Not really. They depend too much on their new shields. Their hulls are not as robustly constructed as they once were."

"You mean they don't build them like they used to?" Nathan said, making fun of the way that the Angla language seemed to always use the most complicated way to say something. Vladimir had once described it as *'reaching around with your right hand to scratch you left ear.'*

"Isn't that what I said?"

"But we'll still have to jump in close to avoid his guns, right?"

"Yes."

"Okay. Abby plot a jump to a position as close in as possible, behind and below him." Nathan turned to face the helm. "Josh, reduce your speed to one thousand KPH."

"Are you serious?" Josh protested. "I've done docking approaches faster than that."

"One thousand KPH, please."

"One thousand KPH, aye."

Nathan turned to Jessica, an idea forming in his mind. "Jess? Can you slave all the rail guns to target as one?"

"Sure."

"Just how good a shot are you?"

"With a rifle? Damn good. With rail guns? If you can get your pilot to get us in close and hold her steady, all I've got to do is put the little red dot on the target. The fire control system will do the rest."

"Can you show her where to put the dot?" Nathan asked Tug.

"Yes, I believe so."

"Abby, let me know when you're ready to jump. Josh, as soon as we jump, you have to pitch over again and fire the mains at full thrust so that we can change our direction of travel as quickly as possible so as not to fall too far behind the enemy."

"I don't know, Captain. Maybe you'd better do it."

Nathan knew exactly how Josh felt. It was the way he felt right now about being captain. "You can do it, Josh. You're already better at flying this thing than I am."

"But I don't know all the tricks. I mean, that guy got over on me real quick, you know?"

"Don't worry about it. You've got instincts. Trust them. That's what flying is all about."

"Yes, sir," Josh answered.

A few moments later, Abby spoke up. "Jump is plotted, Captain."

"Very well. Everyone ready?" Nathan looked around the bridge. Seeing no signs of objection, he gave the command. "Let her rip."

"Jumping," Abby announced.

Another brief flash of blue-white light and the view screen suddenly showed the Yamaro up close and personal, just above their heads as she streaked past them.

"Pitch over one eighty and all ahead full, Josh!" Nathan ordered.

Josh pitched the nose up and over sharply as he rolled the ship over to put her guns on the target ahead of him. As soon as his pitch over was nearly complete, he fired the main engines at full thrust. Even with one thrust port out of service, the other three were more than powerful enough for the smaller and more maneuverable Aurora to quickly reverse her direction of travel and catch up to the Yamaro as she tried to escape.

"Range to target, three kilometers and closing," Jessica reported.

"Pick your target out as soon as you can and open up, Jess," Nathan instructed. "As soon as he figures out what we're up to, he's either going to roll over and deny us a shot or try that braking maneuver again."

"Yes, sir," she answered. She had already called up one of the ship's forward cameras and was using it to zoom in on the target and let Tug inspect it to find the exact point she should aim for. "Two kilometers and closing."

Nathan watched as the enemy ship continued on its course, making no evasive maneuvers whatsoever. "Why isn't he maneuvering?"

"Captain!" Kaylah shouted. "His aft sensor array is in shreds! He can't see us!"

"Hot damn!" Nathan declared, realizing they had just gotten the luckiest break they could ask for.

"One kilometer!" Jessica reported.

"There," Tug stated, pointing at the image on the tactical console and zooming in. "Aim there."

"Target acquired and locked, Captain," Jessica reported. "Waiting for optimum firing range."

"Come on, Josh. A little bit more."

"Five hundred meters."

"A little more," Nathan coaxed.

"Two hundred and fifty meters."

"Close enough. Fire!" Nathan ordered.

All remaining eleven rail guns fired their explosive hull penetrating rounds at the same time, and on the same exact spot on the underside of the Yamaro. The first few hundred rounds tore away at the outer hull enough that the following rounds were able to penetrate the hull and wreak havoc inside the engineering section of the warship. Within moments, secondary explosions began to rock the ship, sending sections of her outer hull spiraling away.

"Cease fire! Disengage and peel off!"

The Aurora dove down and banked to starboard, turning away from the damaged warship as more explosions rocked her aft section.

"Her shields are down, Captain!" Kaylah reported.

"She's slowing as well," Cameron reported. "I think she's losing power," Jessica reported.

"Maintain full power, Josh. Get us away from her guns."

Nathan rotated around in his seat to look at Jessica. "Nice shootin', Tex." Jessica just winked and then looked back down at her console. "She's launching fighters."

"So, this would mean that he's desperate, right?" Nathan asked Tug.

"I'd say yes."

"New contact!" Kaylah reported. "Transferring to tactical."

"What? You've got to be kidding me!"

"It's multiple contacts," Jessica corrected. "I'm picking up at least three more squadrons of Ta'Akar fighters coming from Corinair, sir."

"What the hell?"

"Yup, they're definitely coming in on an intercept bearing."

"So we're caught in between two waves of fighters?"

"Yes, sir. That's the way it looks."

"Any chance we can hold them off with rail guns?"

"A slim chance."

"Damn it." Nathan turned to Abby. "Abby, whenever you're ready."

"One minute."

"What do you plan to do?" Jalea asked.

"I guess we'll just have to keep jumping out of range until we can reposition and jump back into the vicinity of the Yamaro and finish him off once and for all. Then we can just stand off until those fighters run out of fuel and have to land."

"Captain, is there no way that we can capture that ship in one piece?" Tug begged. "Even if she cannot be repaired, the weapons and technology on her could be added to your ship. It would be a big help."

It was an idea that Nathan had already considered. But in light of new developments, he just didn't see a way to make it happen, especially if the Yamaro was actually getting support from Corinair.

"I don't get it," Nathan said. "That ship was bombing them back into the stone age. Why would they come to their rescue?"

"Perhaps to prove their loyalty to the Empire, despite their treatment, in the hopes that the captain of the Yamaro might spare them out of gratitude."

"Yeah, maybe."

"We're ready to jump, Captain," Abby reported.

"Very well..."

"Captain, wait!" Jessica interrupted. "The incoming fighters aren't adjusting their intercept course to stay on us." Her eyes widened as she realized what was happening. "The fighters from the surface aren't coming after us, sir! They're going after the Yamaro's fighters."

"You're kidding!" *Lucky break number two,* Nathan thought.

Although a few of them took passing shots as they streaked by, the Yamaro's fighters mostly ignored the Aurora as they continued on and met the incoming Corinairan fighters.

"Yes!" Nathan exclaimed.

"The two groups are now engaged," Jessica reported.

"What about the Yamaro?" Nathan asked. "Where is he now?"

"He's trying to run behind Corinair, sir," Kaylah reported.

"Josh," Nathan started.

"I'm after him," Josh interrupted as he changed course.

"Captain, if he gets too close to the planet, we won't be able to jump in close any more," Abby reported. "The planet's gravity will make it too risky."

"And he's still got guns, so we can't just run up to him at sub-light."

"But he doesn't know that, does he?" Nathan asked, not really expecting an answer. "Abby, plot a jump to put us behind him again. Let's take advantage of his blind spot once more."

"Yes, sir."

"Comms, hail the Yamaro. I want to speak to Captain de Winter."

"Yes, sir."

"What are you going to say to him?" Jalea asked.

"I'm going to offer him a chance to surrender," Nathan said.

"Nathan," Jalea said, "I highly doubt he would even consider..."

"She is correct, Captain," Tug interrupted. "His honor is at stake, as is the honor and security of his family."

"So, he'd rather die than be dishonored?"

"Death before dishonor. It is the way of the nobleman," Tug explained.

"Well, you may be right. But offering someone an opportunity to surrender is our way. It's something that we consider honorable. In fact, we consider it just as honorable to surrender against inevitable defeat, rather than sacrificing your forces needlessly."

"Also a noble sentiment," Tug agreed.

"I've got the captain of the Yamaro on comms, sir."

"On screen," Nathan ordered. A moment later, the pompous image of Captain de Winter filled their main view screen once more.

"You've done surprisingly well for yourself thus far, Captain Scott. I congratulate you."

"I'm offering you a chance to surrender, sir. There's no need for you or your crew to die in the cold of space."

"My, but you are an overconfident young man, aren't you?" he said with a laugh, after which his transmission ended.

"I'm the overconfident one?" Nathan muttered.

"Jump is plotted," Abby reported.

"Rail guns ready, Jess?"

"Yes, sir."

"Josh, when we come out of the jump, flip us over and pull us in over the top of him. We'll linger there as long as we can before jumping out."

"Yes, sir."

"Jess, concentrate fire on his guns. We need to remove his claws. Maybe that will deflate his ego a bit."

"I wouldn't count on it," she answered.

"Abby, I'm going to need a really fast escape

jump. Even a few light seconds will do."

"Yes, sir."

"All right then. One more time. Jump."

"Jumping," Abby reported.

Again the flash filled the bridge. Suddenly, the main view screen was filled with the image of the Yamaro, not more than a few hundred meters away, and the planet Corinair, which was now filling nearly half the screen.

"Whoa! Up and over, Josh!"

Josh pulled the nose up and rolled the ship over as they swung up over the top of the Yamaro, matching her speed as he did so.

"Open fire," Nathan ordered calmly.

The Aurora's rail guns again began ripping apart the exterior of the Yamaro. Targeting her main guns, which were of no use to her at such close ranges, the rapid strikes of the explosive projectiles shredded the enemy's weapons in seconds.

"She's lost most of her main guns, Captain. Only about six of them left on her forward half," Jessica reported.

"She's launching more fighters!" Kaylah announced.

"Helm, back us away. Jess, re-target all guns on the fighters. Try to pick them off as they launch."

Josh began shaving off speed in order to slowly back away from the enemy ship. Fighters began shooting out of her sides. The rail guns were able to pick off the first few fighters, but their pilots quickly caught on and began ducking down under the Yamaro for cover immediately after launch.

"It's no good; they're too fast," Jessica admitted. "I can't track them all."

"Raise the Yamaro again," Nathan ordered.

Again the main screen displayed the image of Captain de Winter from the bridge of the Yamaro. However, this time, the visual was distorted, as was the audio.

"You have one more chance to surrender, Captain."

"*I am a nobleman. Better to die in space than in a prison cell. You'll have no surrender from me,*" he responded before ending the brief transmission.

"Ready to jump, sir," Abby reported.

"Captain," Jessica said, appearing somewhat puzzled, "the fighters. They're breaking off. They're not coming after us."

"Where are they headed?"

"Out into space, apparently."

"What the..."

"Uh oh," Jessica interrupted. "I'm detecting multiple missile launches on the surface."

"From Corinair?"

"Yes, sir," Jessica answered, just as confused as Nathan.

"Are they targeting us?"

"I don't think so. At least I'm not detecting any weapons lock on us."

"Incoming message from the Yamaro, sir," the comm-officer reported.

Nathan looked at Tug, another puzzled look on his face.

"Put him on," Nathan told him.

The image of a different man came onto the screen. He was standing on the bridge of the Yamaro. He was younger and not as spit and polished as Captain de Winter had been. Although Nathan did not understand the Ta'Akar rank insignias, it seemed obvious that this man was of a subordinate rank.

"To whom am I speaking?" Nathan asked.

"*I am Ensign Willard. I offer our immediate surrender.*"

Nathan had to fight to keep his jaw from hitting the floor. "I thought noblemen didn't surrender," he said. He knew it was probably not the best response as it left his lips.

"*The nobles who previously commanded this vessel have been forcibly detained. I am now in command of the Yamaro. Again, I offer it to you in unconditional surrender.*"

Nathan could tell that the man was very nervous about something. "Very well. We accept your surrender. Power down everything except your flight deck and life support. A boarding crew will be on its way to you shortly."

The Ta'Akar ensign on the screen nodded respectfully just before the transmission ended.

"Now what do you think prompted that?" Nathan asked.

"It could have something to do with all the nuclear missiles that are currently locked onto them," Jessica said, smiling. "Impact in three minutes."

"Comms, contact the Corinair leadership and ask them to abort those missiles. Let them know we are taking possession of the Yamaro, and we will be delivering her captain to them to face whatever charges they deem fit."

"Yes, sir."

"Jess, prepare a boarding team."

"You want us to fly them over, Captain?" Josh asked.

"If you guys leave, who the hell's going to fly this ship?" Nathan said with a smile. "Tug, can you fly

269

the shuttle?"

"Of course."

"Kaylah, are they complying?"

"Yes, sir, I'm showing systems shutting down all across their ship. Weapons were first."

"Very well. Jess, collect their command staff. We'll hold them in our brig for now. Once you get that ship secure in orbit, lock their crew up on their ship until we can figure out how to get them to the surface."

"Yes, sir," Jessica said. A smile started to creep onto her face as she left the bridge. She finally felt like she had a captain.

* * *

"She is seriously injured." Doctor Chen paused to check the readings on the monitor display above Cameron's bed. Nathan looked down at his friend. She was still unconscious. Her face was swollen, her head bandaged, and she was intubated, her breathing controlled by machines. She had a multitude of tubes and wires coming out of her, and there was a considerable amount of padding around her pelvis to stabilize her. Despite the fact that she was stable for now, she looked a hell of a lot worse than Captain Roberts had right before he had died.

"She has fractures of the pelvis and ribs, and a dislocated shoulder. She may also have some brain damage. There was quite a lot of intracranial pressure that had to be relieved in a hurry. And we're still draining blood from her peritoneum, so there's still some unresolved bleeding that we didn't catch the first time around."

"Why not?" Nathan asked, realizing too late that

it might have sounded accusatory.

"She was just too unstable. It was better to close her up and let her stabilize a bit. We can keep giving her blood—there's no shortage of donors on board—and we can keep draining the blood out of her abdomen. But eventually, we have to go back in and find the bleeders."

"But you can find them, right?"

"Probably. But you have to remember, Captain; I came on board this ship to start my residency. I am not a trauma surgeon, not by any stretch of the imagination."

"You're all we've got, Doc."

"Maybe not. Have you considered seeking medical assistance from... What was it called? Corinair? I mean, didn't we just save their world? Surely that's got to be worth something. And if they're as advanced as I suspect, they could probably take considerably better care of her down there, in a real hospital, than I can up here."

"It's complicated," Nathan said softly, as he stared at Cameron.

"Well you need to find a way to un-complicate it, Captain, before she dies."

Nathan stood at her bedside for several minutes, thinking about what the doctor had said.

"How is she?" Jessica asked as she entered the room.

"Not good," Nathan said. "Get everything squared away?"

"Yup. Got all the noblemen locked up on our brig. The rest of their crew is locked up in one of their cargo holds for now."

"How many?"

"Only a couple hundred."

"For a ship that size?"

"Seems a lot of it is automated."

"What about the fighters that were still out?" Nathan asked.

"Most of them tried to bail out over Corinair. Most were captured from what I could tell. But a few may have gotten away. If they did, I suspect they'll try to just blend in and disappear—ride it all out, so to speak."

"Yeah."

Jessica paused to look at Cameron. As tough as she was, she couldn't help but feel something at seeing her friend and commanding officer in such condition.

"Listen, Nathan, there's another problem. Enrique caught me on my way over here. He showed me some news footage he collected over the last day or so. It's pretty crazy." She activated her data pad and handed it to Nathan, showing him the video.

Nathan watched for several minutes before speaking. "This is not good," he admitted, a chill washing over him.

"Yeah, I had a feeling something like this was going to happen after that little incident in the interrogation room the other day."

* * *

Nathan sat in the cargo area of the shuttle. Captain de Winter sat next to Nathan, and the twelve members of his command staff sat along each side of the cargo bay, chained together in rows of six.

Jessica, Enrique, and two marines, all of them armed, had accompanied them on the way down to Corinair, as had Tug and Jalea. All were dressed in the best attire they could muster, which wasn't much considering the circumstances.

"You know, Captain, the Ta'Akar will never stand for this," Captain de Winter said to Nathan.

"What? The imprisonment of a few arrogant noblemen?" Nathan asked. "I doubt there is a shortage."

"No, of course not," the captain admitted. "I speak of the civil war you have sparked."

"If anyone sparked a civil war, Captain, it was you. Did you really think you could bomb an entire planet, and the people on it would just lie down and die?"

"While that may be true, Captain, it is you the Ta'Akar will hunt down, not I."

"No. I suspect you'll meet your fate far sooner," Nathan told him as he rose to move to another seat.

Nathan walked carefully across the bouncing shuttle as it made its way to the spaceport of Corinair's capital city, taking a seat at the far end next to Marcus.

"Captain," Marcus greeted. "Kinda ironic, ain't it?"

"How so?"

"Just a few hours ago, we was shootin' our way outta this place, and now they're welcoming us back with open arms."

Nathan nodded silent agreement.

"Five minutes!" Tug called out from the cockpit. He and Jalea had chosen to fly the shuttle on this trip as well, leaving Josh and Loki aboard the Aurora as her flight crew. Although Vladimir had wanted to come along, Nathan had to leave someone in charge that he could trust.

Nathan had wrestled with his decision to come

down to Corinair for several hours. In the end, the Corinair forces had come to his aid and assisted in the defeat of the Ta'Akar warship that had devastated their world. But other than some communications through official channels, he had not had any direct conversations with any of them. And based on the video and audio recordings gathered by his makeshift Sig-Int staff, he feared what his visit to this world might lead to.

His decision had finally come down to one issue. Cameron was unlikely to survive without better medical care than Doctor Chen could provide, and these people, with all their advanced technologies, were her best hope. When put into the simplest of terms, his decision had been easy.

The shuttle came in smooth and easy, the spaceport's auto-flight systems remotely piloting the ship to a perfect landing in the middle of the tarmac just outside the main terminal building. The ship rolled up to the terminal and made a quick one hundred and eighty degree turn so as to point its rear loading ramp toward the terminal itself.

"We have arrived," Tug announced from the cockpit as he began shutting down the shuttle's systems in order to secure the ship. He had no idea how long they would be on the surface of Corinair this time around, but he was quite sure it would be for at least a few hours.

Nathan stood, as did everyone else on board the shuttle. The two marines began checking each prisoner's bindings to ensure that all were secure.

After checking his bindings, Enrique brought Captain de Winter to the rear of the shuttle and prepared to lead him out behind Nathan and Jessica.

"Enjoy your moment in the sun, Captain Scott,"

Captain de Winter told him. "It may be your last."

Nathan took a deep breath and nodded at Marcus standing at the side of the main rear cargo hatch. Marcus hit the button and the rear hatch began to open, the top swinging slowly away from the ship on its way downward. The smell of smoke, death, and destruction wafted into the shuttle from outside. As the hatch began to come down, Nathan could see the destruction and the crumpled skyline of the city beyond the main terminal building. As the hatch descended below their eye line, it revealed a huge crowd of people massed in front of the main terminal building. There were literally thousands of them all jammed in together. They were holding some kind of artifacts or religious symbols in their hands. And there were signs, lots of them in fact. He couldn't read their language, but many of them seemed to say the same thing. Then he noticed that a few of the signs were written in Angla. The lettering was somewhat different than the English he was accustomed to, but he was pretty sure he could make out the words *Savior, Legend,* and *Origins,* Nathan felt a shiver go down his spine.

The crowd was bordered on both sides by at least fifty armed soldiers. In front of the crowd were several official-looking gentlemen in suits. They were standing on a raised platform that was polished to perfection despite the mangled condition of the rest of the city. Flanking them on either side were at least a dozen more armed men. Nathan was sure these men were some sort of leaders or local dignitaries. Suddenly, a row of twelve military drummers to his left began tapping their drums in a unified pattern and tempo. The row of drum wielding men had been so far back as to be almost even with the back edge of the shuttle. Had they not started playing, Nathan might not have even noticed them.

Again, without warning, another row of men on the opposite side began playing instruments Nathan had never seen before, at least not in person. They were some sort of bags held under one arm, with a lot of pipes coming out. The musicians were squeezing bags that Nathan assumed were full of air with their arms. They manipulated a long pipe that came from their mouths down to the bags of air. The sound they created was haunting: a single, constant base note, with a dancing melody playing over it.

Nathan remembered having seen something similar in recordings from the Data Ark. There had been a country on Earth, before the Great Bio-Digital Plague. It had been called Scotland. It was one of the countries of old Earth that had been completely decimated by the plague and had never recovered. The few that had survived and fled the island had moved to mainland Europe. To this day, only a few thousand people still lived on that island. But that instrument—he remembered seeing it, hearing it.

The haunting music squealed from the instruments as the drums pounded along, compelling Nathan to march forward confidently. It felt as if the music had been intended to evoke that feeling of pride that now seemed to take him over.

Nathan strode down the ramp and onto the tarmac with Jessica, in her full combat armor and her weapon slung over her shoulder, walking beside him and a step behind. Enrique, dressed and armed in similar fashion, followed them, pulling the bound Captain de Winter along with him. As they reached the bottom of the ramp and began to walk forward toward the official looking men, one of the men held up a microphone and began speaking to the crowd. He was telling them something, possibly describing the people that approached.

Tug and Jalea followed next, although in a manner that seemed to be designed not to draw attention to themselves. Finally, the two marines in the shuttle came out next, leading the two rows of prisoners in two chains out of the shuttle and down the ramp, coming to a stop once they were all off the ramp and onto the tarmac.

Nathan and company made their way up onto the platform, stepping up to the dignitaries. Upon arrival, Nathan held out his hand in greeting. As he spoke, Jalea translated. "I am Captain Nathan Scott, of the United Earth Ship Aurora." Nathan's words rang out through hidden microphones on the platform so that the entire crowd could hear them. "I present these prisoners to you, so that they may face charges for the crimes committed this day against your world."

The leader of the group of dignitaries shook Nathan's hand enthusiastically. His eyes were wide, as if he were greeting a celebrity. He began speaking in his own language with such emotion that Nathan feared the man might start crying and hug him at any moment.

"On behalf of the people of Corinair, and of all the worlds in the Darvano system, I thank you," Jalea translated. "You have delivered us from evil, exactly as told in the Legend of Origins. Because of you, there is life. Because of you, there is hope. Because of you, Na-Tan, there is freedom." The man turned to face the crowd, grabbing Nathan's hand and holding it up high above his head as he shouted something at the crowd.

The crowd erupted in cheers at the man's words as he turned and hugged Nathan so hard he thought he would burst. As he did so, the rest of the men began hugging Nathan, Jessica, Jalea, and Tug.

As the crowd continued to roar, Nathan leaned closer to Jalea and yelled in her ear. "What did he just say?"

"He said, 'He is the savior of legend. He is Na-Tan.'"

Nathan felt a knot developing in the pit of his stomach.

Jessica leaned towards him as she too was having the life hugged out of her and yelled, "When Cameron wakes up, she's gonna kill you!"

Printed in Great Britain
by Amazon.co.uk, Ltd.,
Marston Gate.